LAWLESS II

AMARIE AVANT

Edited by
MELISSA HARRISON

LEAVING YOU SIMPLY AROUSED.

ISBN: 9798648501799

❀ Created with Vellum

TRIGGER WARNING

This full-length novel is filled with
sexy, ruthless characters,
graphic scenes,
and *very sensitive subject matters,*
including **explicit sex, violence, and rape.**

∾

Please read at your own discretion.

PROLOGUE

"Watching tears slide down someone's face right before the end—it's all a pleasure to me. But you, my Anastasiya, you're irrefutably beautiful when you cry."

The words float like kisses from an angel across my skin. Simeon peers down from his position on top of me. Gentle, firm lips bathe over the rivers slithering down the sides of my face. His tender mouth presses against the duct tape, a simple barrier covering my mouth. Toxic hate taints his kisses, making them bitter.

Momentary lust sparks in his otherwise dead, dark gaze. He pulls his mouth away from the tape. His mouth is twisted with a dash of amusement, his jaw clenched. Simeon groans, "So beautiful. Still, the tears won't save you."

As much as I loathe the truth, I tell myself, *this is it*—the day Simeon stopped loving me and believing in us. Over the years, I've failed Simeon while he was unconditional, constant in his love for me.

"I'll do the opposite, moya milaya. I'll prolong the pain." Fisting a gleaming knife, he twirls it through his knuckles and over the taunting tattoo: M-I-N-E.

I am his.

He places the flat end of the knife over the warmth of my jaw. He twists the handle until heated blood pools up. His tongue draws over his morose work.

With my soul screaming out my love for him, I pull at silk restraints. A wealth of dedication and tender care was taken when Simeon created the delicate bonds. The maniac in him declined into the recesses of his mind at that moment. I'm unable to free myself.

"When I first saw you after four fucking years, Anastasiya, I wanted to tear you apart." Simeon's deep baritone drones out every word. Though his aura scares the crap out of me, I jut my chin out in defiance. The knife in his hand slides onto a silver tray among a sea of gothic torture contraptions—all shiny, new, and prepared for my torment, the woman he handed his heart to. One glance in Simeon's eyes, and I know he doesn't love me anymore.

This enlightenment festers in my heart, doling more pain than any of his cruel actions.

"I told myself to gut you in half, get back the heart you stole from my chest." His hand skirts across my collarbone to my throat. "Own you like you've owned every moment of my thoughts since you left me at the Black Dolphin." His forehead kisses mine. His breath wafts over my skin.

A whimper of a cry crashes deep within my chest.

"Then I saw you, and just like that, you fucking had me, Asya. And you used your deceptive tears about an innocent baby. . . about how others kept us apart." His eyes gleam with the notion that I've lied to him. "I offered absolute vengeance for our unborn child. You! Were you pregnant? Did the story garner all the sympathy you were looking for?"

Questions consume his eyes as I shake my head no. Simeon shrugs, disinterested in further dissecting my actions. He comes to his full height. My fear-stricken eyes are tense from a lack of blinking. I watch as he reaches into the lapel of his suit jacket. He pulls out a scrap of paper.

"Over the past eighteen days, I've kept this where my heart once was. A subtle reminder you never truly gave a fuck about me, my beautiful Tsarina."

The paper is shoved in my face, too close to decipher the words. Simeon speaks, eyebrows lifting as if from rote memory. "Though it seems I've abandoned you twice, you have to know how much I've always cared. For now, all I can give you are my—"

"My apologies with love." My mind fills in the conclusion as he whispers them to me.

"Any last words?" he asks. Fire lights across my flesh as the duct tape pulls across my lips.

Rushing to explain, I shovel out the truth in one long breath. "Simeon, I didn't write—"

The silver tape is slapped back down across my mouth. Crying inconsolably, I concentrate on Kosta, the *suka* I once called *sestra!* I'd written the note the day before leaving Italy. The first note I'd started to write, I'd rambled, bled my heart out. Then I'd decided how delving into the past always seemed to fuel Kosta's inferno. I scrapped the lengthy letter and left a short note. *This* note.

"It's your writing, Asya. And it pains me to see that you still need to lie. So, you will die for me, moya milaya. And because you will die with my heart still residing in your gorgeous body, I will meet you in death, one day. It goes with the territory of you always being mine."

CHAPTER 1

Anastasiya

Eighteen Days Prior . . .

A spotlight bleeds over the raw beauty of Simeon Resnov. His obsidian gaze, which you can't quite put a name on . . . seductive . . . calculating . . . deadly, tracks across the room. He has a physique honed by years of discipline. A delicious tattoo peeks from his collar. Though he was born in the dark, light loves every inch of him, as do I.

His linen shirt attempts to contain his broad chest and biceps, straining at the seams. His self-assured gait exudes power with each move he makes up the left side of a gilded, grand staircase.

A sea of people surrounds the marbled entrance of the palace. They're enthralled by his every movement. Through lengthy lashes, my gold-shadowed eyes peer up at Simeon. His thick forearms brush the bannister. He leans over to address us all. My fingers rove over the deep, dark peacock feathers at my lower abdomen. The feathers hardly cover my breasts and curves. The dress took from dusk to almost midnight for the seamstress to stitch onto my body. The feathers gather at a train where more material trails behind me than what covers my warm brown skin. Woven along the vein of each feather is a line of diamonds. This decadence sets me apart from even Bratva nobility. All of the Resnov family and their acquaintances, a little Castle Girl like me never compared to, now gawk at me while I stare at him.

In a billion years, they'd never imagined I'd be here—with him. As soon as we landed in Russia this evening, my coronation was announced for half-past midnight. I hadn't a moment to spare for thought, and gazing at the sheer power before me, well, there was nothing to contemplate anyway.

Champagne raised in his hand, Simeon starts with a speech, searching through the crowd to look at me. I cannot hear the words. My brain reverts to a rudimentary form as I gawk at him in reverence. Simeon stole all the breath from my lungs when he was fourteen, and I was a mere twelve. Even when his father's hand balled into a fist to strike, he had this authority about him. It took me ages to say my first words. Partially due to fears that will stay in the dark, partly due to *his* demeanor.

Hard one second. Tender another—and only for me.

And now, he's Tsar.

Simeon finishes his speech with a raised hand, the muscles working in his chiseled jaw. Two byki come to his side. Neither are familiar to me, and one is cuffed to a silver briefcase. The other hands over a silver key as if its contents rival all the Bratva possessions.

While we all stare up entranced by Simeon, Luka is suddenly at my side, elbowing me softly. The man who became my brat years ago whispers his excitement in my ears. His older brat, Kirill, is on my opposite side. Luka's eyes are like a warm lap in a clear pool. Kirill's are an iceberg. Though the brothers differ, I trust Kirill equally because his hard, deadly gaze has one sole allegiance—his cousin, Simeon.

Luka's elbow nudges at my ribs again. "Sestra, now," he whispers. His features resemble Kirill, although his are soft and malleable. He also doesn't have his hair in a long ponytail like his older sibling. Hand at the small of my back, Luka urges again. "Now."

I nod. White noise funnels through my ears. Before I take my first stride, Luka whispers, "She isn't here. Breathe. Enjoy this moment."

Luka means well, but his Sofiya remark discharges adrenaline through my veins. The kind which leaves my breathing shallow. Sofiya is supposedly still *ill*. Nevertheless, the Bratva is aware she isn't of sound mind. Focusing on a deep exhale, I glance over to Kirill. He moves ahead, swiftly commanding each step. Two servants come behind Luka and me to assist with my train. Hushed gasps ribbon throughout the opulent room. *All hail the Castle Girl.*

At the first step, I place one crystal-encrusted stiletto before the other. Head held high, I personify all that I must and ascend.

Simeon's dark orbs glitter across my skin, ceasing the nerves rattling around my bones. The residuals of worry fade away. This could be . . . our wedding day.

I float toward him, imagining that the dark gown, which complements my golden complexion, is pearl white—like I'm a saint, and he is too. I don't give a fuck how many people we've murdered; I'm wearing a white dress one day.

As if reading my thoughts, an angel's smile perches on Simeon's lips, beautiful, deceptive, and promising to shield me from harm.

He clasps my hand and begins to speak. His fingertips trail down my bare spine, and his mouth moves over my skin.

"My empress, my Tsarina, my all." His words float across my shoulder. He signals. My heart squeezes. *Damn, I should've listened to the speech he gave.*

7

The man, who was chained to the briefcase, kneels. Throughout the mansion, every person falls to their knees.

Everyone but the man I love and me.

"Two million." Simeon smiles. His thumb presses over a latch on the briefcase. The silver casing pops open, revealing a crown. "And it still doesn't compare to you, moya milaya. Please kneel."

My insides melt. My heart is laid bare. The servants behind me usher my movements to allow me to kneel in the custom feather gown. Simeon places the diamond crown on my head. His hands clasp my face, his mouth intensely feasting of my own.

It's official.

Less than forty-eight hours ago, I had a slice of birthday cake in Los Angeles. I also made my first female friend, who lacks Kosta's attitude. Today, I belong to Simeon Resnov, and I belong to the Bratva.

~

We descend the steps together. Simeon wears a crown too, though one could tell his only interest resides in showing off his new possession. We hug Bratva-allied politicians, blood, and everyone else worthy enough to be in our presence. Then we are escorted to a ballroom. The crown, which Simeon wore for all of five minutes, is on a plush pillow next to his beloved guns. He sits on an opulent throne in a corner of the room, yet still dominates the entire space. Simeon watches as I dance with a never-ending line of well-wishers.

"May I?" A man whose weathered skin is almost my shade from years of sun steps forward in line. He's slime wrapped in the finest garb.

His fingers latch onto mine, and his hand drops to a respectable level on my bareback. I wonder if Simeon's watching our every move has something to do with it.

"You look familiar," I murmur, praying the quartet will quicken the tempo soon.

"Dah?"

"One of my ses—" I bite down the word, *sestras*. "A girl, who grew up in the same boarding house as me, *ahem*, I believe, I've seen you with her."

"Oh, I acquired a select few of them over my years." His leathery face smooths a tad in disgusting nostalgia.

"That's it." I plant my hand on his lapel and stare up into his soulless eyes. My gaze gleams at the mudak. *Them? You mean us*, I stop myself from saying.

"The porcelain ones intrigued me," he says as if the Resnov Castle Girls were a collection. *Dah*, we were an assortment, but that's beside the point.

"I see." Disgusted with myself, I offer a faux smile. The rich man's presence makes me itch; however, Simeon taught me to listen—listen and allow a person to dig their own grave. The rich man continues to prattle about the Castle and "all the good times." Yes, he's almost six feet under.

"It's a shame, the decommissioning of the Castles, Tsarina. Up until this moment, I assumed you were the reason for such a mistake. My dear Anastasiya, I misjudged you. Would you be willing, for a price? Do tell me if I'm speaking out of turn."

"Please continue," I purr.

"Alright, will you speak with the Tsar? Perhaps he closed the Castles thinking his actions were aligned with your desires."

"I see," I murmur. "You believe Simeon closed the Castles to placate me."

"Dah, your presence has brought back fond memories. I mean, all though you're no longer one of them, Anastasiya. I'm overdue for a new . . ."

The man's words wilt as I glower at Simeon. *Them. Them. Them!* echoes in my ears. A slight smile plays at the corner of Simeon's lips. He nods. I lean closer to the man, bringing my body flush to his feeble flesh. I know he likes them younger, although I feel his arousal increasing.

"You're asking your Tsarina to assist you with obtaining another trinket, dah?" My mouth plays on each word, uttering them saccharine sweet.

Somehow, my words entrance him enough to clutch me tighter. Though this rich man stands before me, I can only envision Oleg, my old headmaster. Their voices and words are so similar. Just a day or two has passed since I begged Simeon to change for me, less bloodshed, less need for revenge. But with thoughts of Oleg, my hand gravitates to the emerald sash tied at the tiniest part of my hourglass figure. The only accessory I insisted on became a last-minute wardrobe adjustment and now a necessity—a diamond-encrusted dagger.

In one fluid movement, I'm to the side of my tormentor, the knife arcing along his throat. Skin severs like wrapping paper. It reminds me of scissors running free over the thin sheets I used, forever wrapping New Year's gifts for Simeon as a child. A blood-red cascade sprays across the floor.

The music stops. The line of men waiting to celebrate my coronation with a dance seems to waver. All eyes are on me. Mine are on the rich man as he clasps at the splashes of copper from his artery. A sort of half-smile plays at my lips. For a few precious seconds, he truly becomes *Oleg*.

"I detest handing out promises." My voice travels flawlessly throughout the ballroom. The soaring ceilings offer a precise reverberation. "You all will understand this promise, this truth. As your Tsarina, I'm not weak."

I kneel, clicking my tongue at the servants' attempts to beautify my every movement. I'd offered them a chance at a break, to enjoy food and drink earlier, but they have yet to leave my side. I look into the dead man's eyes. Though I'm an excellent marksman blind, so as not to see the lives I've claimed, claiming the life of the soulless doesn't haunt me. My bloodied fingertips brush over his lids, closing them.

"I am the . . ."

Mikhail, Simeon's classically handsome cousin, catches my eye. "Just," he mouths as I grit the rest of my statement.

"The *Just* Tsarina. Do not mistake my cordial demeanor! If your beliefs or questions are not in allegiance with the Tsar's, guard them. Make no mistake. What you've witnessed," I cock my head toward the corpse, "was mercy. I'm the lesser of two evils, and yet, discord will not be tolerated—ever."

With my head tilted, I glare at Mikhail as a servant wipes the blood from my hands with a steaming terry cloth towel. A coal-gray suit drapes over Mikhail's muscles. The crinkles in his eyes deepen more as his mouth lifts at either side. "May I have this dance?"

"I . . ." I glance over at the now nonexistent line.

"Seems you've made your point. All the men, captivated by your exquisiteness, fear you now. Bravo." Mikhail tips back a crystal snifter. Amber liquid rushes down his throat. Some sort of residue, like crushed pills, is left at the bottom of the glass. He hands it to a servant then holds out a hand, clearing his throat.

What a mudak. Mikhail's appearance, and insistence on a dance, ruins said point. If I deny any Resnov a dance, I appear either weak in my bond as their Tsarina or . . . worse. And yet this is taboo for so many reasons. Faint redness stains my palm as I hold it out.

"When will you be traveling back to Los Angeles?" I ask in a monotone, his fingers gliding through mine.

"We arrived hours ago," he whispers. Vodka-peppered breath sparks across my skin. "I'm still not convinced of your comfort here."

I peer at his Adam's apple, imagining myself issuing it a few sharp pricks, enough to stop this madness. I want to make him feel something other than jaded over his brother's death. I keep telling myself the brilliant doctor descended to the underworld due to a lack of coping skills. We see lots of death here. While he grew up in Los Angeles, he was accustomed to rainbows and glitter.

"Not every day a woman becomes Tsarina, Mikhail. I'll need time to acclimate myself here. Nevertheless, stop questioning my capabilities. You're well aware of who belongs to me and whom I belong to." I lift the back of my hands to display my tattoos: Sim+Mine.

"Ink isn't permanent." He retakes my hand, his thumb gliding like silk over the branding on my knuckles. "Back to what I know. I initiated plans to return to my life when we were in LA, Anastasiya. I had my mind made up. It included sixteen-hour days in the ER."

"Sounds fulfilling," I mutter, though my eyes glower.

"It once was." Mikhail spins me around, only to pull me even closer. "Then, Luka arrived. The entire time we were in Italy and LA, the two of you have been at odds. Now, he's your brat again?"

"Mikhail, he's your blood cousin. My good friend. You tell me if it's not acceptable for me to call him brat."

Sapphire gems gleam, but the smile in his eyes ends there. "The other day when we chatted outside, I pegged you wrong. I assumed you ran away from a monster—the old, fight-or-flight syndrome."

"I'm madly in love with said monster." I bat my lashes with a grin.

His eyes warm with sincerity. "For that, I'm sorry. But I still have this hunch. You were afraid to return to Russia."

"Yet here we are." I nudge my chin to the old, dead fuck being carted out. "Doesn't look like fear to me."

Mikhail's thumb draws toward my jaw. I drop the sarcasm. "Simeon is watching us. Enjoy the blood flowing through your veins."

"Yes, he's watching everyone." A tipsy, lazy chuckle floats out as Mikhail pins me again. "You have a sprinkle of blood on your jaw, Anastasiya. Anyhow, the beast's consenting to let other men touch you, even for a few choice minutes, was all part of a calculated plot."

"Ha! What *were* you drinking?"

"Really good shit, Nastiya. But we're talking conspiracies."

"Okay, what?"

"Not sure yet. Fuck, maybe this?" Mikhail cocks his head toward maids mopping blood from the marble floors. "Simeon satiates his jealousy by watching men with you. Then he leaves you to eradicate the ones who cross the line, case in point."

"Again, you've underestimated me, Good Doctor. I slit the mudak's throat because he deserved it. Felt good too." *Because it's the closest I'll ever get to killing Oleg.*

His head drops. He grips my biceps and groans. "Nastiya, you don't want to murder anyone. I know you don't."

His hands trail down my biceps and forearms, landing at my hands. "You told me to look up years ago and . . ."

Kirill stands next to us, muscular body stiffened, he clicks his tongue.

"I know you don't dance." I wink, disentangling my fingers from his cousin's. The second I begin to spin around, my servants step forward to move my train. I start to shoo them.

"Please go enjoy yourselves for a little while—" A yelp lurches from my throat as I bump into Simeon's massive chest. I dare not look back. Of course, Kirill hadn't made his presence known to welcome me as Tsarina formally. More byki start past Simeon and walk behind me, leading me to believe they're all here for Mikhail.

The idiot doctor and the rest of us have been here less than five hours. I assumed he had a few more brain cells left than to cross Simeon. Part of me hopes he'll scurry his ass back to Los Angeles before he has a permanent resting place.

In an instant, Mikhail is a million miles away from my thoughts as I stare up. A genuine smile settles over my lips. The joy I feel dusts my skin in a pixie glow. It's as if I hadn't taken a life, not ever, though I know Simeon is elated for that very reason. With a death by my hand, his sex drive soars to new heights.

The man I love crushes me against him. Arousal exudes from his hard body. His eyes roll back, intoxicated, as he grips my ass. "You look so fuckable when murdering, moya milaya," he groans into my forehead. "You cannot be hungry now, nyet?"

I laugh a little, burrowing my face into his neck. Thousands of eyes are still peering at us. "Hmmm, I might already be full of champagne. But unless you're sneaking me away for black cherry pistachio ice cream, I'm eating, Simeon."

"Move," he growls. The charming mask descends as he glares over my shoulder. Finally, the two servants dedicated to my appearance flee.

Simeon leans into me, his eyes never leaving mine, and he takes my hand. His lips feather across my knuckles and the sensitive patch inside of my wrists. Tender warmth spreads from my abdomen and blossoms throughout my body.

I catch the gasp attempting to exit my mouth when Simeon scoops me into his arms. Feathers fall and diamonds crash, dashing along the floor.

"Sim," I seethe. "That was intentional."

His massive hand shields the side of my cleavage where the feathers that hardly supported me before have all fallen.

"You may all enter the dining room for dinner," Simeon calls out. He strokes my cheek and then presses his lips to mine. Our kiss is long and deep. An animalistic hum vibrates low in his throat. I lean into Simeon's body, captivated by his aura. His lust is rising, fast.

Against the haven of his muscular frame, I let the heat and freedom of the night crash over me in a blissful wave. My dark fairytale has come to life.

CHAPTER 2

Simeon

Politicians, judges, and members of my family danced with my irreplaceable jewel and survived, well, most. Not to say I haven't claimed more lives in a single night. This evening was a test for my Anastasiya and me.

For me, I had to still the blood lust in me, cease the jealousy, and focus on the crowd. I needed to confirm that all who were present tonight were indeed loyal to the Bratva.

For Anastasiya, well, she passed. She had no fear in marking that pizda's life. Whatever he'd said had to have been immoral, and she responded accordingly. I need for her not to second guess her decisions due to the moral compass growing in her soul. It means I'll have less training for my little Tsarina.

Her honey eyes flit around as I carry her through the palace. Her vibrant, golden skin flushes at my touch. How was I to know the fluff and strings holding her up were as delicate as the small of her backside?

"If someone sees half of my breast, Simeon," she warns.

I place her down in an abandoned corridor. The sound of music, laughter, and chatter is so close. Thick lips set in a line, she crosses her arms over her chest.

"Then what?" I pluck at a feather. More plumes and diamonds cascade to the ground. I place a hand along the wall over her shoulder, leaning down, taunting my gorgeous prey. "What will you do?"

"I . . . will . . ." She nips at my bottom lip. "Fight you."

My fingers play along the strap of feathers at her shoulder. Not even a yank is necessary for the string beneath to snap. More tickling feathers fall from her, unwrapping her like a present.

"Fuck." I breathe deep.

"Fuck what?" she moans, glancing along the empty corridor.

"Me," I order, snatching her chin and bringing her gaze back to mine. Out of all the romance stories Anastasiya begged me to read to her, I cannot piece together anything more worthy than the sight before me. I clasp her breast, paw at it, let her nipple pierce at the inside of my palm.

"Simeon Resnov, how are you speechless?" she murmurs, her brain in overdrive. "I threatened you. Please shut me the fuck up. The good way."

My hand clasps her throat. "You mean, the good way as in I choke you out and screw your pussy? Or the good-good way where my cock assaults your mouth?" I press my lips to hers. "And you choke on my cock, then choke a little more on my cum."

A mesmerizing haze floats around us.

Her head falls back against the marble wall. She moans. "Can you do both? Please do both, Simeon. Fuck me deep, spill your cum in me, on me, all . . . All over me, Sim, please."

My hands go to her jeweled crown. I fist them, bringing her down to her knees. When I crowned her earlier, I had never been more aroused—harder than these millions of dollars in diamonds. I couldn't defile Asya by fucking her mouth to an audience, but I can now.

Anastasiya's fingers fly to my belt. I take on a wide-legged stance. She has my cock out, her breath warming over it in seconds.

"Nyet," I groan. "Just the crown of me, moya milaya."

Her mouth widens as much as possible, enveloping the bulbous head. My legs plant wider.

"That's good. Suck me like you're hungry, baby. Just the crown. Then bring me to your tonsils, Anastasiya. All tongue, nyet fucking teeth."

Her lips are soft, plush, and siphoning me deeper into her mouth. Anastasiya follows every caveat.

Her tongue skims the long length of my shaft, flitting as she goes.

My cockhead is in her tight wetness. The back of her throat is comparable to her pussy. I bang my cock against her, punching at her tonsils. My dick assaults her mouth, plundering faster, harder, deeper. Each onslaught to her tonsils wedges my cock into the tightest, heavenly grip.

Asya groans, sending tiny thrills and vibrations along my rigidness. The beast in me takes over. I corrupt her plush lips, sending cum down her throat, across her cheeks.

My blessing—her little fuck face.

Anastasiya lets the cum mask her face. Her fingers trail through the glob of cum along her cheeks. She scoops it into her mouth like her favorite ice cream.

"Simeon," she mews as I pull her up to her feet. "I'm so happy, so happy we found our way back to each other."

"Good. Good, because I would've found you from here to the end of the fucking earth, girl. Now clean your crown, it's a little dirty."

It's almost three in the morning when we return to the festival. Anastasiya is now wearing another custom-made dress for her coronation, a long-sleeve, floor-length champagne satin dress. The crowd has taken to the gardens behind the palace. I slide my arms into a fur coat as the two servants who've followed Anastasiya around provide her with one. I take it from them, and they make their retreat into the shadows like earlier.

"Please eat something," Anastasiya calls after them. "You scare everyone." She blinks meaningfully at me, then sips at her champagne.

"Let me get you warm." I remove the champagne from her lips. A little spills, and I lick the trail descending her jawline then assist her into her jacket.

"Wait." I place my chin in the crook of her shoulder while holding her from behind.

A loud explosive shoots off in the distance.

"Simeon!" Anastasiya gasps. Fireworks dance through the sky, glittering in her eyes. I press a few strands of hair away from her gorgeous face and can't stop myself from kissing her again.

"I plan to marry you one day soon."

She gulps, voice trembling. "Are you asking—"

"Nyet. When I do, you will say, *dah*. None of this English bullshit."

"Oh? I don't have a choice." She glares up at me through the thickest of eyelashes. Her attempt at anger only makes her more beautiful.

"Not a chance in hell."

I never thought I'd be anywhere near this happy after she disappeared. Clutching her hair, I delight in her mouth, holding her so tight she groans against my lips. Now she's returned, I'll never let her go.

"Asya, I rushed this evening, placing the crown on your head, but I'm learning to slow down." I clasp her cheeks as fireworks continue to blast around us.

"Don't slow down, Sim. Marry me tonight." She lowers her gaze. "You were planning on it after your release from the Black Dolphin—"

"Asya," I groan.

"Because you planned to be gone from me so long that flowers wouldn't suffice."

"You're so crazy, moya milaya." I cup her cheeks and press her lips to mine. "Before you disappeared, I spent all the time I had in prison determining how I'd propose."

Urgency flashes across her face. Or was it something else? My eyebrows pull together. Darkness descends, drowning out her face. Then with the burst of another firework, more bright lights shine above.

"What is it, Asya? Talk to me." I shake her shoulders. Then my hands fall into fists at my side. For the past few days, I've warned myself not to try and bully the truth from her. But this time, when sharp white fireworks spear the sky, Anastasiya eyes me with a baffled grin on her face. Maybe I'm reading too much into nothing?

～

The next afternoon, my cousin, Mikhail, is sprawled on a bed in one of the lavish guest rooms in my palace. Chunks of vomit are in his blondish-silver hair and face. Aside from the discarded tie on the floor, he's slept in his suit. I sit down on the chair a byki pulled out for me.

"Look at this pizda, can't hold his vodka." I shake my head, then nudge my chin.

A byki gives Mikhail's bristled jaw a few slaps. He grouses awake.

"I assumed you slept through natural disasters because you

invested hours upon hours in the ER, Kazen." I glance at a bottle of pills next to a silver flask. "But sleep may cost you your life one day."

Mikhail groans, coming to a seated position. "Simeon, I have a massive headache. Can you pause with threatening my life? Or follow through."

Kirill blinks at me a few times. Out of all my family, he and I are the most alike. We either simmer in dark contemplation, or we pounce.

In one motion, I'm out of my chair. I grip the lapels of Mikhail's crummy suit and snatch him up to me. "You're my blood, Kazen. Give me a good reason why I should put you down, dah?"

He struggles. My curled fingers tighten his collar, constricting much of his breathing.

"Don't test the devil, Mikhail." I push at him, and he falls onto the bed then pops back up.

"Malich is one of my top favorite uncles, so you have choices. Keep those eyes in your head or test my authority. Fight me and die. Would you like that, big Kazen?"

"Simeon, wha-what are you talking about?" He runs a hand over his face.

My eyelid twitches. So, he's playing oblivious.

"I've awoken to a hostile environment. Sim, I don't understand."

On the edge of the bed, Kirill sits next to Mikhail and loops an arm around his neck. He gives our older cousin a few pops. Mikhail tosses his elbow to Kirill's rib. The two start off the bed and begin to wrestle when I order them to stop.

"Nyet," I growl at both my older cousins. "If Mikhail wants to test me, I don't require any help. You're my older kazen, and I beat your fucking ass when we were kids, play fighting. But we are no longer young. Mikhail, you're blessed and loved still. Keep the little space you have in my heart." I knock at my chest. "The instant I contemplate your feelings for Asya for too long, not

Malich or any of the Seven will stop me. I will snatch your heart out of your motherfucking chest. Do you understand, blood of my blood?"

Mikhail's groggy gaze widens a little. He stands up, stretches, then pads across the floor to pull back the satin drapes. "I'm still trying to understand the hostility, Simeon."

I smile, flicking my wrist. All the men in the room head toward the door. Kirill is the last one to leave.

I resume my seat.

There's this rule.

You don't fucking sit, not in the presence of your enemy, especially when they're standing. But I have all the confidence in the world I will own Mikhail's death—if we cross that bridge. With a gesture, my older cousin claims the seat at the edge of the bed.

"I've never coveted anything belonging to you, Mikhail." I smile at him. I never expected to have to educate a family member in that regard. Well, aside from Anatoly. He was the single parasite in our dynasty, and he was cut down by none other than me. "Asya is a stunning woman. It shocks me even to have to mention it. You're taking certain liberties; those liberties will be the death of you."

"I haven't tried anything with the Tsarina," he mumbles.

"I'm well aware. Still, you've placed me in a position in which I have to address you. She's mine, Mikhail. Don't make me out to be the man you knew my father to be. He would've had your life on speculation, Kazen. One little glance, and you're dead, dah?"

Mikhail sighs, and an alcohol stench assaults me full force. "I worry about her—"

My forearm slides across his throat. "Because I love you, I will grant you something else to worry about. Would you like that?"

His heartbeat thumps against my skin. The desire to kill is almost enough to consume me. "Would you?"

"Y-yes," he gasps.

"Good." I breathe easy. I wouldn't fight Mikhail to the death or issue a few custom-made hydro bullets between his eyes. *Nyet.* I'd tear the mudak apart without any regard to my love for Uncle Malich. I'd spent all night dreaming the perfect death.

The *how* has always led to my satisfaction. I head to the door, drumming my fingers along the knife in the back of my blazer. "Kazen, brush your teeth and wash your fucking ass. Then let's play a game. Not one for little boys but grown men, for sport. Dah?"

CHAPTER 3

Anastasiya

A jostling at my shoulder snatches me from the dream. I pop into a seated position, the handle of one of my beloved Colts fitting my palm. As I cock the hammer, Luka dodges away from the bed.

"Oh, just you," I murmur, engaging the safety, though continuing to palm the pearl handle. Power seems to funnel through it, settling me. If our lives were a story, we could've closed the book last night with fireworks splaying across the sky, Simeon claiming me in the haven of his strong arms. In a perfect world, the Tsar and Tsarina lived happily ever after. But we all know of the demise of the last true Tsar.

Anyhow, in my perfect world, the epilogue would transpire like so: we killed some people, had a child (not replacing the one who died but created another new life), killed more people, and brought more children into the world, loved them. Then somewhere along the lines, Simeon and I healed together and memorialized the tiny soul lost to us.

The end.

A worthy epilogue to our sordid life. An exemplary second chance romance. But it's not. Real-life has tribulations, and our love never stalled between said tragedies.

So, the story is still playing out. Enter Villain number whatever. A more worthy opponent than any of our past enemies.

Sofiya is Simeon's mother and the reason we were apart for four years. She's the under-signer of my unborn baby's death.

"Just me?" Luka waves a hand, garnering my attention. He sits wide-legged on a silk chaise across the way. "Who were you expecting? An enemy? Anastasiya, us bykis are thorough in securing the grounds."

A sly smile dons my lips. "Don't feel slighted, Luka. I meant you rather than Simeon. Where is he?"

"Oh, I get it." Luka sighs. "Nightmares about Sofiya."

"Sim made last night perfect . . . until he asked me to visit her."

The diva grins at me. "When are *we* paying my manipulative aunt a visit, Asya?"

"Day after never." I let my head rest, kissing the cushioned headboard. "Hey, why are you so insistent I play a game of Russian Roulette."

"Sim won't murder you, Asya. You're a good person. You won't attack her, not without asking your questions, wishing the best. Human nature at work."

Heaving a sigh, I murmur, "I hate that, Luka. Hate how I wish the best for her."

"Still! You'll gather evidence, present it to Simeon."

"Yes!" My head bobbles in a nod, attempting to keep me above water. "I'll ask my questions, ask if Anatoly coerced her, and I'll allow Sim to handle *it*." The end of my statement strangles out. *But I wanna handle that bitch myself!*

"You can do it." Luka offers a therapeutic smile to which I roll my eyes.

"Mother Sofiya was the only good thing he had in this life. She was constant—until Simeon murdered her brat. Fuck, even I disappeared."

"He understands now, Anastasiya. And my aunt isn't the only good thing. He's got me and Kirill. You will never meet a man more loyal than my brat. The twins—"

"Dot and Beam?"

"Dah, you call them creepy, I call them loyal. Simeon has good family. We will support him—however he handles Sofiya. Speaking of family . . . Mikhail might die today."

"What?"

"Hey, I hardly grew up with the guy. Sure, he's my cousin, but he was more estranged to us than Vassili and even Yuri and Igor."

"No, Luka. I mean what as in . . . *Oh fuck*. He's not thinking." I rub a hand over my face. "Cover your eyes."

A faint smile forms on Luka's lips. He slaps his hands on his knees and gets up. "I'll come back. Simeon might enter this room after washing his kazen's blood from his hands. He'll forget my attraction to my own gender and fly into a second rage. So, I decline the compromising situation."

By the time he's to the door of the massive suite, I've already shrugged into a shirt and jeans. I run past him. Luka laughs.

"This I have to see. My next statement cannot be considered treasonous, but some advice from your good friend. Saving Mikhail's life might cost you your own, Tsarina."

"Don't," I grit.

"Besides, Simeon is probably disposing of his body right about now. It looked like Mikhail was walking the plank when they left this morning." Luka winks.

∾

I felt sorry for Mikhail Resnov. Simply put.

I was to blame for his attempt at a connection. At least my dysfunctional mind had been when I flirted with the slightly older

Resnov. It was a single encounter—years ago—*in Vegas*. He symbolized Volk, and I hate the part of my brain, which reacts without prompt because of my old owner. I've told myself Mikhail's gravitating toward me because of grief.

After showering and completing my morning routine, I find Luka in the massive dining room. I pluck up his second slice of toast and settle next to him. With a faint smile, he pats the side of his mouth with a linen napkin like true royalty.

I shove his arm. "Luka, they're both your family."

"I know Mikhail's my kazen," he groans.

When I reach over to snatch a slice of melon, Luka swats my hand. "*Ahem*, why do you keep stealing my food?"

"Why didn't you request a plate for me?"

He cocks his head toward the opposite end of the table. At least fifty seats down, there is a silver dome. Holding in a chuckle, I retrieve the plate and settle back next to him. "Simeon has enough betrayal in his life. This is a misunderstanding."

Luka pats my cheeks, and I swat at him. "You're too gorgeous for your own good, Anastasiya."

"Pah." I point a piece of speared pancake at him. "You haven't given me a compliment since I tore a hole in the dress moth—Sofiya," I pause to grit, "designed and had a tailor spend a thousand years making for me. You only said that because I was afraid she'd give me the spanking I never received and sorely deserved."

Before placing a mug of coffee to his lips, Luka mumbles, "Speaking of the devil."

"I'm speaking to you." I clear my throat, then close my eyes and bite my lip. I shouldn't have brought up the sweet memory. All the good ones from my younger years lead me back to Sofiya.

If the term *parents* were tangible, I'd douse it in gasoline and light a fucking match!

After finishing the fluffy confection, I set the plate aside.

Luka grips my bicep, rubbing it with his thumb. "Do it now."

"No."

The friggen Prima Donna holds steady. I clutch a steak knife in my hand.

"Not fair," he growls.

I twirl the base of it in my knuckles "You've known me as long as Simeon, Luka. It's my timing or . . ."

He laughs a little. "Or The Tsar's timing, dah? Don't pretend as if you always get your way. Only with me. And it stops today."

Luka presses his hand over the knife, and we're up in seconds. "Do it, now." He enunciates every word.

"Okay. Now." I rise from the seat, conviction slamming through my bloodstream. "Now. We're going now," I grit out, stalking along the vast corridor toward the foyer.

"And start speaking Russian again," he counters.

I glare back at him, my pace quickening.

"Too much?"

"Dah," I snip out. Although I was born into this life, I still can't force myself to play the part—the Russian girl. I've denied my mother's African heritage all my life, not sure why I never rejected my father's. Maybe it was because I grew up here. But with people I care about, the façade is down. And I deny my native tongue.

"Keys," he orders to a byki standing guard near the front door. Seconds later, the byki returns with a set of keys for one of the cars in the fleet along the way.

An Aston Martin SUV lights up. He steps around to the passenger door. When I don't make a move to slide into the awaiting seat, Luka clears his throat.

He glares at my hesitation. "We're visiting Aunt Sofiya and getting answers."

Mouth set, I climb in.

Minutes later, Luka navigates along the row of luxury vehicles. Ahead, more courtyards split the road in half. He drives the lengthy wooded lane leading to the edge of the land. To force Sofiya from my brain, momentarily, I toggle onto my email app on my phone.

My mouth tenses. Kosta still hasn't responded. When we first escaped to Cape Town, Kosta and I bickered to no end. In Miami, my Sestra was a little easier to stomach. The only difference was we had more than a twelve-by-twelve-foot area to live in. Since everything went down in Italy, the stubborn suka hasn't responded to me.

"Slap on a smile." Luka reaches over and nudges me with the back of his hand. "Today, you meet with one witch. No need starting the meeting already disheartened by another witch."

"I—"

"You don't owe Kosta shit." He begins to slow as we approach the wrought iron gates. "Kosta saved you from your headmaster when you were children—she made the sacrifice."

"Ha, I gave you the short story. She's done more for me." While Simeon dealt with some business on the jet ride home yesterday, I confided more in Luca than I had anyone. I guess it was a practice of sorts, preparing me to talk to Simeon.

"One thing distinguishes Kosta from martyr status," Luka starts in retort. "It slipped the suka's mind that she made a conscious decision to sacrifice herself for you. *Again*, emphasis on *her choice*. Listen, I'm a Russian man, but I understand how women like their choices, maybe even more than the next man."

"Whatever, diva." I start to chastise him then calm myself. "That's not all Kosta did . . ."

We come to a stop at the main gates to the palace. A byki exits the hut and leans in, resting his elbows on the driver's window. "Morning." He lowers his head at the sight of me. He's torn between the proper greeting of Bratva royalty and something else. A ribbon of apology is in his gaze as he says the customary hello to me, then adds, "Please wait a minute."

"Do you see who is in the passenger seat?" Luka asks.

"Dah. I still have orders," he huffs.

Luka zips up the window, and the byki moves away.

"Moreover, when are you telling Simeon about your headmaster?"

"After I see Sofiya. Which would've been never, but you're a pizda. So, tonight," I strangle out. I hadn't meant to share so much with Luka before Simeon. I couldn't even bring myself to mention the mudak's name to Luka. How the hell will I ever be able to say Oleg out loud to Simeon?

"Tonight is good." He shakes out his nerves. "Wait until I'm out of the general vicinity."

"How nice of you."

The byki taps on the window.

"What the fuck?" Luka growls, lowering his window.

"Kirill is in charge while the Tsar is away. Open the back door."

"Did you tell Kirill his more-than-competent brat is accompanying the—"

"Dah, Luka. I value my life. The door, please," the byki groans.

Twenty minutes later, we've arrived at a townhome where Sofiya is held against her will, for her sanity's sake. A faint dusting of snow blankets the massive roof, which stretches like a cloud across the sky. The byki opens the door for me. Again, he offers an apology for his presence, and I smile then push back my coat, letting him catch a glimpse of my twin pistols.

"I'll stay here." He clears his throat.

More byki are on the scene at the front door and inside when we enter. An older man is sitting at an antique settee, a cup of tea in one hand, as he reads a psychological journal.

"Mr. Garbovsky." The byki begins making introductions.

"I remember you." Garbovsky smiles a row of caffeine-tinted teeth. Other than this addiction, he seems high society. "You brought Simeon lunch on a few occasions."

"Ye-Dah." I smile.

"Before you meet with Mrs. Resnov, may I have a word with you?"

I nod slowly.

"Privately, if possible." His gaze tracks over the additional men in the room.

"You are all relieved," I call out.

Each one, including Luka, nods their respect before exiting the room. I close the door and take a seat in the stiff chair adjacent to him.

"Sofiya mentioned your coronation this morning. It triggered her honesty, softened her a bit, too. She cried and mentioned you were the daughter she never had."

A boulder drops into my throat.

"She shared how much she's grown to care for you over the years, Ms. Anastasiya. And how you had a traumatic experience with Anatoly . . . similar to what she's endured in his hands in the past."

"She said that?" My eyes gloss with tears.

"Sofiya has fond memories of her past as your caregiver. How she brushed your hair when you were a little girl. How much she doted on you and watched as you grew into the young lady her son loves fiercely—these are all her words." He pauses to smile. "Her memories, including you, have had a positive effect on Sofiya. Thus, I'd like to include you in a few family sessions. If you'd be willing?"

The therapeutic, smoothness of Garbovsky's voice captivates me. I wipe a stray tear. "I'm willing."

"I will take you to her now. Please keep your discussion to about fifteen minutes or so. Then I will return to discuss her sessions going forward." His words seem to echo in my ear, followed by white noise as he arises. We exit and are led to a court-yard at the center of the home.

"Ah, she has finally returned to her gardens," Garbovsky says. He glances around the area.

"Where is Simeon's mother?" I ask, but it comes out more of an order to a byki seated on a wrought iron bench, ornate in the shape of roses.

Brown eyes peer through me.

Head tilted, my senses heighten.

The mudak is snoring!

I jar him awake. "Where is—"

The byki jumps up and bows.

"There she is!" Garbovsky's chipper voice grows farther away.

The byki stutters out an apology as I follow after Garbovsky toward a small greenhouse. He opens the door, and I enter first.

Sunlight shines down on Sofiya's silver, silk tresses. She seems to be fussing softly about how her red roses are frostbitten. When she turns around, her mouth pulls into a smile. "My daughter, Anastasiya, you have returned . . ."

My eyes widen in shock. "Mother," I gasp the words, falling to my knees before her.

The thick stem of a red rose glides along Sofiya's wrist. With her gaze locked onto mine, Sofiya's movement is autonomous. The sharp thorns of the rose dig into her flesh, ripping at her sensitive skin. Soft droplets of blood fall to the ground as the dramatic suka smiles and slashes at her wrists. "My precious daughter has returned."

Fingers trembling, I beg, "Stop, Mother, please."

"Hush, Mother knows best. Just a tiny prick. How many times have I told you roses love blood?"

Though it's on the tip of my tongue to tell her that she'll bleed to death, I'm seized by her cold blue gaze, pupils awash in a sinister glow.

The single rose with its thorny vine Sofiya used to dice at her lifeline shimmies to the ground. I'm gathered into her arms. All my senses fail me save for my sight. I'm aware she's embracing me tightly because of vision alone. I'm aware she's crying because I'm viewing rivers gliding down her porcelain skin.

Then my hearing returns, Sofiya's lies funnel through the white noise. "I've missed you, Anastasiya."

The moment becomes real, and I'm clutching her as tight as she is me. I never knew my mother, and for a time, Sofiya Resnov settled into the perfect place. There is no dysfunction, only love as she offers a hug only a mother would give.

"Sofiya!" Garbovsky rushes toward us. He yanks at the linen sleeve of his shirt.

The connection I have to her breaks. I blink, and her dark blue eyes gloss in tears. Blood is streaming down both her wrists into a bed of roses.

The byki's mouth forms his next apology. My eyes close, and I squeeze the trigger. The bullet pierces the mudak's head.

"You should've watched my mother," I whisper. *Because her death has my name on it and no one else's.*

CHAPTER 4

Simeon

I fucked up, made impossible promises. Aside from crowning the head of my love, I agreed to slow down. In a sense, I have, and I will continue to align myself with Anastasiya's desires. Her pace.

The end of the Resnov Castles had been an easy compromise. I detested the entire sex trafficking business.

But her other two requests.

Nyet!

She appeared so innocent when requesting I let Volk—aka our president—live. *And* she'd been vulnerable when asking me not to seek revenge for our child.

But what she doesn't know won't kill her.

Killing the president had become a requirement the day we crossed paths. Though, I've consented to taking my time in that regard.

Killing any of Rudolf's family who knew about him assisting

my disease of a father in Anastasiya's disappearance, *that* is my plan today.

Rudolf was a soldier of mine, Luka's lover. He was also missing when Anastasiya needed him most four years ago. After leaving the Black Dolphin, his death by fire never satiated the beast inside of me. I tortured five of my byki, whom I considered loyal that day.

Now, I have an inkling one of his family members knows something. Has to.

I'll own the death of an entire male lineage before I allow this new, brimming hate for him to rest. I'd let the youngest of Rudolf's family leave and the women, not the whores. Whores talk. So, here they will stay, in addition to Rudolf's closest in age siblings and his father. His mother died a few years back, so she's granted her reprieve as well.

Rudolf's actions caused the death of a sweet, little baby I never knew I had. A baby would have softened my soul. His deception with Anatoly and the Armenians will be unearthed all because this world spins on torture and mayhem. And Mikhail is here to help me do it.

He will learn the lesson of his life too.

Anastasiya is calling me, yet again. It's as if she's aware she made a bargain with the devil.

Condensation puffs from my lips as I shove my ringing cellphone back into my pocket.

I look up and say a prayer of sorts. *Dah, you're a mudak, Sim. However, this is for her. She will thank you once all is said and done.*

The windows are at least fifteen feet from the ground, not offering an escape, not even relief from the mind. Sunlight scissors the air above, unable to touch down into the darkness.

Sticky blood is beneath my leather boots. I've taken off my shirt. Though I don't mind the pretty, little red specks, my hobby has tired me out.

Faint sobs come from the figure crouching on the ground.

"You're covering that hideous face?" I chuckle. "At the expense of me harming your spine. What's more important? Your vanity or this here column." I run my index finger down the man's trembling spine. "Helped you walk when you were a wee boy. All those nerve endings are leading to the most important organ in your body. But conceit has exposed it. Mikhail!"

My cousin jumps at my side. Eyebrow cocked, I turn to look him up and down. He's dressed from head to toe in a makeshift hazmat suit created from plastic bags. Our actions in Italy became less than nothing compared to this morning.

"You're dressed for a ditch." I assess his garb.

After dumping the first of Rudolf's relatives, Mikhail took the plastic bags to cloak himself.

His lungs cave. "Well, I'm seeing an even more brutal side of my younger cousin. You've exceeded my expectations."

I stare at him, unblinking. "Good."

I crouch down to the trembling ball of terror. Whimpers float unheard across the room. Rudolf's cousin is less than a man now, no pride, not an ounce of confidence. There's not a flicker of faith behind his lost gaze.

With a shake of my head, I stand to my full height. When I place my hand on Mikhail's shoulder, an underlying fear reverberates into my palm. "You may cease playing God. This one has no more stories to tell. No need keeping him alive."

Mikhail starts back. My hand clamps into his shoulder. "But don't you dare leave."

"Simeon, this is—" Mikhail wrestles from my grip, his face sliding forward. Hands on his knees, he retches next to the cowering man's face. An apology begins to lurch from his mouth. He can hardly turn around before another round compels him.

"Stop," I bark at my cousin. I step away from the chunks of vomit marring such gorgeous crimson liquid. "Retrieve my dagger, Kazen."

"I can't! I'm a fucking ER doctor, Simeon. What we did in Italy was child's play compared to this! This . . . this is a sacrilege of the basic human race."

My fingers glide through Mikhail's hair, and I yank him up. He punches out, but I slip the gun from inside my blazer out, nudging his chin. "I've given you the chance to fight me before, Mikhail. I'm already satiated. The dagger, please."

My cousin glares at me.

I cock back the hammer. "My dear mother is the reason I said please. It's instilled in me." I let go of his hair and shove him away.

As if rousing awake, the cowering figure begins to beg, "Please!"

Ignoring the crying, I watch Mikhail dig through my black bag of delights. His arm jets away from the open bag, the tips of his fingers dribbling in blood as he mouths, "Fuck."

I smile. "You think me a barbarian, don't you?"

"Simeon, I've had it already with your antics." Exerting more caution than before, Mikhail sifts through the bag. He fists a serrated knife and heads back over. Eyeing the gun I'm fisting in my hand, Mikhail hesitantly hands over the knife.

As the man on the ground continues to cry, the blade lunges into his spine. The begging dies out.

Now, my phone is ringing again. I rub a hand onto my slacks and answer. "Dah?"

Anastasiya groans. "Oh, thank God, you finally answered."

"What is wrong?" I grit. Don Roberto Dominicci slams to the forefront of my mind. Before I slaughtered the Dominicci house, he'd inquired if there was a woman in my life. Less than twenty-four hours ago, I publicly declared my true love. Now, she's calling, voice wrought. "What is it?"

"Your mother."

Nyet. I wriggle my jaw.

"Sim, baby, Sofiya hurt herself again. I'm with her now."

Eyes closed, I wipe the knife on my leg and place it back into the bag. "I'll be there soon."

CHAPTER 5

Anastasiya

"*She's manipulating you,*" Luka had said. My brat gathered me into his arms when Simeon arrived, a devastated look on his face. Nobody but the two of us saw straight through Sofiya's dramatics. Fog plumes around me, and my friend's words dominate every corner of my psyche.

Luka and I left Simeon at his *ailing* mother's side hours ago. I had expected him to return by now. The dual rain spouts of the shower fall like hot tears. I'm craving his arms around me. Knots tie in my stomach as the water pelts my skin, and I let Sofiya's first taste of deception pull me under.

The room I grew up in after leaving the Resnov Castle had sweeping, ornate chandeliers. A rich wood canopy adorned the center. I'd say crystal trinkets cluttered the rest of the area—but there's no

such thing as cluttering a two-thousand square foot room. At almost sixteen, I had selective mutism, only speaking to my token friends.

I delighted in the times Simeon would come and read to me. He'd started off a million miles away, his strong voice carrying to me. He seemed to know my triggers, especially not wanting to be touched. By now, our platonic relationship left stars in my eyes.

But he hadn't come to me this evening. Sofiya's husband, the man Simeon called the epitome of weak, had left a while ago. Desirous moaning and shouting had ensued; Anatoly's shouting, Sofiya's grunting, and a bed carved of wood scraping across the ground of the third floor.

In frilly, lace pajamas that popped against my darker skin, I sat at the vanity. I clutched a silver brush in my hand. My thoughts were a whirl. It was easier to transport my mind elsewhere while the siblings went at it. I didn't have the courage to question the Tsar and his sister.

The door burst open. Through the mirror, I watched Sofiya enter. A silk robe adorned her flush skin.

"Simeon is angry with me."

Dah. I spoke to my mother lots, but not when Sofiya sought a pity party. Then I bit my tongue. They had a routine. The siblings would fuck, and their son disappeared. He'd return with blood smeared or speckled across his gorgeous, brooding face, and he'd be satiated.

Clutching the brush handle tighter, I contemplated, put your child before your disgusting needs. Because they'd bought my freedom, I stared up at her with a look of respectful empathy.

"Simeon doesn't have an assignment this evening," Sofiya purred into my ear. Her fingers glided across the back of my hand. I let go of the silver-plated brush. Simeon's mother plucked it up and began to brush my tresses. "You have such gorgeous hair, Anastasiya. I have always loved how unruly it is. Then when straightened, it's spun silk."

My forced smile brightened at her compliment.

"As I was saying, our Simeon doesn't have an assignment this evening, moya Anastasiya." After each stroke of the brush, she'd glide her fingers through my fresh-pressed hair. "And he doesn't understand girls like us."

I caught her gaze through the mirror.

"Anastasiya, we love men who are different."

We love men?

We.

Love.

Men.

Should I love a man at my age? Kosta had tarnished the stars in my eyes already. She'd made me realize Volk wasn't my knight in shining armor. Sofiya was tempting me with old, taboo sentiments.

"Simeon is like his father." She smiled softly. "Their vices are in their powerful hands, Anastasiya. Simeon is seventeen now, you know. He's a man, one of power."

My mouth lifted, though I was confused as to what she was inferring.

She paused and placed a hand on my shoulder. "Nyet, don't speak yet, my child. Holding your tongue has always been your allure. Go to him now, Anastasiya."

I blinked a few times. Nobody knew the feelings I had for Simeon. He treated me like a little sister. What was she suggesting?

Her fingers bit into my shoulder, thin lips lifting at the edges. "Go, sweetheart. Now."

And I did.

At the door, I grabbed a robe.

"Nyet, sweetie," she called after me.

I glanced down at myself, my tanned legs on display. Simeon had always respected me. As a matter of fact, I'd have to stop myself from pouting when he took on the 'big brother' stance after I showed him a new dress. I didn't have much up top, but the frilly stuff around my chest and ass area puffed out.

"You are decent, my child. Go." This time the silk of her voice had fled, and it was all order. I exited my room for Simeon's. His room was just as vast as mine, though swallowed in masculinity, and the saddest of blues.

Simeon sat on the ground near the lengthy wall, which was filled from ceiling to floor with books. He was staring at his hands, and as his mother had said, they did wield power, although empty. Deadly dark eyes caught sight of me. A fraction of the animosity in those smoldering orbs fizzled out.

"I'm not reading to you tonight, Anastasiya. Go," he growled.

"Go. Everyone has their orders for me," I thought. I'd grown accustomed to our banter, but Sofiya warned me not to speak—something about her scared me. In trepidation, my bare feet stalled on the marble flooring. My gaze pleaded with him.

"Fuck," he growled, letting his face fall to his chest. He grabbed tufts of his dark hair. "I remember to the very day, the very fucking hour, I asked you to fucking stay, Asya. I don't mean go, go. Just return to your room, girl, please," he said, voice tense.

I stared. I could feel sadness seeping into my skin. Simeon was not a good person. He only loved his mother. But he tolerated me.

"Shit," he groaned. "Only you are capable of making me say please. I haven't done that since then too, and before that, never."

It was as if one false step would make Simeon forget the deal he made with the devil to save my life. At the opposite end of the bookshelf, I reached out to grab any book.

Simeon stole the space between us before my fingertips brushed the smooth leather.

His hand scooped my waist, and he snatched me to his powerful body. His movements were so quick that I stumbled over my own feet as he hauled me over toward his dresser.

"Anastasiya, you're aware of the routine now. The servants leave. That suka they call my father slinks away. Anatoly arrives, dah?"

Neck elongated, I nodded. Simeon yanked me back farther to him. A new type of fear settled in the pit of my stomach. Not the sort Oleg instilled in me at the Castle when I denied Volk. This was a delicious fear.

Where was Simeon headed? What was his intent?

While he stole much of the air from my lungs by squeezing my midriff, his other hand trailed down my jaw. "Anatoly didn't leave a single order for me. I don't have anyone to—I have no mission tonight." His gaze wavered over me. This was a time where Simeon still shielded *me from the devil in him. I knew he found relief in the Tsar's gruesome assignments.*

"I'm not a mudak like him, who expires anyone, just because. And we all know my capabilities."

I stared at his reflection in the mirror. Simeon glared back. Tonight, Mr. Hyde was skimming beneath the surface, and I was already madly in love with Dr. Jekyll. Mesmerized by Simeon, my mouth was agape.

"See this hand?" He continued to stroke at my neck. "It's usually buried in blood by now. Warm, soothing blood. A gun weighing my hand won't do . . . moya milaya. I crave something more intimate."

More of his body pressed against me as he reached over to grab a pair of scissors. The pointed tip slid down my neck, stopping at the pulse.

"You know how to stay away when Anatoly is here." The muscles beneath his jaw worked in anger. "For your safety. Do not cross paths with me tonight if I'm still around."

I blinked a few times. The truth froze in my light brown gaze. Dah, the demons in Simeon were more prominent when his father and mother sought each other.

"Fear vibrates through you." He slammed the scissors on the countertop.

Goosebumps lit across my skin.

"Heed those instincts, Asya. Go!"

~

"You're home." I jolt at the sight of Simeon on the edge of the bed. A dewy flush radiates across my skin from my luxurious shower as I step out of the en suite bathroom. The memory of him that one night still fresh in my mind. I'd been deliciously afraid, and I had never run so fast in my life. I had almost stalled the nerves curdling in my veins, but I knew what he craved.

Sex.

To this day, Simeon doesn't like to fuck when I'm afraid. I know that now. From that day on, Simeon had never tried me underneath the roof of his mother's home. Though I suspected Sofiya anticipated our connection would cool the beast in him.

The same smoldering hot, sultry desire radiates off him now. He's angry, and he wants to fuck. He's fisting a bottle of Resnov Water and downs the potent vodka.

"Sim, I have to tell you something," I murmur.

"Nyet. I've engaged in all the discussions I'll tolerate today," he grumbles. Those obsidian jewels blaze over me, and the hardness of his voice fades. "Listen, we made a promise less than seventy-two hours ago for me not to be so domineering, and you opened up to me more than ever. Though I appreciate you opening up, Asya, can this discussion wait until tomorrow?"

Sofiya screwed with his head enough for the evening. Four years have passed since Sofiya tossed an ax between us. What's another night? I nod slowly.

"Good. Tomorrow, I'll be the attentive, *Just* Tsar to my little Tsarina." A faint smile softens the edges of his lips before he cocks his head commanding me closer.

All of Sofiya's manipulations are blown to smithereens as I take his offered hand. A jolt of energy rushes through me like he's made of lightning. His metallic, testosterone-filled scent floods through me. Someone's death was on his hands today, and I can't quite connect the importance. Instead, his scent fills me with safety and desire. Hands laden with strength frame down my curves. His fingers stop on my hips, bruising my ample shape. Nails clutch my skin, and his mouth kisses and bites against my lower abdomen. Titillatingly slow, I arch into him. My frazzled brain is unable to determine what hurts more, the bites or the kisses. Each touch spirals through my soul, making the oxygen shake out of my lips.

"Simeon," I gasp, as his hand juts up and claims my breast.

"Shhh . . . Tomorrow we can discuss anything you'd like. In the next week or two, I promise to take you on a holiday. The two of us. Wherever the fuck my woman desires, dah?"

"Mmmm." I moan as he kneads a nipple between his thumb and forefinger. "Take me to a tropical island."

"Leg up."

In a swift agile movement, my left leg hooks around Simeon's neck. His fingers bite into the inside of my thigh, pain dissipating when his mouth plants there. He kisses his way up to seal his lips against the ache spreading across my throbbing folds. All the air is stolen from my lungs.

Simeon mops my sex with an electrically charged mouth. His other hand twines down my other hip, fingertips biting hard into my skin. The pain is enough to still the trembling in my weak limbs.

I lift my other leg off the ground. A violent wave crashes into me as Simeon descends to his knees and places my body down to the rug. His growls vibrate against my slick inner and outer folds.

Panting in air, I beg, "Simeon, fuck me."

Our bodies join together. The girth of him stings my slickness. The length of him digs deep inside of me. Simeon takes on a hard, punishing pace. With each thrust, my arched back slams against the floor. I'm drowning in kisses richly seasoned from the pleasure between my thighs.

"You're so fucking beautiful," Simeon groans into my neck. His voice surrounds me, seems to dig deep into my soul, stroking an urge I wasn't aware I had. The pain of him fucking me relentlessly on the ground shatters, and all that's left is me calling Simeon's name.

CHAPTER 6

Simeon

A primitive groan rises, my hips working like a piston. I'm soaring into the depth of Anastasiya's orgasmic ocean. Thrills shiver across her gorgeous curves, and she grunts out the rest of her wetness.

"Oh, oh, oh . . ." she groans, unable to form a true word.

Purple, oxygen-deprived lips beckon me for a taste. I reach down and feast on her mouth, her heart slamming at my chest. With Asya still breathless, I crush her breasts and ample body to the hard floor. My teeth sink into the meaty flesh of her ass. My hand claws at the back of her neck. The perfect arch of her ass causes my lips to plant at her tiny, puckered asshole. My tongue flickers over her exposed lips, licking the succulent sweetness she made.

I settle on my knees. If I were a fucking vampire, blood would be running down my chin. Instead, the saccharine taste of her sex drips over my lips and jaw. Licking it all up, I assault her pussy with my dick. My hand continues to claim the back of her neck as my member is swimming in her once more. I gather her hair into my fist, forcing her into a greater arch. Momentum surging, her quivering pussy is ready to squeeze my cock for dear life in another orgasm. When I let Anastasiya's hair go, she's mewing like our sex will be the death of her.

"Once more, moya milaya?" I trail a kiss along her shoulder as she bobbles her head. "Breathe."

"Please," Anastasiya purrs.

Laughter bursts from the depth of my abdominals. "It will have to hurt . . . and I really need you to cum before you pass out. So, breathe."

My sweet, little heart places her palms along the ground and pushes her ass back. Her luscious breasts are slapping around with each thrust. Swallowing air, she glances back and licks her lips. "I love you, Simeon. Hurt me."

My fingers trail over her wicked cunt as it puckers between her thighs. I press my lips to it, kissing the heated pulse of her fat, achy lips. Fuck, I could eat her pussy for every meal.

I blow at the pain, created from the force of my cock ramming so deep. With full force, I slam a hand onto the side of her ass cheek, sending it jiggling so hard that her cunt massages at my tongue. A quick succession of smacks at the same spot gives her warm skin a peach tone, and her lower back sags more.

"Good, you're catching your breath." I offer a wicked smile. My hand rubs at her throbbing flesh, and she sucks in more air. The pain of being swatted has her lungs full enough for me now. I reach over, grab my belt from my slacks, and slide it around her throat. When I yank on either side, my cock soars into her wet, swollen heat, pummeling her cervix. Each pound rocks through Anastasiya's core. Her walls stretch to accommodate, creaming with each slaughter. Before the carnal beating could steal her last ounce of oxygen, I give one last energized thrust. With a vengeance, I cum. My Tsarina's tight pussy meets me with the same renewed passion.

"Simeeeeooonnnnnn . . ." Her scream is enough to shatter the windows.

She's so wet. I fall into her wilted body as she gasps for air. Moving to my side, I bring her tiny frame on top of me.

She sniffles into my chest, burrowing herself closer. In a trembling, mess of a voice, she declares, "I love you. I love you. I love you, Sim."

Stroking at Anastasiya's hair, I kiss her forehead. "That's right, Asya. You love me, and I love you to death, girl. You're mine, now and forever, my little Tsarina."

"Remember our first time," she murmurs against me, a dreamy look on her face.

"How could I forget?" I pepper her face with kisses. "You look drunk."

"Ha, more like you banged out my brains." Red heat flushes up her cheeks, and she hides her face into my chest. "Simeon, I love you with all of me. Let's stay like this forever."

Time passes with me holding Anastasiya in my arms. Even when I was a caged animal and mystery surrounded her disappearance, I carried her with me. Now, I'm carrying her exhausted frame to bed.

More hours pass by. I'm contemplating how to revive my mother when Asya begins to whimper. Consoling her sleeping frame while nightmares pull her under is far from my mind after my mom's latest suicide attempt. I cup Asya's cheek, saying, "Wake up, moya milaya."

A last whimper seeps through Anastasiya's thick lips before her lashes flutter. A moment of terror seizes her eyes. Then they're liquid honey at the sight of me holding her near.

"What happened?"

She closes her eyes and presses near. "Bad dream."

"Tell me about it, Asya."

"I'm trying to sleep." Her eyes pop open again, shooting a warning before they close. "Remember the time you tried kicking me out of bed. You learned your lesson, Sim."

"Nyet, girl. I remember waking you up one time when you were snoring, happy fucking snoring, and you tried to kill me. This isn't it. *Talk*," I grit. Though I made a promise not to order Asya around, we must find a middle ground. She was just crowned my Tsarina, sheltering her is out. "Talk!"

"Dammit, Simeon!"

Anastasiya pushes away from me, and I zip my arms around her, bringing her body against mine. Her curves fit like a puzzle, soft and plush against my brittle stoniness.

Fisting the back of her hair, I bring her groggy gaze to mine. "I need you here, whole."

"What are you talking about? Why won't you let me sleep, mudak."

My hands frame her face. "Last night, you slitting that old fuck's throat, was it to appease me?"

"Fuck you, Sim. I'm not a robot, fulfilling your orders."

"Then what?" Her attempts to wrestle away are fruitless. "Asya, You've been playing the moral card. Enlighten me!"

"He was a Castle benefactor who didn't deserve to live. You satisfied, Simeon? I'm sleepy."

"Good," I press my lips to hers in a hard, searing kiss. "Keep your wits about you, Asya. When you feel uncomfortable about a situation, you act. I don't give a fuck if it's at the sake of a man's life. Instinct first. Deliberate later." I clear my head. I'd meant to talk about the dreams, but I have a feeling this all ties in together. "If you have any doubts, share them."

"I am," she sighs.

"Earlier tonight, you mentioned we need to talk."

Anastasiya's hand flies into the air, and I catch it. I pin her beneath me. "You're awake now, dah?"

"Wow. From a demon to a genius. Perfect observation, Simeon. I was dreaming bad dreams, so what! You can bully me later when I have a knife in my hand, you know, tip the scales in my favor a little. Though, I'd prefer a gun."

Light sparks in her eyes. The last part was a joke. I stroke her hair. "Your dreams. What of them?"

"Hey, you put pussy before connection. Right now, I'm placing sleep on the same scale. When the sun rises . . . I'm begging you!" she seethes through gritted teeth.

Half of me wants to shake the life out of her. Force out more truth. While I mentioned her instincts for the sake of her not second-guessing them, mine are blaring. I'm missing something.

But all in due time.

"Your dreams, Anastasiya. I have never throttled them out of you. Don't make me now."

Her eyelids close, swallowing rich, sparkling honey orbs, full to the brim with sadness and . . . Disgust? Confusion?

"Talk to me, moya milaya."

"Grrr! Okay, I had a nightmare." She starts into a seated position, legs folded over.

"I gathered. I woke you. Tell me."

Anastasiya shrugs. "Sim, can I collect my thoughts?"

"Spill them." Or I beat them out of you.

"Or what? You strangle them out of . . ." It's as if she realizes she's deflecting. She shoves a hand through her crimped hair. "I was in a room with this thing." Her voice reaches out to me, wrought, and laced in fear. I bite my tongue. My fists are so tight they are ashen. *Shut the fuck up, Simeon. Listen.*

"What thing?" I clip the rest of my query.

"An abomination."

I chuckle. "You're sleeping with one, Asya."

From her glare, I stop the attempt to lighten the mood.

"Simeon, you're a beautiful creation. The devil was the most attractive angel, right?"

"You're calling me . . ." I pause, grasping how I've played into her desire. "Don't change the—"

"Alright," she grits. "It was a girl or a woman. Simeon, she was like a robot. Bruised all over."

"Who caused it? How did you know her?" I ask.

"It's only a dream, Simeon." Anastasiya flops back onto the bed. I climb on top of her.

"A dream?" My eyebrows knead in thought. "Was it because of that girl you once saw? The one with the collar and the Middle Eastern owner? What was her name, Kosta?" I sigh heavily. "Did our actions that night give you bad dreams, Asya?"

Her gaze falls.

"I understand our actions scared you in the moment. You cared for her, and what you asked for, I obliged. Was the torture your dream?"

"No, Sim." Her voice floats over from a million miles away. She clears her throat. "You took my virginity that night, so definitely not."

The regret threatening at my tightened chest evaporates. "So?"

"It was a dream." Anastasiya's silk palm slides down my chest to my cock. "Bad dream. Will you make me feel better?"

"Then why are you shaking like a leaf, eh?" My eyebrow arches. The back of my hand skims the side of her cleavage.

"I—"

"I hate fear in you, moya milaya." I mop her breasts with my lips, my tongue gliding over the taut nipple. "Right now, I will fuck the fear out of your body. Because you've asked it of me. But when the sun rises, you *will* tell me the truth like we agreed upon."

CHAPTER 7

Anastasiya

"Simeon," I groan into my cellphone. The silk sheets crumple beneath my clutch. He'd promised me a tropical island soon. I covet the notion of escaping this world with him after I share Sofiya's deception. Now, his side of the bed is empty. "You offer endless orgasms, then leave me cold in the morning?"

A beat passes. "I'm headed to Syria—for us."

"Why? And no literary prose, Simeon. No using your doctoral degree in literature on me. Besides, you tried to force me to talk at an obscene hour. Come home; I'll chat now, under my terms."

He's smiling through the receiver, almost. I can feel it, yet undertones of intensity ride along. "Dah, I was a bit forceful last night."

"You were *old* Sim. *New* Sim crowned me. I'll talk to *that* Sim, as long as he's home in the next half hour."

Simeon chuckles softly. "Asya, if I bring you back the bloody head of a mutual enemy—"

"You don't . . ." My voice drowns. *You don't know my enemies, not yet, Sim.* "Which of my demands did you break?"

"The unnecessary stipulation." There's shuffling around in the background. Car doors are slamming. Simeon has a fleet of byki, and they're all prepared to do bad things. I grimace. Luka's old lover, Rudolf, had no part in our baby's murder. I'm certain the number of men surrounding him isn't a threat to Volk's army. So, I can assume he didn't go after the president. So, which of my rules did he break?

"Which one?"

"Anastasiya, I will have all the answers for *us*. This is for our mutual benefit. Then you and I will visit any destination on the globe."

Throat stifled, I manage. "You're searching for more information about our baby?"

"Dah." His retort strikes like usual. It's as if the last few days and all of his promises are seeping through my fingers. "I lost him or her, too."

I sigh. "This is about Rudolf then. Well, he had nothing to do with it, Sim."

A door seems to shut so hard glass shatters.

"What are you doing?" I sigh.

"Got out the car. Needed space." Simeon grumbles, adding truth to my imagination. "At your request, the majority of Rudolf's family returned to their homes. Only a token few were kept. The twins had his big brat overnight and gave word that Rudolf had an Armenian friend."

"You mean tortured? I'm sure they didn't have Rudolf's older brother over for dinner in one of your guesthouses?"

"Dah. I met him about an hour ago, and now he's dead," Simeon replies in a lethal tone. "The friend is in Syria. Say nyet, and I won't bring the mudak back for the two of us."

"Hard no, torture the bastard yourself." A tightness stitches my chest into a tight knot. "Because he could be innocent, Sim. I have continued to tell you why Rudolf wasn't the offender. He was my friend. Luka loved him. I sent him away that morning so he could prepare for their anniversary, *genius*."

"Will you wear the dress I chose for you for dinner tonight? We can have the chat about your dreams, and I'll oblige you, Asya. I'll keep the Armenian alive for a while, pending our chat."

"What dress?" I groan, the scent of us surrounds me and obscures all of Simeon's faults.

"The tailor made a few drawings. I chose one. Should be ready for you soon."

"Oh, God," I groan. "Is this the life of the Tsarina? I have to stand for fittings and wear dresses. Damn you, Sim. That was a strategic move to keep me out of your way today, right?"

I can hear the smile in his voice as he replies, "Black cherry pistachio ice cream will be your dessert. You'll be mine."

My body turns conspirator. The surface of my skin flushes in desire at the thought of being his craving. "Ha! I might not allow you to brainwash me with your tongue, Simeon. While you're away, I assume I'm still on lockdown?"

"For your safety."

"Alright, let me give you my orders."

I can almost hear him chuckle.

"Spare the Armenian's life until I say so. Send the person who's been in charge of acclimating the girls back to orphanages to me. I have questions about the adoption profiles I read over yesterday."

"The liaison, Faina, will visit you for lunch, and the Armenian will be in our cells by nightfall. You may wear the dress or nothing at all tonight but divulge all your worries. I may not grant all your wishes if they deviate from my own; however, I promise to listen, moya milaya."

A beam brightens my face. "Hmmm, not sure if your honesty is refreshing, but thank you, Sim, for scheduling the meeting. I'll be transparent, tell you everything." *Then you'll leave Rudolf's Armenian friend alive and focus on your mother.*

~

I n the passenger seat of the same Aston Martin SUV Luka drove yesterday, Simeon's promise echoes in my ears. Luka and I snuck out of the palace without any additional byki. But not until I begged him to. I needed to see Sofiya again, try to comprehend her story before I tell Simeon the truth. Tonight, I *will* purge. We're parked parallel to the townhome. Fresh snow dusts the shoulders of two byki in front of the stone structure. The soldiers eye us warily.

"My Tsarina." One bows. His eyes stay on the snowy ground as he adds, "I believe our Pakhan required more escorts for you."

"Thank you for your concern." I grin, moving my leather jacket to the side to flaunt my Colts. "I brought my two babies. This suffice?"

His eyes flicker toward mine and then down again. Hope, uncertainty, and fear of his life flash in his orbs for a second.

Luka places a hand on his shoulder. "My brat is the commander. I'm more than competent with the Tsarina. Move."

"Thanks," I mumble.

Luka rolls his eyes. I'd begged him before we left not to bring another byki because if my conversation with Sofiya didn't go well, I refused to ride home with a stranger. He'd tried to tempt me by finding a guard I'm familiar with, and I threatened to visit Sofiya on my own. My friend hoped for the best, so he nudged his chin and settled for a complacent mask instead of annoyance.

My fingers glide through his. "Can you not disappear while I talk to her this time?"

Luka gives my palm a firm squeeze. I start up the stairs with him behind me. A byki at the top of the steps gestures toward the double doors at the end of the hall. We enter a grand bedroom with opulent tapestry. The doors to the balcony are open. Sofiya is on a lounge chair. A throw blanket covers her bandaged wrists. I close my eyes for a second, hoping not to feed into her deception.

A few feet away, Garbovsky sits. The tip of his nose is red. His thin lips pinch together. Across from them is a panoramic view of an all-white forest. Vibrant, lustrous blood red buds are the only color, sitting stemless in a crystal vase of water.

"Mother Sofiya," I call, letting a smile slide onto the edges of my lips. *Please be all Anatoly's fault. Please don't give Simeon a reason to be disappointed.*

"Moya *docherniy*, daughter, you came." Water fills her sapphire orbs, and I pray she's genuine. "And Luka, you're as handsome as ever."

"Sir, may I?" I gesture toward her therapist.

He stifles a tremble and stands. "Of course. Please, either one of you send for me or a guard prior to leaving her side."

I nod. Noise funnels through my ears as Luka responds to his aunt's inquiries. She removes her arms from beneath her blankets. Her fingers glide across gauze as if imploring us to view the self-mutilation. "You're one of my only true family, Luka. You and Anastasiya. The two of you had nothing to do with this."

It curdles my stomach to collect Sofiya's hands in mine and soothe her. "You loved Anatoly so much."

"Dah." She brings our joined hands to her face and sobs.

Luka chews his lip in trepidation then claims Garbovsky's seat. Shit, he'll go all sorts of Prima Donna on me when we leave. I flash him an apology.

"Simeon did what he thought was right . . . he never understood your connection." I start to segue into more about Anatoly. Sofiya nods.

"That is true. Moy syn was confused. He only saw his father strike with an iron fist, rule as a Tsar must. The two of you will continue my Anatoly's legacy. You and Simeon will—"

"I apologize for my interruption, but I have to know. Mother

Sofiya, you were a-at m-my home," I stammer, "with the Armenians. I believe they were Armenians. I'm sorry for cutting you off,
but I need to know." *And I don't give a fuck about Anatoly.*

"They were Armenians. . ."

Her infinitesimal voice trails off, hardly meeting my ears. Or
maybe it's the blood rushing against my eardrums.

Licking my lips, I further inquire, "Did Anatoly coerce you into
assisting them?"

"Luka, will you," she arches an eyebrow, her gaze flitting
toward the door.

My friend glances at me. Emotion is wrought in his eyes,
mirroring my tangled reaction. Though it pains me to, my chin
dips in a slight nod.

Luka stops behind me, squeezes my shoulder, then retreats into
the house. My attention returns to Sofiya. The glacial wind sends
silver tendrils over her pale skin as she watches Luka close the
door. Then her lips curve into a sneer.

"I assumed you were too traumatized to recall. You
shouldn't—"

"I shouldn't what," I grit out, hands on my hips.

"*Recall*, daughter." She cuts each word, lips screwed up. "Anatoly
hadn't the slightest hand in that day, Anastasiya."

An ice wind surges through every muscle in my body, immobi-
lizing me.

"You were such a pretty flower, a rose, comparable to my
prized blood roses. Yet, I had pruned you all wrong."

Her fingers curve gingerly around the cluster of buds. She
plucks at a silky red petal. It falls between us. I crush it under my
boot.

"See, you understand quite well, moya *docherniy.* Your disposal
was necessary. Unfortunately, those idiots didn't follow through
with my orders."

My hand cleaves to the Colt beneath my leather jacket yet stays weighted at the back of my belt. Sofiya's empty eyes threaten me to follow through.

"I have nothing to live for, Anastasiya. Your presence ruined everything for me!"

I gargle on the word: "How?"

Blood rushing through my vessels moves so swiftly I cannot hear her twisted, jaded lies. I clamor to the doorframe, images of Simeon flitting through my mind. *If I kill her, he will torture me to death!*

On troubled legs, I head toward the bedroom door and out of the room. I grip the banister, my breathing labored, and start down the stairs. The floor below swims before my vision. Sofiya hasn't moved a muscle from her lounger on the balcony—and her filthy heart still beats. My only regret is that if she takes a short drop from her balcony, she might break her legs and not her scrawny ass neck.

Luka is starting out of the door when he turns around. "What the fuck, Asya?"

"Get me out of here," I growl low. "Get me out, before I strangle the life out of her, and suffer the ramifications with Simeon, later."

He calls out to the nearest byki, issues a few commands for them to go up the stairs. They're asking if Sofiya is all right, if I'm all right.

"Check on Sofiya," he barks. "Women's issues." He nods to me, shielding me with an arm.

We start out of the house and down the passageway to the SUV. Luka opens the door and ushers me inside.

"What happened, Asya?"

"Get me out of here before I kill you too!"

"Is she . . ."

"No!" I toss my fists at Luka's chest. His eyes seer over me again, and he slams the door.

I pull out my cellphone and dial Simeon. In my opposite hand, I weigh my colt. "Please answer or I might . . ."

The driver's door swings open. Luka hops inside as the voice-mail comes on. He bites his tongue.

"Simeon, I need you so bad right now," I strangle out. "Call me."

"What happened?" Luka parrots as I click the off button.

"Drive fast, or I might jump out, go back, and . . ." I hold up my shaking hands. All the love in the world is at the tips of my fingers. As an adolescent, I wondered if I loved Simeon more than myself at times for his role in setting me free. After our first fuck, I knew the truth. His love was my madness, my sanity, my all. "Drive faster, Luka," I growl in Russian, using the language I've spurned for years.

"The roads are slick!" The luxury SUV purrs as he steps a little harder on the pedal.

Bending the corner, Luka slows. Soft pinks break through the ultra-white flurry of snow and trees. My eyebrows knead together at the sight of a tiny gated area, leading to another road. On the gate are pink-painted padlocks in the shape of a heart. It's like a whimsical, petite version of Padlock Tree Park in Moscow. The image is dashed as Luka bends another corner. Tears blur my eyes.

Simeon and I had a locket there, and now, I want nothing more in the world than to shatter his mother's heart . . . like she did mine.

"Drive faster!"

"I can't!" Luka retorts, fisting the steering wheel. The pensive setting of his mouth and attentive look on his face cease my whining.

The rear tires veer to the left, though Luka hadn't turned the wheel. In an instant, we're flying around in circles. The side of my temple shatters the passenger window. The SUV tumbles over the slick asphalt.

Trees and blue skies.

Gravel and snow.

Trees.

Snow.

My vision is jostled from earth to the heavens with each flip. The airbags deploy, twisting my face sideways. My vision is obscured by the thick, airy cloth. The vehicle slams down an incline into the forest area.

My spine all but cracks when Luka's side of the SUV concaves, wedged against a massive tree. Whimpering with each move, I reach around, slide my gun beneath some of the material, and shoot. Then I do the same with Luka's airbag. Blood bubbles from his lips.

"Brat," I groan, every utterance escaping my trembling lips. "S-say you're alright, ple-please."

Luka's neck is twisted in an unnatural position against the steering wheel. When his eyes pop open, wet, hot tears drench down my face, burning at my cheeks. Everything hurts, and looking at him, my pain cannot compare.

"I-I can't move, sestra," Luka wheezes.

Warm, stickiness drips into my eyes, causing my vision to swim in redness. Blood from my temple mingles in with the tears. *Get up, Asya, no time to be weak.*

I mumble, "Give me a moment, Luka. I'll help you."

With a *thunk*, the passenger door whips open. Cold air trickles over my bruised body. In relief that someone had seen our accident, I drop the gun to the ground. The weight of it is too much for me to bear. An unfamiliar masculine voice calls out. He doesn't have a Russian accent, British maybe. Yet, this stranger identifies me—*by name.*

CHAPTER 8

Simeon

When Anastasiya called this morning, I'd been leaving the factory where the twins had kept Rudolf's older brother *comfortable* overnight. Now, I've climbed out of the backseat of an SUV, inside of an open hanger. The pilot is speaking with Kirill, and he's utilizing lots of gestures. People succumb to hand motions when they're at their wit's end. What the fuck is his problem? Kirill moves away from the jet and the pilot I'm not acquainted with and heads toward me.

"What the fuck, Kirill? Where is Tim?"

"Tim's too drunk to drive here, let alone fly, which isn't the problem, Pakhan. Traveling to Syria is."

"Who the fuck is he?"

"Again," Kirill groans, "Not the fucking problem. You called me sixty minutes ago. Every second since, I've attempted to gain clearance to land in Syria."

I curse underneath my breath. "We've landed there a lot. Get access from an airway we've used before."

"I've tried," he grits out. "Luka told me Chutin gave you drones and a horde of peace offerings since you've become Tsar. I'll ask—"

"Not an option!" I cut in, forking a hand across the bristles at my jaw. The mudak was never a friend of mine. He can shove all those drones up his fucking ass. "You had ample time to make this happen."

"With all due respect, I've been kissing an entire country's ass, so that we aren't *shot the fuck down* by entering its airspace. We have yet to gather the appropriate authorization. The few commissioners I spoke with, they're working on a backlog. That's where Chutin comes in. Make a friend in him, Kazen."

I run my knuckles over my bottom teeth. Following Anastasiya's requests were impossible. Our child deserves this, and so I force down the guilt gnawing at my gut.

"Get me into Syria now!"

Kirill's cellphone vibrates in his slacks. He pulls it out. "Excuse me, Tsar, this looks like the one last hope I had. They're calling now. May I?"

"Answer it. If the person on the other end of the line hard balls you, asking for more capital, threaten their entire lineage!"

CHAPTER 9

Anastasiya

A mass of swelling flesh mangles Luka's features. His face slumped against the steering wheel, Luka's only movement is that of his shocked gaze and tensed lips. "Who are you?" he asks the stranger.

"Nobody," replies the British man. My gut screams that he isn't just a helpful bystander.

"How do you know my name?" Each word shudders from my lips with effort. The pounding in my head refuses to cease, but I spit out, "We're *Resnovs*."

"I'm well aware, luv. Sorry for hosing down the road back there. I know it was already frozen, but I had to get your attention." The Brit reaches inside my door. Something pricks against the side of my neck.

He injected me with a substance, which causes an autonomous response. Liquid fills my mouth. I can't gulp it down fast enough.

"The name's Trick. Don't worry. My job is to deliver you," his British voice purrs against my cheek. My fingers shake profusely. All the muscles in my body seem to be shutting down. All the power left sparks at my nerve endings. "It's your typical drug, luv. By the way, you won't recall a thing once you fall into a nice slumber. I use it when I'm *knackered*. Best sleep of my life, I always say."

His leather-clad hand picks up my Colt. He places it into my palm and nestles my finger on the trigger. Devoid of consent, I'm training the gun toward Luka.

No, no, please stop! Screaming jars at my brains but won't break free. Tears fill Luka's eyes. Unable to move, he watches us.

"Well, mate, I'm the man who has been paid dearly to transport your gorgeous friend here. And because my primary gig is assassin, someone has to meet their maker. So, it'll have to be," the gun goes off. The power in the recoil is enough to jolt my limp wrist. "*You.*"

Trick scoops me into his arms. My body weighs heavily into him. My face lulls against his hard chest. He stands there. The snow-capped trees around us are dwarfed in comparison to the Brit. He's omnipotent, superhuman. Something in his eyes is sad, though. As his gaze tracks over my face, contentment shines through.

He reminds me of Simeon. The world did something to him, and now his enjoyment resides in the darkness. He won't kill me. And he's already claimed to be the delivery boy, so what enemy has caused this. A ghost of a smile forms on Trick's thin lips. He has secrets that he refuses to tell.

"You're a strong one, eh." He clicks his tongue and readjusts his hold on my body.

As he trudges down the incline, frigid cold causes tears to crystalize across my cheeks. He places his mouth a fraction away, the warmth of him removing the burning chill on my skin.

Absorbed in assessing the Brit, I notice how he's no longer trudging. I can't swivel my head around, but from my peripheral, there's a road. We've traveled all the way down the incline to the next opening. SUVs line the area.

"You said she'll forget?" A voice as familiar to me as my own reflection in a mirror calls out.

"That's right. Usually takes about five to ten minutes for 'em to be totally knackered. This little lass is a beast." Trick praises me, squeezing me tightly again.

Kosta is in my face, holding up a piece of paper.

Trick rolls his eyes. "What is this? My job is done. How about you have the girl-fight when the score is even, luv?"

She shoves the paper against my nose. Vision starting to fade, I focus harder. "You wrote this to me, Anastasiya. The truth while you stood at my door in Italy for the longest. Then you left that piece of shit short little note in its stead. I rather like this one!"

"I'm a tad unamused by your need to argue." Trick stiff arms her. "She's falling asleep, *and she will not remember, lass.* So, fyi, you remind her about me later, I'll kill you in ways you can't fathom. This may be personal for you, but this is just a job for me. It's time to get moving."

"No need for threats. I'm almost to my point." Kosta's angry eyes flash at me again. "I found the real note. The truth must've fallen from your pocket when you left the hostel. But don't worry, that pathetic apology you left me, well, Simeon will find it now. Seems fitting since you left me twice. Now you left the mudak twice, suka!"

That day comes to the forefront of my mind. *I'd fleshed out every misdeed on the notebook paper I received from the Italian who had a room across the way. Kosta had always been my weakness, and I'd apologized for more than was necessary. Then I balled it up and placed it into my pocket. The note I left read,*

"Though it seems I've abandoned you twice, you have to know how much I've always cared. For now, all I can give you are my—"

Kosta's words are still ringing in my ears before I'm drowning in darkness.

Kosta should've understood no matter what happens, we gravitate toward each other. I didn't want to rectify all my wrongs on a piece of paper. I wanted to be woman enough to apologize to her face once and for all. And if she didn't care, as Luka had claimed, then fuck her.

Guess the joke is on me.

CHAPTER 10

Simeon

With my spine wedged against the butter-soft leather seats, I watch the colorful city I love so much shift past in a blur. Gray vapors start to surround the jet as it levels out in the sky. I'm en route to Syria, to more answers surrounding my child's death, and all I can think about is Anastasiya. Instincts urge me to reach out.

I wrestle my cellphone from my slacks to see the damn screen shows "do not disturb." "Fuck," I mumble. I'd mindlessly pressed it after our chat because she was safe. And I didn't want to hear her mouth until I gave her answers.

But she's left me a voicemail. I press the message button. All the while, I continue to remind myself the woman I love is safe. Ligaments in my frame become rigid. Listening to Asya's distraught message, I'm slammed back into the moldy, dank cell in the Black Dolphin, where I waited and waited for her to visit.

"Stop the jet," I order a byki.

"What is it?" another byki inquires.

"Kirill, dial Luka," I order, attempting to return Anastasiya's call. Anxiety torments the pit of my stomach. My woman's previous voicemails were shock-filled worry dedicated to my mother. This one scared *her*.

It doesn't ring.

"Kirill," I grit out, testy. Out the windows, the city, which had whirled away, has returned into view.

"I'm waiting, boss . . . Fuck! My brat's mobile went to voicemail."

While he disconnects and dials again, the jet begins to shift around. I order calls to our forces at home. Kirill mumbles about an incoming call, then curses under his breath.

"What?" I growl, as the nose of the jet begins to guide toward the strip again.

"Nothing, boss. It was Faina, the liaison. She's arrived for her lunch meeting with Asya. But the entire compound is blocked off."

I try the front gates myself.

"I'm tracking my brat's phone." He pulls the holder from his shoulder-length hair and gives the blond strands a nervous shake. "There's less cell service in the theater. That's it. Those two always watched movies together. Luka's intelligent. He reaches out when necessary. They have orders not to leave the grounds without a detail. In case, I'll track his phone."

My cellphone lights up. My body slightly jolts as the wheels of the jet kiss the ground. "Tsar, I'm sorry to say," a byki speaks into the receiver. "The car Luka used yesterday isn't in the lot. I'm waiting for all the servants to finish a sweep of each room . . . but I thought you should know that. Please forgive me."

"*Of course, you're forgiven because when I see you, you're dead.*" I hang up the phone, then unlock my belt and climb from the seat.

Kirill reaches the door first and activates the lever. "I have Luka's cellphone location, Anastasiya's too. They're together, Kazen. No movement. Maybe they had a blowout."

"Where the fuck are they? Asya loves to defy me. Are they headed toward one of the Castles?" I attempt to calm myself. Maybe she couldn't wait for Faina to discuss what happened to the girls?

"Nyet. An hour away from us . . . about five minutes from Aunt Sofiya's. There's a clearing in the road." He gestures toward another byki. "Grab the pilot. Let's take the helicopter to get there sooner."

~

F isting my cellphone, I allow my eyes to rove over freshly impacted snow as I'm seated in the backseat of yet another car. The chopper landed a few kilometers north at a clearing. Beam was in position to transport us the rest of the way.

I glare at Kirill. There's no implication of a blowout—or any signs of a vehicle. Mother Nature has been known to turn tragedy into beautiful, white serenity. But my gut warns bad shit happened here.

"Boss," Beam murmurs, slowing down around a snowy crook.

I glance through the windowsill. A fleet of *politsyia,* police vehicles, are parallel parked at the side of the road. The only proof of a car crash is from the uniform officers uncovering scrap metal. Based on the number of vehicles, the majority of them have taken a hike down the summit.

"I'll handle it," Beam suggests, opening my back door.

"Now, why the fuck would I sit here and wait?" I grit, my hand claiming his throat as I climb out of the car. A pale ruddiness descends on his face as his breathing continues to be restricted. "You see me getting out of the car. Then you shut the fuck up. I ask, you speak! I do, you motherfucking follow. Dah?"

The second I remove my vice grip around his throat, Beam issues a swift nod. He then doubles over to hack. Eyes are on us. The *politsyia* bagging fragments and capturing photos pause to

67

stare. A few lower their heads—this isn't an altercation for them to handle.

"Who's in charge?" Kirill clears the air.

The *politsyia* closest to us nods his head in a sign of respect. "My apologies, Mr. Resnov. We arrived on the scene approximately twenty minutes ago. Some of our men are still attempting to reach the car. Given the circumstance, we had yet to know the vehicle belonged to you. Our men are still working their way down the crest. It looks bad . . . Should we leave?"

Should they leave? Bratva and *politsyia* affairs seldom cross. I have my higher-ups in the department. And there are those who do not appreciate the Resnov presence.

Puffs of condensation are emitted with my command, *"Leave."*

The politsyia whistles to the team, working along the impacted snow. "Let's pull out," he says.

The private farthest from us, shouts down the bevy, "Let's g—"

His order is cut off by another command from down below. The request is for. . . *homicide.*

Dazed, I start down the decline. My boots slip, and my hands cling to the snow. Kirill jolts past me, then sinks into an even deeper snowdrift. His face, ghost-white, mirrors the horror spinning through my veins.

"Fuck," I grit, righting myself. I gain speed and run down the mountain. With each step, my shoe sinks a foot.

"Move, suka!" I shove the back of a struggling *politsyia* in front of me and continue to trek down. I weave around trees and grip at branches along the way.

About fifty yards below, cops are surrounding a piece of metal, custom pearl black, measuring two feet in any given direction. My Anastasiya is tiny, but even she couldn't fit inside. Blood funnels through my ears. My heart jolts in my chest.

"Who the fuck is dead?" Kirill grabs the first cop by his collar, rattling him.

"A male, approximately twenty to thirty years old."

"And the girl?" I growl.

"Nyet, girl."

～

An hour later, the majority of the *politsyia* have left the scene. The body was identified as Luka Resnov. Not a second later, I bashed his brat between the eyes, sending a postal Kirill straight to sleep.

"I need fucking order and answers." I grab one of the byki by the face, my fingers digging into his jaws. I shake his head with me, "Dah?"

"D-dah, Tsar."

I've already assessed the scene. One single bullet. Had an enemy murdered Luka, the hunk of shit that was craned up the slope would've been riddled with bullets. *Take the queen* pops into my head. The most sought-after crash specialist in Russia is assessing the scene. A Bratva detective is reviewing Luka's body but the words continuing to whirl through my mind are . . .

Take the motherfucking queen.

CHAPTER 11

Mikhail

I'd prepared to leave Mother Russia, a place which I've never referred to as 'home.' The country where monsters named Simeon get everything, even innocent jewels named Anastasiya. Though I thought it was unfathomable, my father, Malich, saw fit to bury our mother here. After a visit to her grave, I'd downed my favorite cocktail, pills and scotch, packed, and surfed my phone's internet for cheap airfare to L.A.

Swinging the duffle bag over my shoulder, I walk out of the palace. A few feet away, I stop and stare up at the fortress.

"Where the fuck are you, Anastasiya?" I mumble to myself. Perhaps she's out governing, tainting her soul in Simeon's delights. I wanted to say goodbye. My mouth tips at the thought. The cool evening sends a shiver through me. "No goodbyes, Mikhail, and not because of it sounding sappy. You planned to play Russian roulette with your life again."

I had deliberated while packing one single duffle bag that I'd kiss her. Kiss the fuck out of her. Cross my fingers and hope the similar feelings swarming through my heart sparked in Anastasiya's too. I'm not a wistful man. The first and only item I've stolen was my father's stethoscope while crawling around. From that day forward, concrete evidence ruled my life, the rush of adrenaline from the ER. Sex with beautiful women did have a place in my *downtime* list, not love.

Closing my eyes, the trappings of success and reasons Anastasiya stayed fade from my view. I meander over the powdery ground to the bodyguard nearest the fleet of import vehicles.

"Hey, may I have a ride to . . ." My voice trails off. We stare about half a kilometer out. An SUV coasts along the lengthy road. Second thought, I'll ask whoever is driving. My last name should at least bum me a free ride to the airport. I'll sleep on the plane and head straight to the community hospital to begin my shift. There's no need to hear arguments from my mentor about flaking out on another opportunity since Igor's death.

The luxury vehicle stops right in front of me. A familiar bodyguard exits the driver's side, opposite to me. "You, give me something to sedate your kazen with now!"

My eyebrow cocks. *Simeon? Sure, I'll have him in an induced coma for the next hundred—*

The SUV jolts around. Glass crashes outward from the backseat. I jump back as a foot goes slamming out of the back window.

"Sedation, now!" The driver orders, opening the back door. He heaves forward, and I start around the limo-tented windows to get a good look. My cousin, with the thick neck and no brain, is being dragged out of the backseat.

Kirill shouts, "My brat, my brat—"

The driver forces his body onto Kirill's upper area. Another man is kicked on the opposite side of the vehicle. They maneuver around, holding him down. With the swiftness of a doctor prepared for the ER, I retrieve a vile from my bag, and I administer a dose of propofol. While Kirill continues to wriggle around, I stab him in the neck.

The driver slides out of the car. Huffing, he falls to the ground.

I hold out a hand.

"Thank you, Mikhail," he stands. "Shit, I could use a little of what you're giving."

"What's happening?" I ask.

He shuffles a shaky hand through his hair. "Luka's dead. Anastasiya was taken."

"*Missing*," the other bodyguard grits, climbing from the backseat. "Killed Luka, fled is what she did. History repeats itself."

"What the fuck are you talking about?" I stroll toward him. "She's your Tsarina! What you're saying is treasonous."

"Listen, the Tsar, Kirill, we all saw the scene. We all observed the crash area. An enemy would've left a ransom note or a little token: the girl's head, toe, a fucking tattooed finger. Something. Four years ago, the Tsarina left . . . good men paid the price for her weakness. Luka was her brat, and she mur—"

A shot slams through his skull. The driver places his gun back into his slacks. "You'll be my witness as to his lack of loyalty, won't you, Mikhail?"

"Tell me everything!" Discarding my duffle bag on the ground, I pick up Kirill's legs, and the driver grabs his shoulders. I wish I had laced and downed a few more glasses of scotch before heading back toward the lion's den.

CHAPTER 12

Anastasiya

Peaceful darkness invites me to stay in paradise. Essential oils permeate the air and funnel through my lungs. Throat vibrating in a delicious moan, I peel my eyes open only to preview heaven on earth. Candles flicker. The bed of clouds melded to my frame has exceeded the tranquility of the one Simeon and I shared at the palace.

"Hmmm . . ." I groan, captivated by invigorating tingles in my muscles. Had I just been given a massage? Simeon promised a tropical island, and yet I don't recall the purge of sharing—What did I need to share? "Sim—"

"Nyet," is issued with a leveled breath. "Awaken my little krasivaya. We mustn't mention such atrocities anymore."

Gasping in air, I jolt into a seated position. A white, lace gown brushes abrasively at my skin, burning from the fire shining in the eyes of the man staring at me. A man who once coaxed my innocent heart years before I met the family I was predestined to hate.

"Atrocities?" I gulp, fixated on the specific word, and not the blaring truth. Candlelight flickers across gleaming tapestries, ornate walls, and glittering jewels. The four-poster bed rivals the one I share with Simeon, and he is nowhere around.

"Make no mention of *The Young Resnov*." Volk removes his hands from the pockets of his suit. The material drapes over lean muscles. More crinkles have aligned his attractive face.

"Anastasiya," he murmurs. Desire flashes across his molten blue eyes. He settles on the side of the bed. My arms start to lunge out at him and then are yanked back by manacles.

"What has the Young Resnov done to you, krasivaya?" Warm concern drenches over his face as he glances at tattoos on my knuckles. "Blemished your skin, claimed you like an animal. You're safe now."

"No," my voice grows hoarse. "I was safe, okay?"

Volk's pupils dilate. His mouth is a fraction from my mouth. Bile churns down my throat as his lips crash onto mine. His tongue slithers in monotonous rhythm. Volk's breath skirts across my jaw as he pulls up for air.

Still in shock, I implore, "Will you let me go? You've always cared for me. I must return home. Simeon will be looking for me."

Volk laughs a little. "He cannot find you. Although, it's possible if the Young Resnov contains his emotions and utilizes his intelligence—*he will die*."

"*Irek*," I grit the Volk's true name. President Irek Chutin, the man whose power exceeds that of any Bratva. "Irek, I didn't ask for this."

As he ponders my words, Irek's lips suck into his mouth. "You have choices, Anastasiya. Most essential—reconcile with the man who loved you *first*."

"I was a little girl!" I gasp. "It was wrong!"

"Those are lies force-fed to you, Anastasiya." His hands claim my face, lips targeting mine.

The previous bout of disbelief doesn't latch on. I growl, "Truth!

I was nine when we met. The thought of kissing you a second ago makes me want to drink industrial cleaner!"

Irek runs the back of his hand along his wet jaw. "The Young Resnov came to see me once. He had a tantrum, started a fire. Aside from having my life flash before my eyes, he made me realize something."

"What."

"I learned how I'd never be over you. There was a girl that night, too, when that savage came by. She resembled you in age, mannerisms, looks. Notwithstanding her mixed heritage, she lacked your spunk, albeit she learned to submit. To say the things you said, to fear me as you did."

"I never feared you!"

A fond memory softens the fine grooves in his face. "You feared my disappointment, Anastasiya. That if you didn't regurgitate precisely what I taught you about a certain piece of art, you'd no longer have my love. You were perfection. You passed the test."

Again, I reach out to lunge at Irek while he rises from the bed. "What test?! My life is not a game, mudak!"

Irek unbuckles his belt. His eyes sear into mine.

"What's your plan? To hit me because I'm the same breed as Simeon? I love him. I hate every part of you."

"You love the Young Resnov, yet you won't speak Russian? Ha! Hit you? Nyet." His barely there lips move into a devilish grin. The nickname, Volk, had come from a naïve, young girl's need to recategorize a man she once adored. But he is the fucking Wolf.

The monster, the scum. I lunge my knees together to shield a part of myself from him. Irek had a claim to my soul years ago, though he never touched my virtue. My sex belongs to Simeon.

"If-If you touch me," I choke out the words, "I will kill you, Irek. Not a single man on this earth will stop me from tearing you in half! Don't you dare touch me." *Please, please, don't touch me. Simeon, where are you? What happened?*

Irek unleashes his belt, lets it fall to the ground. In a debonair

75

manner, he removes his cufflinks. A low, pleasing hum of enjoyment emits from his abdomen.

"Remember the well-educated young lady I trained you to be, Anastasiya."

Clothing tailored for him alone slides to the ground. Continuing to hum, Irek removes a small set of scissors from his pocket. He gestures toward my gown. "May I?"

"No, please, n-no," I croak. *C'mon, Asya, fight him. Do something, save yourself, you stupid suka!*

With meticulous care, the fine, hand-sewn lace shreds down the center. The humming stops. Irek licks his lips and unsheathes my breasts. The warmth of him slithers across my nipple. Rearing my chin back, I headbutt him. Too frantic. I've connected with his jaw. All the stars meant for him dance before my gaze.

"Uh oh, you shouldn't have done that," Irek replies in a playful tone. He climbs from the bed, grabs his belt, and twirls each end around his fists. I scream as the leather strap confines my throat.

The pressure applied to my throat teases, pulls at my oxygen. Wetness blurs my gaze as Irek aligns his body over mine. This is my last chance to save myself from him! I'm bound, but the mudak cannot silence me.

"Irek . . . please. *You* love me." My lips tremble on each enunciation. Gathering conviction from deep down in my soul, I repeat, "You love me. I am not a Castle Girl. I am not one of them. I'm the one you have loved so much. So, so much."

Irek stops shoving my legs aside. His forehead falls, only to kiss my jaw. His breath skirts across my skin in a heavy sigh.

"I am not a Castle Girl," I sniffle.

"True. Your value far exceeds those whores. You've been corrupted, my love," Irek murmurs in my ear. "Only I can fix you . . ."

Crushing my eyes closed, I wait for him to invade my body. I suddenly have one last desperate thought that might save me.

"Our first time," I strangle out. "You want it to be special."

Oxygen depleted lungs squeeze in my chest. Then I choke on air like I've come up from a thousand miles below the ocean's surface.

Irek moves from between my thighs. His lips are a tight line. His gaze dances over my nakedness before settling confidently on my pupils.

"Forgive me for my momentary lapse in judgment, Anastasiya. After all these years, our first time should occur under mutually favorable circumstances. Once you are reinstructed, we will have our special night."

Without warrant, my lips tremble at the thought of what could have been. He almost stole a part of me that I've only ever granted to Simeon. Irek clears his throat, redressing. Tears flood my eyes. I blink back blurred vision because I'm still *in* his presence. What's to determine that the Volk won't break?

"Let us resume our proper course." Irek moves across a room as grand as the Resnov palace to the double doors. The illumination is faint, yet I perceive two armed guards in the hallway. Irek speaks with one of them. Then from the shadows, sauntering into the room is the Resnov Castle Girl whom I love more than blood.

"Kosta!" I jar at my confines. "Help me, sestra."

"She . . . does . . . *not* . . . remember." Kosta's lips pull into a vicious line.

My eyebrows stitch. "What don't I remember?"

"I saw you taken this morning, sestra," she declares, sauntering forward. "Actually, I saw you earlier than that. It was from afar when the Brit assisted me in entering the palace, undetected."

"What are you talking about?" My eyebrows pin together.

"Eh, a note that I left at the palace. But more about that later." Her sneer raises into a full-on grin. "Earlier, what I did bring to your attention, before your bout of amnesia, is how I'm done with you, Anastasiya. How you love Sim—"

Kosta falls to her knees. A bullet pierces between her eyes. The trajectory sends blood and skull fragments splattering across the linen at the foot of the bed. White-blonde tresses fan away from her scarred cheeks as the rest of her body catches momentum. The side of what was the rest of her face slams against the glossed wood floors.

Irek places a gun into a carved box. "She was a plague, krasivaya."

I sob. "Why?" Apparently, portions of time are missing based on whatever Kosta was talking about before . . .

"Kosta reached out to my associates, indicating that you needed me. I flew her in from Italy of all places." He pauses, a condolence smile inserted at the edges of his mouth. "Kosta assumed seeking my assistance would serve as some sort of punishment for you. But I'm here to rectify my wrongs. Nobody will stop us. Not the Young Resnov . . . or any assets at his disposal because today doesn't exist. Every satellite, every server that picked up my profile, even my own security network, is being reconfigured to a day in the near past. Then there's the tricky part of actually accessing this false data since it's all encrypted."

"What do you mean?"

"That I covered all my bases. You were never here. With regard to anyone using technology, searching for you, you've vanished." He claps his hands together. "Now, I will help you become the gorgeous girl we all once knew."

I bite down on my tongue, too infuriated to say a single word.

"Now, your training must resume."

My pupils expand as a nightmare comes to fruition behind Irek. A tendril of fear wraps around me, igniting into an inferno at the horror. Throat clamped, I strangle out one single word, "Oleg."

CHAPTER 13

Simeon

With the most sought-after P.I. in Russia and forensic engineer, I have all the answers conceivable. All of them point to Anastasiya.

The investigator arrived on the scene about an hour after the *politsyia* departed. He and his crew were provided all the details the sergeant left behind. The handmade bullet in Luka's dome was a precise match to either one of Anastasiya's custom Colts. Now, the rest of my faith rests on the forensic engineer's last assessment of the clunk of crap Luka was removed from.

I'm seated at a desk in my office. Crash photos lay scattered atop it. My eyes are weary from processing hundreds of them. More to go. Fuck, this looks bad. My head tilts up toward the vaulted ceiling. I issue out a long heave. "What the fuck happened, baby?" I mumble, refusing to believe the love of my life is dead. She didn't kill Luka either.

But from the outside looking in, Asya murdered blood, a Resnov. *But she's my Tsarina.* This has to be a setup. The Table of seven, nix my mother, had no qualms with any of the moves I've made over this past year. Anatoly's termination wasn't my lightning in the bottle or tied to my security as leader. Dominicci's downfall was a turbulent move. I pushed the limit, reaped the rewards. Now, the only woman I will ever fall in love with is missing.

"She's my enemy." The foreign statement settles around me. I wrestle the desk drawer open, grip the neck of a bottle of Resnov Water, and open it. The vodka becomes a smooth scorch to my throat.

She has to be somewhere, afraid . . . but . . . what if? Maybe she did do something stupid. She's crazy, but she's always been my kind of crazy. I tell myself the day I placed a crown on her head and called her my little Tsarina didn't overwhelm her. It did not result in this catastrophe. I force myself to believe someone else tossed a literary *red herring* into our love story.

My mind is reeling. I swig more vodka. At the knocking at the door, I grunt.

Dot enters and bows before me.

"Dah?" I growl.

"Dominicci is recuperating as expected. None of our byki stationed in Italy can attest that he had a single hand in this. I've reached out to our brotherhood, none of our enemies are bragging—"

"Or acting in a manner which would imply they have Anastasiya," I cut in. Beam slinks into the room, positioning himself next to his twin. My eyes seer into Dot's, and I growl, "What of *your* president, Chutin?"

Dot clears his throat. "We-we have hackers attempting to infiltrate security videos at his homes—"

"And?" I cock a brow. I lift my gun, weighing it in my palm.

"His vacation homes are impenetrable, let alone his political offices," Beam interjects.

I point the barrel at him. "Was I addressing you, Beam. Dah or nyet?"

His voice lowers. "Nyet. I apologize."

I gesture with my gun, and the twins arise. Aside from Kirill, who's conveniently sedated, these two mudaks are my best. As they exit, Mikhail hesitates at the threshold.

I target his forehead. "Do enter, Kazen."

He rolls his eyes, takes a few uneasy steps before stalking into the room. "I was about to give Kirill another dose when your door finally opened."

"Did I request updates?"

"Can you put that thing down, please!"

I cock the hammer, and a bullet flies from the chamber. Catching it, I hold it up for Mikhail. "These are custom-made *hollow tips*, Mikhail. Do not insult me. Where were you today?"

His blue eyes narrow slightly, then he teeters out a chuckle. "I'm a suspect now? Or have you forgotten I'm family? I'm concerned about finding Anas—"

"Don't," I growl from deep in my abdomen. "It's Tsarina to you, Mikhail." *And to everyone else, therefore, I need to find her and straighten this situation out.*

"How can I help, Simeon?"

"You haven't answered my question."

"Oh, sure, about my day." Mikhail plops down in the chair across from my desk. "I bought flowers in town, saw my mother's grave. Thought to head home—"

"Dah. You had a flight." I glance at my Rolex. "Leaving in approximately twenty-three minutes."

"Why question me? How about you find our Tsarina?" He sighs. "Listen, you're my cousin, Simeon. We've never engaged in a real disagreement until last week. We had a simple misunderstanding. How can I help?"

"Doctor Resnov, you have no skills here. No benefit unless it's saving a life. When I find out what happened to Asya, you'll become necessary via keeping the tortured alive. You may go."

Something flashes in Mikhail's eyes. I'm about to threaten his life when Kirill stumbles into the room. He falls to his knees. "Tsar, I have to make a request."

"Don't speak." I start out of my seat. If I were to have a full-blooded brat, I'd mirror Kirill. Nobody harms a single hair on the head of someone I love.

"What's wrong, Cousin?" Mikhail asks.

Kirill looks from him to me, biting back hard tears. His loyalty to the throne is wavering.

I stand before him and help him up. I plant my hands at the back of his neck. "Kirill, you're my right hand, dah?"

"Dah." His chest rises, skin burning hot from the rage.

"You had to take a short nap after witnessing our little Luka, and you know how much I love my kazen, dah?"

His thick neck becomes more constricted as he nods.

"And I know how much you love your brat, and you require justice. We all do. If I let you stay awake, will you assist in finding Anastasiya? She must not be touched, Kazen." My hands swing from around the back of his neck to his throat.

"What the fuck are you doing, Simeon?" Mikhail gasps.

I squeeze tight. "Because if my Anastasiya returns harmed in any way under your orders, Kirill, I will bring you back to life after a thousand times of me killing you and kill you again."

"Sim, Kirill would never . . . We all love the Tsarina."

Mikhail, a good doctor, a bad judge of character. Men like Kirill and I feed on vengeance. I let Kirill go, pushing him back. He doubles over, rubbing at his throat and hitching air into his lungs.

"Tsar, you will always have my honesty," Kirill grumbles. "If I see Asya, I'll kill her."

My eyes close briefly. *Nyet! You're my most efficient asset and most trusted byki, Kirill.* Seconds later, the ponytail elastic holding Kirill's hair falls off. He hits the ground, unconscious. Gritting my teeth, I shake the sharp needles shooting through my knuckles. Our eldest cousin blinks a few times.

"Mikhail, I stand corrected." I gesture toward our insensible cousin. "Utilize your capabilities. Keep him asleep."

His eyebrows pull into a line. "He's angry with Nas—Anastasiya?"

"Mistakenly confused, albeit very angry." I wave him out of the room. Mikhail grips Kirill's limp hands and starts back toward the door.

CHAPTER 14

Anastasiya

Mutism, as a child, stopped me from staring into the empty pits of the Invisible Thing's eyes. It restrained the need to vomit the entire lining from my throat when Oleg conquered Kosta. Once Simeon came along, I, instead, died of the shyness of his presence. His confidence. His capabilities. All of him enraptured me.

Now, I'm incapable of crawling into the corners of my mind.

Now, this fucking nightmare descending around me won't break.

No waking.

No hiding.

A female servant uncuffs me. The two bodyguards who were outside the door hold guns targeted in my direction. The servant removes what's left of the white, lace dress, leaving me bare and ashamed before Irek's hungry eyes. Oleg gawks, not tearing his gaze away even to blink.

"Enjoy the sight of her," Volk warns Oleg. "This is the last time you will see my Anastasiya undressed."

Oleg has yet to speak. Zealous glee glints in his eyes. Though older, he still has a build like Simeon. His suit drapes over fine cut muscles. Manic intensity surrounds him as the servant slides a thermal over my shoulders. Her touch is delicate. Oleg's eyes follow her movements, stopping on my nipples as the material brushes past there.

Resisting my body's urge to run, I square my shoulders and stare into the eyes of the man who ruined Kosta. He almost ruined me too. Irek clears his throat, detesting the connection Oleg and I share.

Again, Oleg's eyes square at the apex of my sex as the servant slips a pair of panties on me.

"Lady, you disgust me," I murmur, lifting one foot after the other to accommodate her.

Her eyes meet mine for a fraction of a second, yet I'm the one who glances away. Years ago, I allowed Oleg to harm Kosta. I never fought for her with the same vigor she fought for me. Oleg plundered her mouth on many occasions and screwed her in my presence. I was about as complacent as the maid who's finishing me off in jeans and boots.

The maid reaches for a goose down jacket when Irek clears his throat. With submissive, tiny steps, she exits the room.

"For the next month or year," Irek licks his lips, "let us all hope not an entire three hundred and sixty-five days transpires with you under Oleg's wing. Anastasiya, you will spend your time in training."

A bodyguard moves forward and places handcuffs around my wrists. The click echoes in my ears.

"Year, with him . . ." I stare at Irek, horror reflecting in my gaze.

The president lifts the back of his knuckles to stroke my cheek. I flinch. His eyes narrow. "Precisely why you must follow Oleg's training and return to me sooner."

He steps back, nodding to my old headmaster.

Oleg stands the same height as Simeon yet lacks his soul. The man I love has these gorgeous dark eyes filled with depth. Oleg's mirror a churning, deadly ocean.

He removes coins from his pocket and drops them at my feet.

"This is the price of a Resnov Castle Girl when I make a bargain with a Chutin." He bares all of his teeth in a sinister smile. "For decades, the Chutin men purchased the finest the Resnovs had to offer. Some of their chattel were a worthy investment. Some were not."

Irek laughs. "There's no such thing, Oleg. My grandfather, father, and I coveted our little games. Even when our Castle Girls depreciated from $20 mil, or so, to being worth mere coins, as Oleg indicated."

"A Chutin handpicked another Castle Girl, purchased her, allowed her to live in the Castle. While I," Oleg bows for effect, "had a little fun with his chosen."

"Sought how breakable you were," Irek says. "The reason you're here now, Anastasiya, is because you passed the test. Had you caved to Oleg's advances; you'd have failed. I'd have discreetly signed over my contract to Oleg. The Resnovs don't take kindly to tampering with their product. It was a stipulation in the contract. Who would I be to have Oleg tortured until the end of time for reneging on his previous employer's requirements? Thus, once the contract with the Resnovs ended, and—"

"I was taken from the mansion for good," I murmur. "You would've sold me to Oleg."

"Dah and nyet. You would've appeared to have left the Castle at the end of the contract timeframe. But were sold to Oleg for a mere dollar."

I gulp down bile. "You're so rich. You'd buy a woman for enough to feed a third world country, then allow Oleg to harass and frighten her. If she doesn't have the will to stop his advances and caves to Oleg's desires, you'd throw her away. Give her to this mudak! Well, technically, I broke, Irek."

"You did not!"

"Kosta redirected his tormenting!" I chortle. "You think of me more highly than you ought to."

Irek cocks his head, a flabbergasted smile on his face. "You do not understand the game, Anastasiya. I'm rich as sin, beautiful. This ritual was initiated by—"

"Your piece of shit father and piece of shit grand—" I snap.

Oleg's fist stops a fraction away from my mouth. I'm no longer staring at the barrel of two machine guns. The guards have leveled their weapons toward him. One even nudges his jaw for effect.

"Remember, Oleg, we've changed the rules for her. No touching." Irek wags a finger. "Sweetheart, you were my first Resnov possession. I was about the age you were when we met, eight or nine, when I learned of my father's amusements."

"Shut up," I groan. Venom swims through my veins.

"I had no idea which I preferred when we crossed paths, breaking you or my first dollar. I'd never seen such a futile amount of money. Then I fell in love with you, and you loved me too!"

"Never." I yank at the handcuffs. Irek's thumbs glide down between the metal and my torn wrists.

"You remember the first time I touched you—"

"Fuck you," I scream.

"We were at a gala. You'd torn tiny moons into your palms—"

I jolt my foot out. Irek is diverted by one of his guards, while the other wrestles me back onto the bed. His knees plant onto my thighs, and his upper body levels into mine.

Irek continues, "I allowed the Young Resnov to have you because you stopped seeing me, Anastasiya! You stopped being you!"

"Fuck you! Die!" I shout, as his guard warns me to calm down.

"I went on to other girls. Spent millions. Received a few dollars for defectives, which left Oleg satisfied as well. Our discreet arrangement worked, Anastasiya. I'd have left you alone for the rest of your life except for Kosta. She convinced me that the Young Resnov manipulated your brain. *Which is evident!*"

I hiss, declaring my hatred of him.

"I'm here to save you. The sooner you learn under Oleg's direction, we can return to the life we built. Visit galas, make love under the stars—"

"What about your *wife?*"

Irek pauses for a moment. The creature holding me down shuffles out a breath.

"What about your wife?" I groan, voice dry.

"What about her?" He starts toward the door and stops. He heaves a sigh, appearing much older than his years. "Anastasiya, you've disappointed me. Now, you must depart. You have my word, Oleg will under no circumstances harm you. Nor will he be alone with you. A detail will protect your person at all times."

"Who will protect you from me?" My voice trembles.

Irek's hands claim the intricate doorknobs. Flickering candles near the double doors dash into nothingness as he leaves me in the hands of the devil.

CHAPTER 15

Simeon

Half-past midnight, light bleeds across the palace corridors. Servants and byki alike are completing a clean sweep of over one hundred rooms. All staff received strict orders not to enter the bedroom I share with Anastasiya for all of two nights. Stepping into darkness, I pull the doors flush behind me. My hand finds the light switch, and then I'm drowning in a few token memories.

An image unfolds where Anastasiya is in our bed, awakened by a nightmare and panting for oxygen. Then I see us on the floor, me fucking her so good her shouts break into mewing sounds.

Visions of her fade. Four years ago rushes to the forefront. I watched tortured bodies, inhaled the stench of burning flesh. The unquenchable rage takes over. I owned the deaths of Rudolf and a select few of my byki. But I was never satisfied.

My fist slams into the marble slab wall, each hit pounding at my knuckles.

"Where the fuck is she?!"

I should've coveted peace. When I wasn't Pakhan, revenge didn't matter. My life was of no importance as long as Anastasiya was around me. Vindicating my mother shouldn't have taken precedent. Blood smears across the marble. I bash my fist again, hearing myself agree to my father's Black Dolphin mission.

"Shouldn't have gone." I slide down the wall next to the master-piece of chaos I've created. Massive chest heaving, jaw clinched, I consider my options. The obscurity around Anastasiya's disap-pearance, this time, is overshadowed by politics. Once aware of this catastrophe, the Seven will require revenge, and I demand the truth.

"How can I play fair?" I slide my mangled, bloodied knuckles across my bristled jawline. Finding answers and ceasing the Seven's interest in how Luka died will cause me to become . . .

"Don't fucking become that mudak," I grit out. To my left, my blood trickles along the veiny marble slab to the ground.

Anatoly had no qualms with murdering a byki without cause. I've always justified my reasoning.

Anatoly annihilated his own blood, no hesitation.

If Kirill or anyone else in my bloodline sets Anastasiya in their crosshairs . . .

I.

Will.

Slaughter.

Them.

Uncle, aunt, kazen, half-siblings. Anyone.

A psychotic laugh vibrates against my abdominals. "Well, you'll have to find her first, Sim. Find her, to keep her safe."

Gripping the ground, I start up. My vision slightly blurs from the disequilibrium and vodka coursing through my veins.

"I'll find Asya," I say with a grunt, standing tall.

Sticky blood dribbles on the ground as I pull out my phone. I dial Beam.

He grumbles a greeting.

"Line everyone who was on the grounds yesterday out front. Firing squad style." I click the off button, sauntering along the side of the bed. I press my hand against the marble. *Be a little like Anatoly . . . get shit done.* I consider the motto as the wall protracts. Before me are military-grade weapons.

"Too much like your fucking father," I murmur, breath imbued with vodka. My hand trails over a bazooka. With Kirill comatose and only a select few aware of Luka's death, I can bide my time with the *doctored* evidence targeting Asya for his murder. However, too much firepower will pique the Seven's interest. I still have to believe whoever abducted her wanted to cause discord.

An IWI Negev settles in my arms. The light-weight machine gun was a gift I received a few years ago. When I step back a few paces, the wall zips shut.

I'm starting to turn toward the door when I notice a slip of paper on Anastasiya's nightstand. I lean the machine gun nozzle on the ground, handle against the ledge. The neurons in my brain fire in rapid succession, eating the words faster than I'm able to decipher them. My head tilts, eye twitches, and I start from the top.

My cellphone buzzes. I glance at the screen. It's Beam. My request is complete. I slip the phone back into my pocket. Bloody prints soil the paper, as I fold it neatly and place it into my lapel, right where my heart once resided. For now, I'll still kill anyone against my Tsarina. This letter means nothing because she still has my heart.

First light glints over the shoulders of a line of servants and trusted byki. At least fifty personnel stand along the court, shoulders fallen, gazes fatigued. Fog exits their mouths as they shiver in nightgowns or thermal long-sleeve pajamas. Dot, Beam, and a few other trusted byki stalk the line of prey, prepared to carry out my command. The palace steps are my dominion. My unblinking eyes track across morose faces. They've stood in the same spot for hours as I've studied their every demeanor.

Patience is a caveat for the torturer. You can watch someone. They are well aware that their lives are in your hands. They wait patiently, their eyes begging for their lives. Their lips are trembling —because they understand that they are not at liberty to speak yet —to beg, plead, or die.

Morning daylight shines down.

Snow falls.

A few women slink down into the slush. Just before a gun is leveled into their faces, another loyalist hefts out a hand to assist them at my request. The actions become humdrum.

The peacoat I'm wearing is no match for the stark chill. Asya's letter in my pocket is the gasoline, the match, and the mother-fucking fire. My most trusted stalk back and forth with the antici-pation of tearing into any one of the shivering mudaks who are lined up.

Too many hours have transpired since I last held Anastasiya close. The feel of my lips on her forehead as I climbed out of bed in the early morning, is our last memory together.

My last memory while she slept. Finally, my voice booms over the horizon. *"Who entered my room without consent?"*

The pizda in me is still hopeful Asya's letter was created by a world-renown forger.

"Pakhan," Dot grits. "Looks like this one has something to tell you."

He grips the back of the neck of a maid. Her knees buckle

beneath her, and she stumbles into the snow. Her already shaking body flushes gray and purple from the frigid ice.

"Good," I murmur. "What would you like to tell me, sweetheart?"

"I," she begins in a stutter. At my subtle nod, Dot's knuckles wash white. Her teeth bare to the pain of his attempts. "At first, I believed our Tsarina had returned to her room yesterday."

"When?"

"After lunch, sir."

I tip back my vodka bottle. *Empty.* The glass shatters against the frozen steps as I growl, "Please continue."

"I thought it was Anastasiya. But it was not. The woman had to be about the same size. I did note she had a streak of white-blonde hair. I cannot be too sure it wasn't her entire hair color. She wore a covering over much of her."

White-blonde hair, white-blonde hair, I turn the minuet description around in my brain. "And you didn't think to share the news with any of the guards?"

"Dah! I went straight away to the first guard." The instant she speaks the name of a guard, he calls her a liar. "I'm telling the absolute truth, my Tsar."

Dot lets go of the back of her head, and her forehead kisses the ground as she bows fully.

I'm out of my seat and down the steps.

"The suka told me nothing, Tsar!" The byki clinches his fists at his side. While I head over, his gaze lowers as custom. He continues to refute the maid's report.

"I do not have time for conflicting statements." I gesture toward Dot. "Be nice to our maid."

The sound of a shot rings out from his area as the knife in my hand glides into the byki's torso. Warm blood sprays across my fingers. In a guttural tone, the byki admits he didn't get a good look at the woman before she left.

"Not a good look at all?"

His body begins to waver, as the knife slices through him. "Ny-nyet."

"Did you warn any of your other consorts? Request assistance from the byki surrounding the palace?" I inquire, lifting the blade slowly. "You're not a lone ranger."

He struggles. "I . . . did . . . not, Tsar."

"That's right. You took the safety of your Tsar and Tsarina for granted." The knife continues to hook and slide up his torso to his chest. Kicking him in the abdomen, I pull back, retrieving my knife, and the dead byki falls to his death.

"That is all for now." I flick my wrist. Men and women alike jump into action, falling, tripping, to enter the warmth of the palace. I gather my closest byki.

Chewing my lip, I consider the dead maid's words. White-blonde *hair*.

"Anastasiya had a roommate at the castle." I snap my fingers then slur, "Kosta. They've connected in passing throughout the years. Asya visited South Africa with Kosta. Perhaps they were in Miami together." My gander slides along their tensed, cold faces. "Who retrieved Asya's belongings in Miami? Confirm if there was any proof two women lived there instead of one."

"I'll gather the men who stayed behind, sir." A byki nods his head.

I flick my wrist, and he does an about-face, heading toward the double doors.

"Beam, look through the Bratva files. Kosta's previous owner went by an alias, Khadar—"

"Should I—"

"Nyet, shut the fuck up. I haven't given you an order. Khadar is dead. The one who sold her to Khadar is the Sheik of," I chew my lip in thought, "Sheik of Abuli. Pay him a visit—commence with kindness, gage him."

"Okay," Beam says.

The wheels in my brain are on rapid-fire. I grab his shoulder.

"New plan. Any man sets their eyes on Anastasiya and Kosta, that man may have Kosta's life or death, or both. I don't give a fuck about her. Bring my Tsarina home unharmed and be greatly rewarded. Understood?"

Beam asks, "May I schedule a conference with the Table of Seven. See if they can spare more men? Abuli is a huge nation."

"Not necessary. My family is mourning Luka," I lie. "Outsource and pay any fees necessary."

Beam and Dot share glances before the one twin heads off.

"You're all relieved. Half of you oversee the grounds with the rest of these incompetent fucks. The remainder of you, aid Beam or Dot."

Sleet pelts down. Dot stands back, running a hand over his face.

"You may speak," I order.

He nods his appreciation. "We aren't telling the Table of Seven about Anastasiya's disappearance or Luka's death."

"Nyet."

"She is *our* Tsarina." He bobs his head again, icicles clinging to his mustache and hair. "When she returned, Beam nor I had faith in her, Pakhan. But you're *our* leader. We will find her safe. I'll have a hacker on Chutin soon. I promise you that, or you may own my death."

Dot heads toward the steps, and I let the pelts of ice fall on me. Reaching into the inside of my lapel, I slip out the letter once more. Though I've memorized it, seeing is believing.

CHAPTER 16

Anastasiya
One Week Later

Traveling from Irek's vacation home to Oleg's crummy compound took hours. My old headmaster didn't see fit to have Irek's guards place a cloak over my head. He'd promised that once he was done with me, I'd beg to return to Chutin. The mudak expected a cowering, sniveling fool in me. I made a mental picture of everything, down to the road in which Oleg resides.

My prison is a five-by-five-foot cell with a small bed and an overworked mattress. I'm sure it's in close proximity to other rooms, the horror rooms and caged areas. But mine is just a room. Stark walls. Picturesque windows. I was different all because Irek Chutin has his requirements.

Two of Irek's guards are on shift rotating day and night to keep Oleg from me or me from running—*which*—I haven't the slightest idea.

With cuffs confining my hands behind my back, I stand near the window. It expands half the area across from my bed. A clearing is outside, and a hatchet is stuck in a wood stump that my palms are itching to touch. A half a kilometer away, pillowy snow-white trees jut into the sky.

All magnificence and a reminder of my confinement. What would be worse? One of the cages Oleg has threatened but has no right to make use of? Or this?

The gorgeous sight constricts my throat as I long for Simeon. I'm torn between the thought of Simeon saving me or my meeting Simeon in death one day. Our happily ever after must have a better outcome in the afterlife, right? Or fighting to survive and still dying . . . harder.

Where the fuck are you, Sim? I contemplate, pinching the sting from my eyes by shutting my lids tight. The serene outdoor view dashes from my vision. Symbolic freedom plunged into darkness.

"You waste food!" Oleg's stomach-curdling voice calls out from the open door. It's never shut. This nightmare is my life.

Blinking, I try my best to resurrect Simeon in my mind. To love him. To hate him for instilling this desire to save myself.

"I don't shit money like those mudaks!" Oleg shoves a bowl of gruel and oats into my face. Defiant, I turn my head as he continues to argue. "The Resnovs gave me my resignation years ago! Irek's only paying me to train you. Just you. Meaning once you're gone, I have to—"

"Become gainfully employed?" I hear myself sneer. The full lips donated to me by a nameless woman curve cruelly. "Sell your own ass. I can still hear you telling Kosta to lick here, tease there, suck that!"

Oleg shoves at my shoulder. With my balance tied to the binding of my arms behind me, I stumble a few steps, then move into a wide-legged stance. "Oleg, I suggest you suck a dick a day. Perhaps that'll keep you fed."

"Will Simeon Resnov still love you were I to carve that

97

gorgeous face! Better yet, tear you in half from your belly button to your precious pussy?" He reaches forward to poke a finger at my abdomen. My knee juts up, aimed toward his groin. My momentum and reflexes are not so polished. I meet all air.

"Descend, foolish girl. Beg your host for forgiveness." Oleg laughs. He unzips his pants, his appalling shaft at attention. "You won't eat the oatmeal?"

A guard, leaning against the wall, takes an interest. "Oleg," he tests.

"I'm aware of Chutin's irrational rules! Anastasiya will be my toy forever at this rate." My headmaster grunts, massaging at his cock. He holds the bowl right beneath it.

"I've lost my appetite." I begin to roll my eyes, but the bastard is already shooting his seed into the bowl. I wink. "Wow, how quick."

The glaze in his eyes as thick, gooey spunk spirits into the bowl begins to lessen. I laugh harder, and Oleg slides the bowl of slop onto the ground before my feet. At the clatter of the tin bowl, Oleg stops it with the top of his boot.

"Down on all fours, now!"

His hands wrap around my abdomen, and Oleg's tongue slithers across my cheek. Head tilted back, laughter bubbles from my soul.

"I-I'm su-supposed to f-fear your touch," I stutter, chuckling. The past couple of days teeming in threats and no actions have driven me to tears and laughter. "Impossible."

His domineering stance causes Baldy, the older of Irek's guards, to chirp on his walkie-talkie. He's no doubt sending for the younger guard with the chipped tooth, which I've named 'Chip.' Usually, while one man observes me, the other is asleep.

Unaware, Oleg's knuckles flex.

I taunt, "Defy Chutin. You could have my submission the traditional way. *Hit me!*"

"Bring this suka to her knees!"

"What's next?" I bark.

Baldy snorts. "Oleg, she doesn't want to fucking eat your cum-laced oats! It's absurd. Chutin would be livid!"

"Nyet?" Oleg arches an eyebrow. The younger soldier has entered the room, and he gestures between the two of them. "Per Chutin, no infliction of pain, no penetration! Now, you two idiots bring the Resnov Tsarina to her knees!"

Chip fork's a crooked tooth over his bottom lip. He places a firm grip on my arm and pushes me to my knees.

Baldy sighs. "What sort of training is this, Oleg?"

A sinister smile dances at the edges of his lips. "Nyet penetration!"

Yellow rain zips toward my face. My lips cleave shut. The stench chokes down my nostrils. The soldier releases me in fear of Oleg's aim.

My old headmaster's shriveled cock zips around in circles. "I'm writing my name."

I lunge forward, falling onto my face, hands bound behind my back. He grips my hair and slams the bowl of oatmeal down on me like a crown.

"You didn't want to fill up with nourishment, Anastasiya. Now, I've blessed your hair." He mops the goop around in my mane.

Chest heaving, lips snatched tight, I silently cry. *I'm not the Invisible Thing*, I repeat to myself. Grunting, Oleg moves to the ground, laying in the puddle with me. Like a lover brushing away dirt, he removes the oats and semen masking my hair. "I can't hear you. Break for me, Anastasiya. Cry for me . . . louder."

My throat is clogged, and my mouth opens without provocation. Weeping gurgles through me. No amount of self-hatred or threats to myself will stop this. I'm no longer bound by hysteric laughter. Instead, I cave to a fit of body-wracked sobs.

CHAPTER 17

Anastasiya

I was almost seventeen. I sauntered down the steps in Mother Sofiya's home. As I gripped my cellphone in one hand to speak, my words echoed across the opulent void. "Luka, have you arrived at the physician's office?"

"They couldn't see—" The sound of my brat belching, caused me to pull the receiver away from my ear.

"Are you okay?" I started in the sitting room and tried the doors to the rose garden, ensuring they were locked. I listened to his hacking and then hung up. Damn, I was about to tell him to return. That I'd make soup for the first time in my life, take care of him, as he'd cared for me.

Tapping the cellphone in my pocket, I considered calling Simeon. Mother Sofiya had relieved our byki and servants this morning. I didn't want to call him. Last time I wore a form-fitting dress, he hardly looked at me. Today, I had put on a skirt the second Luka left for the hospital, hoping Simeon would stop by. Now, I felt like a selfish brat all dolled up.

It was apparent Simeon only saw me as a little sister. Sofiya's encouragement last year had gone to shit. Simeon hadn't tried to touch me since *that one time when I attempted to console him after his parents screwed. Now, he attended the university, surrounded by gorgeous women. Simeon had a lot of ass to choose from. And I was slinking around in a tight skirt and felt like a donkey's rear end.*

I started down the cream-colored corridor, checking windows, locking doors, telling myself not to call him. Not to manipulate Luka's misfortune into a teen girl's crush.

My phone rang.

"Sim," I breathed.

"Luka texted me an hour ago that he left. Your instructor doesn't come on Tuesdays, and my mother is away." His intellectual assessment became hard and clipped as he asked, "Why didn't you call me?"

"Because you have class on Tuesdays." Lit, Communications, and the one psychology course with Garbovsky that you're taking because your mother is a nut case. I'm also sort of a stalker. And what's with the angry tone? *I cleared my throat instead of sharing my thoughts.*

"Secure the house, Asya."

"Simeon, don't bark orders at me," I gritted out. It always took a few seconds for my desire to subside, and I matched his usual clipped tone. But beneath it all, I'd swear I was sexually frustrated, and I'd never done the deed. "I'm a grown—"

"You're a girl, Asya," Simeon bit out. "How many times must I remind you, this world isn't safe—"

"Are you speeding?" I cut in. This world had to be safe for me because no matter how dark it was, only in this universe would I be tethered to Simeon. After all the hatred I had for a Resnov, my heart beat for one.

"Dah, I'm speeding to you."

I almost smiled, my imagination at work. Though Simeon seemed tensed, he was, after all, coming to see me. Setting aside girlish thoughts, I cleared my throat.

"There's ice on the road. You're half-an-hour away," I groaned, stalking toward the front door. "You're not invincible."

His tension seemed to abate. There was a rare lush drone to his deep, steel voice. "Maybe I'm invincible. Ten minutes."

Dah, he was invincible and dangerous.

A danger to my soul. I bounded past crystals on pillars, feeling beautiful. "As I said, you're not. Wait, Luka texted you an hour ago . . . while you were in Lit?" I slammed my lips shut, warmth spreading across my cheeks. God, he knew I knew his schedule. *Hell, I goaded Luka and pretty much knew all the days of the week he got laid, too.*

"I drive fast."

Smiling, I reached for the door. My fingertips brushed the knob when it turned and bumped into my hand. I stepped back a few paces, staring up into the stark eyes of Simeon's father. Whereas Simeon had a lush dark mystery surrounding him, Anatoly Resnov's aura reeked. A demonic, pulsing force surrounded his broad shoulders.

"I-I'm on the phone with Simeon," I trembled out.

Arm snaking behind my back, Anatoly slammed me against his chest. He took the phone and pressed the off button.

Nausea twirled me like a spindle. He'd never been close to me, not like this. His vodka breath teased over my nose and cheeks.

"I never visit my Castles, Anastasiya. Too much temptation." His callused hand pawed along my cheek. "None so tempting as you."

I found myself nodding profusely, warning myself to speak.

"This isn't the Castle, Tsar. I'm in love with your son," I rambled. Simeon had shared one of his psychology books with me. Build connections with your tormentor. That would be my tactic. "I love Simeon, with all of me . . . and he loves me."

"Does he?" Still clinging to me, Anatoly closed the door behind him. Over his shoulder, I glimpsed a traverse of byki in SUVs outside. "Fuck words, Chak Chak."

I glared at him. Because of my caramel complexion, he was comparing me to a dessert. "I'm not sweet."

Sharp, white teeth chomped close to my nose. "I bet you are. Now, how has our abomination shown you his love? What has he done for you, Chak Chak?"

"Support and understanding. Simeon cares for me, Anatoly. I know everything about him, and he knows everything about me." It was sort of a lie. Simeon never needed to know about Oleg; however, I had a point to drive home. *"Simeon shows his love. You know, like a parent is there for their child. Love, support, guidance. By the way, he'll arrive soon."*

Anatoly ran the backs of his knuckles over the side of my breast, gripped my hands before I could run, and spun me around. Oh God, I'd dressed like a whore. Sofiya would applaud my attire was it her son and not her brother who snared me.

Our movements became a dance. I would lash out. He would grip my wrist, kiss my knuckles, suck my fingers into his mouth and bite. My leg lifted in a fit of rage, and I found purchase to run off. Anatoly grabbed my thigh. He lifted it and slid it over his hip, pressing his groin into me.

"You want to pound my cock, Chak Chak?" Anatoly's hand claimed my hip harder.

"Anatoly, your son and I are in love—"

"You sound so innocent." Hand gripping my throat, he slammed me against the wall. The edges of my vision hazed over. "You will love this."

~

Crying had stolen me from this sordid reality. Only my dreams didn't offer me amnesty. I sleep in a puddle of urine. Humiliation marinates into my flesh and settles there. Tears salt across my cheeks. I'd awoken before Simeon arrived.

The side of my body, having laid on a cement slab, aches when Chip arouses me awake.

"Girl," he calls out. "Girl . . ."

My eyes flicker open. His shiny boots are before me, outside of the realm of my shame, and Oleg's drying urine pool.

"Can you?" He gestures for me to rise.

"She can't. Not with her cuffs behind her." Baldy grunts, hefting my bicep. Chip reluctantly grabs the other. The two soldiers drag me across the tiny bedroom into the en suite bathroom. I step onto the cold, porcelain square tile with grimy grout. Chip turns on the shower with caked dirty rings around the tub. He folds his lean arms and rests his shoulder against the wall, refusing to look at me.

Baldy settles on the cover of the toilet. My mind taunts me. All I do now is dream or think. I have all the time in the world. My thoughts keep going back to before all of this—before I woke up with Chutin. *What happened? What had I been doing?* I had finally remembered that Luka and I had been to see Sofiya. Or was that another day, when she cut her wrists? Time is hazy in my brain. A thought comes, then it is muddled and slides away.

Where the fuck is Luka? My brat and I were together before—

Something's wrong with my brain. I wrestle with my restraints, desiring to yank at my haggard tresses.

"The longer you're here, little Tsarina, *we are here,*" Baldy declares. "I have a daughter your age! Comply, so we can all return home."

"Home?" I sneer. "Not until I kill him."

Baldy grips my chin in his hand. "Implying I have a child your age doesn't mean I give a shit about you. You might have been the Resnov Tsarina. But before that, you were owned by them. *Castle Girl!* You're a sex slave. *This* is your calling. Lucky you, Chutin's giving out second chances."

"Fuck Irek." I grit, fighting at the cuffs holding my wrists behind me. "The second I set eyes on him, he's dead!"

Shaking his head, he yanks me up by the shoulder and forces me back. My calves hit the porcelain tub, and my ass falls into it. Hot water soothes my tattered ego. The stench rises from my skin.

Chip clicks his tongue. "Don't."

Baldy flinches toward my face, and I offer an unbothered blink.

"Your patience is wearing thin, same for Oleg," I say. "Which one of you mudaks breaks first? The second either one of you lose control, that's when I'll have your fucking head!"

"You have superpowers?" Baldy grits out. "I hit you, and a supernatural force aides you in retaliation. Is that it, huh?"

Chip clears his throat, and Baldy stands at ease.

Holding out a bar of soap, Chip mumbles, "To wash. You comply, okay?"

I nod. Baldy removes my restraints as Chip hands over the soap. The bastard made a mockery of superheroes. They were never a source for my daydreams as a child. But now, I know my way out. Shower time affords me the most freedom. I'll use it to my disposal.

CHAPTER 18

Simeon

Glass crashes to the ground, and shards scatter across the room. A priceless, oddly shaped artifact that has been in the palace longer than my life is no more.

"You're telling me you went to Abuli ten days ago. Not a fucking trail leading to Anastasiya. Nothing?" I grit out, glaring at Beam.

"After a few days, I leveled with the Sheik."

I point my gun at him. "You shared with that mudak why we were there?"

"Dah. Might sound illogical, but he was growing suspicious, and I trusted him."

"All that air in your fucking brain." I shake my head, cackling at the thought of how dead this mudak would be if I followed my father's lead. "You trusted him, Beam?"

"I did. He handed over access to airline files: commercial and private. He gave us access to satellites. I combed over the security footage. He used the Resnov Castle service for thirty years and asked if I needed anything else. Tsar, the crew and I didn't find anything suspicious, and no one resembling the Tsarina entered or exited his country."

Chewing on my knuckles, I contemplate other means for the Sheik of Abuli to hide the woman I love. Then I laugh a little, shove a hand through my dark hair.

"That mudak likes young virgins," I tell myself, fingers curling around an almost empty vodka bottle. The Sheik does not need Asya.

I see Anastasiya, and all of me falls to my knees, psychotically bewitched by her. Like a fucking drug, I'll never get enough of her. Sure, she left a letter.

Fuck her letter.

Fuck her.

She will forever belong to me, and I will have her returned to my possession. I deserve the truth from the woman I love. Why she left, and why she killed her brat. But I have to use my brain.

I glare at my team. Daily and nightly updates have been provided. Still, I placed all my eggs in one basket. I banked on the Sheik. But I still have Chutin.

"Does anyone have anything essential to finding Asya? Any-fucking-thing?" My unhinged gaze tracks back and forth. "Where is Dot? I called a meeting, where is that mudak!"

A byki catches my gaze. Flicking my wrist, I give him consent to speak.

"He has a hacker in one of the guest rooms. She's viewing script. Has almost broken through Chutin's firewalls."

I smile.

He gulps.

Two days ago, Dot had a potential hacker here.

The mudak left in a body bag, unable to fulfill his obligation.

~

L ater in the evening, the Armenian whom I had the urge to meet ten days ago has arrived from Syria. The textbook on the Armenian history of torture I'm skimming through is discarded. I fist the highlighter in my hands as his tanned body falls to his knees on my rug.

Removing my cufflinks one at a time, I fold the sleeves of my linen shirt, watching him squirm. The gag in his mouth doesn't concede to the begging and pleading his wild eyes are doing.

Standing before him, I pop the tip of his nose with the highlighter. "Don't be so afraid," I click my tongue. "I will not have your death today." *Anastasiya requested that I wait for her before finishing off Rudolf's friend. I'll keep you barely alive until that very day.*

Gripping the back of his hair, I pull until his Adam's apple lulls uncomfortably in his throat. "I dedicated my time to reading about the Ottoman Empire. How the Turks almost obliterated your people."

He cuts me with a hard gaze.

Before I can reprimand him for glaring at me, a knock comes at the door. I shrug a little.

Dot enters, the widest grin on his face. "Tsar, we have access to Chutin's videos."

"Where?"

"All over—"

"Nyet, you fucking idiot! Where is the laptop?"

"My hacker is working her magic, saving aerial views as we speak. I'll take you to her."

I turn toward a byki. "Feed the Armenian his eyes. If he shares any pertinent info about what happened to Asya four years ago, you may stop with one eye. Nevertheless, one or two, *make him eat them.* Dah?"

Without awaiting a response, I head out of the room. In the elevator, Dot mentions the girl is retracing data from Chutin's security systems, and how it's easier to dissect real-time videos.

We enter a guest room, a small figure in a hoodie hovers over a laptop. Various wires are twisted around, connected to a bevy of television monitors.

My hard gaze scans each video, displaying various areas of different homes. There is footage of the outdoors, some of which is tropical, some desert. The mudak appears to have residences on every continent. A lump forms in my throat.

My obsession is somewhere . . . hidden by Irek Chutin, and I will have her back.

"Where is she?!"

"No facial recognition," a tiny, very young voice snaps. "Based on this photo." A dark brown hand lifts up said photo while the other one continues to type. "Can't chat. Square Head, update *him*. I'd rather not be murdered for insubordination."

I gather that Square Head is Dot by the way his lips bunch together. Then he shares how half the screens are in real-time, and the others are "rewinding," per the girl.

"See these timestamps?" Dot narrows his eyes. "The lettering is tiny as fuck—"

"Move. Language!" the hoodie says again.

My jaw clinches. Were she not tapping into Chutin's database, I might consider having her head for the snarky responses. I move around, glance at the screens for the timestamps. The twenty-four-hour clock is sliding back swiftly on one.

I catch the kid's side profile. She's African descent and young.

Too fucking young to correct for her mouth.

"I'm fourteen. Stop staring, or I *will leave my zone*."

It had been on the tip of my tongue to offer her the fucking stars, the moon, the sun for information on Anastasiya. Instead, I step back a few paces. This is not the proudest moment of my reign as a Pakhan.

"Maybe you should return to the Armenian?" Dot suggests.

"Great suggestion," she retorts. "Maybe the two of you should follow through with that."

"I'm not leaving, kid, and if . . ." *You'd like to see another day.* I close my eyes. The bully Asya made me out to be when she gave her ultimatums in Los Angeles slams to the forefront of my mind. "You will be greatly compensated, girl."

"I know." She has the last word.

For the first time in ten days, my mouth curves at the edges. *Anastasiya, I refuse to let you go. Give me a fucking sign, moya milaya, because I will have you happy with me.*

I contemplate on the letter, and how her disappearance may not revolve around anyone but us.

Dah, happy with me. Or dead with me.

CHAPTER 19

Anastasiya

The cold chill of night frames the soggy wet clothes sticking to me. Oleg's aim had been to strip my pride. I'd held onto my convictions even while showering fully dressed. Look where it's gotten me, sniveling and sneezing.

A tiny space heater on the ground clicks on and off, further cutting into my affliction. Each click a boisterous taunt. Warm air floats in the opposite direction, toward a snoring Chip, sleeping on the chair near the door.

"Haaaa—" The sneeze begins to tear through my soul. I jolt my hands toward my face. At night, the manacles are re-secured with my arms in front of me, offering my stiff muscles some rest. A pain like a match strike sparks fire along my restrained wrists from the force of shoving my hands to my sniveling face. Teeth chattering, I fall back to Anatoly.

Simeon's father entered the house. Unrequited delight glimmered across the predator's face. While I struggled, he continued to pull me flush against him.

The devil's lips crashed down around mine, sucking all the air from my lungs. My neck became putty in his hands. My tonsils pulsed to his powerful grip. He spoke. "Shhh . . . Asya, I'm tallying every second of your insubordination. Shut up about love. You haven't convinced me that you've been fucked. So, I'll do you the honors."

Anatoly's clutch between my legs began to rip and tear my panties to shreds. My throat had swollen shut. Every fearful breath hitched through my nostrils. His teeth bit my tongue, forcing his entry. A finger strained past my tight resistance.

"You're not even wet!" he gritted, twisting his finger deeper into me. His nail scraped at my insides. "Oh, but as I suspected. Untouched. My cock will break you in half at this rate."

Anatoly pulled out of me, and I sucked on air. His finger slammed down my throat.

"Get you wet for me," he growled. My teeth latched onto his filthy finger. The back of his other hand sailed across my face. The force sent me reeling into a glass-vaulted cabinet. Gripping my bicep, Anatoly jerked me hard enough to loosen my spinal column. Blood dripped from a cut at my lip. He situated my legs around his waist and crushed me against the wall again. He slipped his wounded fingers in his mouth.

"Nyet," I groaned, throat throbbing, head pounding.

"If you continue to cry, I won't make it feel good for you too."

The tender petals between my thighs lit on fire at Anatoly's attempts to stretch me wide.

"Stop. Sofiya will—"

"Never mention her!" Anatoly's head reared back. His temple started toward my face, issuing enough force to break my nose. As his forehead was meant to slaughter my entire face, an arm claimed his throat.

"How many times have I told you that you're dead to me, Father." Simeon's bicep strained around Anatoly's throat. A terrible rage burned across his mottled, taut skin. Not toward me, but toward his father, and toward this dark world that almost claimed me before he had. His eyes were on me, and yet, I doubt he saw me. All he saw was another life to claim, this time, not on behalf of his father.

"You knew I'd kill you." The left side of Simeon's mouth curved in a sinister smile. "Don't fear, Father. Not yet. You die when I say so."

He sent Anatoly's body reeling away. Jeweled hands clamored to the floor. Anatoly wheezed and sputtered, much as I had before. Simeon's boot crunched against the side of his rib.

"Okay, moy syn." Anatoly spat up blood.

Simeon slammed his foot into Anatoly's back. "In what world is it okay for a son to claim his father's life, huh?" He kicked Anatoly's rib. "Turn over, suka. LOOK AT ME!"

Anatoly rolled onto his back, lips inflamed, face a mask of blood. Simeon's foot slammed down onto his face. My body shook so hard that I flailed, catching myself at the wall again.

The man I loved wiped the bottom of his boot on his father's suit jacket. "You're staining my motherfucking boots, Anatoly. You undeserving, mudak. How dare you." He shoved a finger in his face. "I can't even stomach your presence long enough to consider torturing you."

Simeon slid a knife from his back pocket, his knees landing on his father's shoulders and arms. One hand around Anatoly's neck, he held the blade against his throat. "A shame. You deserved my worst—"

"Sim," I shuttered out a breath. "You can't."

Lashes fluttered upward. Cool eyes glinted in my direction. "Stop me, moya milaya."

"He has men outside! So many of them. The second he dies." I shook.

"She-she's right, moy syn," Anatoly gritted. "Your mother isn't here to save you."

Simeon snarled, "You think I need my ma to save me?"

"I've always said," he gulped in consternation, "Moya Sofiya—"

The knife glided into the side of his neck like butter. Simeon cocked a brow, "Milaya?"

"Don't," I called.

"Ha, Sofiya calls you the smartest motherfucking Resnov there ever would be. The day you came into this world, I should've tossed your little ass into a ditch. See how long you could fend for yourself!"

Anatoly's hand gripped the knife, chewing near his carotid artery. He *chucked up blood with a wide-toothed, crimson smile. "Moya Sofiya kept you alive."*

I don't know how I floated over to Simeon, but I fell to my knees. "You had a plan, Simeon. Now isn't the time to execute it. You're smarter than all of these mudaks. Continue to work on your plan."

That plan had always diverged from the Castle Girl, who craved a knight to whisk her away.

That plan always included Simeon murdering his father.

This was not that plan.

This was all our executions if Anatoly didn't walk out of the house.

"Dah," Simeon closed his eyes for a second. His forehead was resting against my face. "But he had his fucking fingers inside of you. I'm executing my plan today, Asya."

A hand jars at my shoulder. I want to return to the dream, maybe try to rewrite its course. Because seconds later, men broke through the doors and beat Simeon half to death. My eyes bite shut. I concentrate on Simeon.

This time, I'll fight with Simeon. He almost died. I didn't care if I died for him. I would fight.

Chip groans. "Your stomach won't stop growling, and you won't stop whimpering."

I continue to bite my eyes shut, but he grips both shoulders, shaking them vigorously. He whispers, "Open your eyes, girl. Eat. It's a fucking apple. It's safe."

Through the dark of night, I connect with his light blue eyes and shake my head. "Take off my cuffs."

Chip shoves the apple beneath my pillow, whispering, "You're too stubborn for your own good, girl." He reaches down toward the heater and turns it in my direction. His cold, trembling hands zip his jacket to beneath his chin. He resumes his position next to the door. Heated tears burn my eyes.

"Sim, where are you?" I mouth.

CHAPTER 20

Simeon

Though it seems I've abandoned you twice, you have to know how much I've always cared. For now, all I can give you are my apologies . . .

—With love

"Anastasiya," I murmur, thumb running over the ink of her signature. A forensic analyst isn't necessary to confirm her handwriting. "She left me twice . . ."

Another week has passed. Seventeen fucking days since I last laid eyes on her, held her close, ensured her safety. Before I sent the young hacker away on a different assignment, she had been able to retrieve entrance into all Chutin's security systems. She had images of him from an entire month preceding Anastasiya's disappearance. I currently had bykis analyzing everything day by day. It was a lot to go through. Political dinners. Sex with his wife, sex

115

with the harem of whores. Tea with all the powerful men in the world, aside from me.

I chew my lip, contemplating that. He's an angle I'll never stop pursuing, not until his spirit flees this world. I'd broken two of Anastasiya's stipulations.

Continuing to target the Armenians, the blind fuck in my basement has yet to break.

I slip my phone out of my pocket and call a number I've always sent straight to voicemail. The man himself answers on the second ring.

"Young Resnov." Chutin's voice dips in curiosity. I remember the day we met. He'd called me that stupid name. "To what do I owe the pleasure."

"You've attempted to kiss my ass since I became Tsar, and I've ignored you." I wriggled my jaw to cut the tension. "I wanted to apologize over tea." *Which does not indicate that I'm apologizing, nor will I.*

"Kiss your ass? So uncouth, like your uncle. I had high hopes we'd mend the relationships our grandfathers once held. Nevertheless, you're offering tea."

"Dah. When might I expect you?"

"And you're calling me yourself. I've grown accustomed to that cousin of yours as the liaison. The one with the striking blue eyes."

My head tilts. Is he referring to Kirill or Luka? It's been over two weeks, and Luka's family is still not aware of his death. A world-class mortician has my little cousin on ice. "Who the fuck are you referring to?"

There's silence for a moment. "Tsk, the one with the ponytail."

I narrow my eyes, and I ruminate over any connotation in his voice. Kirill has the ponytail, and he's slept this entire time. Is Chutin aware that Luka's dead?

"Well, I'm sure that I can fit you in toward the end of the week. My secretary will advise."

"Good." I hang up the phone.

An image of Anastasiya is fresh in my mind. My version of perfection was inside of her: mind, body, soul. We had just embarked on forever before she left that unforgivable letter and ruined things. All I want to do is get her back.

With me.

Dead.

Or alive.

Those are the only thoughts roaming through my mind.

CHAPTER 21

Mikhail

The slight tremor of rustling awakens me. I jolt to my feet, forcing myself to discard the screaming tension in my neck from lying on a lounger. I rub a hand over my pants. I'm dressed in jeans, fully dressed. I groan.

"You're still in mother-fucking-Russia," I tell myself. Two weeks later, and reality still hasn't penetrated. My eyes adjust to the darkness. It's an opulent room with brocade textured walls. And there's a body in an extravagant bed. It clicks. Kirill.

I've kept him asleep for over two weeks, and now he's got one handcuff loose and working the confines of his other wrist.

"Stop!" I grit.

"What are you saying, Mikhail?" Kirill grits out in Russian. "I do not speak English."

Fumbling over the words, I issue it again.

"Sounds a little better. Though, you *do not* order me. Unless it is death you seek. Give me a moment, and I'll assist with that." His chuckle is tense.

I stumble toward a gun on the dresser and hold it toward him. "You're my family, Kirill. Readjust your handcuffs, okay?"

"Do it for me." He lets his free hand fall. His blue eyes mirror mine, although with a sinister gleam.

"Why does everyone fucking test me?!" I head toward him; gun still leveled out. Kirill reaches forward with one hand. I launch my forearm into his neck, pressing the gun against his nose. "Act like an animal. I'll shoot you like a motherfucking animal, Cousin. I'm done playing civilized!"

He sighs. "If it weren't for the blood coursing through your veins, Mikhail, I'd kill you."

I nudge the gun harder into his neck. "Same for you."

I start to assist Kirill with putting the handcuff back on when he twists his arm to the side. With the butt of the gun, I slam against his nose then his temple. It's not enough to render him unconscious, but enough so he'll stop resisting. *One day, I'll fucking snap!*

Kirill sniffs back the blood in his mouth. I settle onto the edge of the chaise.

"Where's my injection?" His eyebrow lifts. "Or will my brat receive the memorial owed to him?"

I lick my lips. "Luka was about the sanest of you all. Simeon was as close to him as he is to you."

"Dah." His eyes lower.

My gaze follows the Tsar's lapdog's every move. *What happened? Why exactly was Kirill put to sleep? Why does he blame Anastasiya? Where the hell is she?* A battery of questions flits through my mind.

"Sim is looking into what happened to them," I mutter.

"Them? You mean Luka and the *suka*?" His laughter dies into a hard sob.

I pierce my tongue with my teeth, bite copper, and warn myself: listen and do not interrupt.

119

Kirill shakes his head, fallen, soiled tresses curtain his face. "I'm murdering Asya. Might get tortured half to death. Maybe the Seven will grant me leniency."

"It's treason to threaten Nastiya's life."

"Nastiya?" Kirill juts his chin. The matted blond mane covering much of his face finally parts ways. "Sim know you have your own pet name for the Tsarina? Asya manipulating you the way she did my brat?"

"Shhhh." I wave the gun. It's the middle of the night. Though I stayed in Russia to see Asya returned, I've followed Simeon's orders of keeping Kirill in a comatose state. "How could you even fathom she meant Luka any harm?"

"Everybody knew my brat was queer," Kirill grits. "But Luka wasn't just gay. He loved women, one woman. *Her.*"

"Kirill, you're projecting your grief. You need someone to blame. The Tsarina is missing, and Simeon will find her." *At the rate he's fucking going, I'll leave this place and find her myself.* "She was taken."

"You're such a pizda, Mikhail. That girl had Luka wrapped around her pinkie finger at the age of thirteen. He did anything for her. I've always believed him falling for men was because he pined for *what belonged to Simeon.*" Kirill glares through me. "Maybe four years ago, they started something—"

"Started what?"

"A relationship. Then she felt torn between the two. Things became tense while Sim was in prison, she fled. When she returned for Simeon, she and Luka—"

"Not plausible."

"She and Luka," he reiterates, snarling, "caught eyes again or something. Luka, my sweet brat, said something, did something, and she grabbed the wheel."

"Sounds like a Lifetime movie." I chuckle.

Kirill blinks.

Shrugging, I admit to having only seen a commercial for one. I put down the gun. "Alright, Kirill. I believe you."

The second he starts tinkering with the handcuffs, I replace the gun with the syringe and jam it into his neck. "You need a few more nights of sleep. Doctor's orders."

Around two a.m., the conversation with Kirill claws at my brain. Anastasiya belongs to Simeon, and it's his right to find her. Why hasn't he? I stalk out of the room I've shared with Kirill and gesture to the nearest byki to station himself at the door. Then I start down the hall, heading toward the room that mudak shared with the woman he never should've claimed.

I bang on the door.

"Mikhail," another guard says.

"I'm speaking to my cousin *now*!"

"But he is not there."

"Then where is he?" Anxious rage scorches across my skin. "Did he find her?"

"Nyet. Come." He nods his head.

Almost ten minutes later, I'm standing at a door on the third floor. Prisoners are kept on this level. How is Simeon's need for revenge more important than finding Anastasiya? Does he have a potential culprit, or someone who may be privy to her whereabouts inside?

I pull the handle, and open the door, shoulders squared, prepared for answers.

Through narrowed vision, I glare at Simeon on a low-seated couch. A leather-bound scroll is in his lap. He chews on the end of a gold pen, but his eyes are all over a maid. Her skirt is hemmed a lot shorter than the others, and her ass is in his face as she wipes at imaginary dust across the room.

"What the fuck are you doing, Simeon?" I grit out. Anastasiya is lost and either he's relishing in the show or . . . or he's deep in thought. I can't fathom how much I've grown to hate this cousin of mine, so I refuse to believe the latter.

Simeon shakes his head, finally acknowledging me. "My dealings are not your business, Kazen."

Pure rage tightens my jaw. "Enjoying your peep show?"

His dark eyes roll away from me.

"Why aren't you searching for Anastasiya, Simeon?"

"Girl, come," he orders like one would an animal.

With mile-long legs, the young maid drops her rag into a bucket on the floor and saunters to him. Standing up, Simeon twirls his finger. She turns her back toward him, eyeing me with a wink. Disgust burns red-hot up my esophagus as Simeon's hand twines up the center of her chest and clasps her throat. "Mikhail, you're so devoted to my woman. Allow me to show you what the fuck I'll do to my little Tsarina when I *catch her.*"

I gasp. "Catch—"

"As in Anastasiya ran off. Nyet abduction."

"What?" I snarl.

The whore's face pales white as does Simeon's knuckles as he claims her harder. His other hand roams over her low-buttoned blouse. "I'll gut that pretty little heart out of Anastasiya's chest, Mikhail, and own it forever."

"I see." My mouth twitches into a smile. I nod my head. At this precise moment, *Oleg* comes to fruition in my mind. Asya mentioned the name in her dreams, and because I give a damn about her, that's where I'll start. With a slight salute, I do an about-face and exit the room, closing it behind me.

"Never deserved her," I mouth. Though I have no intention of leaving Russia until Anastasiya's found, it is time I left *this* hellhole. First stop, Aunt Sofiya, because that bitch hides behind an all-knowing smile.

CHAPTER 22

Anastasiya

Eighteen days in, and I've counted every second. A pit of degradation surrounds me. The stench creeps into my nostrils, permeates my skin, mattes my hair. I glower at Oleg. He lets another photo from his collection slip from the tip of his fingers as he sits across from me on the floor.

"These are all the delights we're unable to delve in, Anastasiya," he says.

Images of more Invisible Things than I could give names to are piled between us.

The yellow rain has settled into my skin, coated my clothing. Finally, I open my mouth. Curiosity supersedes the need to keep quiet. "Is she dead?"

Another image drifts from his hands. The view is of an androgynous person, scars along every inch of his or her naked flesh.

"Is she dead?" My shout catches the eye of both Baldy and Chip.

"Who?" Oleg's vibrant cerulean gaze claims my honey orbs. I stare on. "Oh . . . the one in commission when you and Ghost Girl —*ahem*—now dead suka caught my attention."

I gulp. Ghost Girl must be in reference to Kosta. "Where's the other girl?! You killed her?"

I cleave to his body language, the slight curve of his mouth, the subtle rise of his gigantic chest. I cling to everything. His response will be my fuel. Today, I save my life. He flips through the stack and pulls one out, dropping it in front of me.

"You killed her." I declare again, breathing in more of the stench I currently live in. My eyes burn as I stare at the Invisible Thing.

"You're mistaken, Anastasiya." Oleg paws at my cheek. I hold steady, and he gasps. "Nyet flinching? Nyet spitting in my mouth—"

"I didn't—"

"You were but a girl, though a temptress."

My jaw tightens. I'd never been more afraid in my life, still haven't, when Oleg cornered me in that classroom. I'd spat *at* him.

"Best taste I ever had. Do it again."

"Oleg, tell me the truth. You murdered her," I growl. *Give me fuel to do what I must.*

"I'm no murderer." He shrugs and taps the photo. "The one who accompanied me during my visits with you, well, her heart stopped beating one day."

"How? Was she tied up when it occurred? Locked in a cage? Being raped by you?! How?"

"She died in the midst of doing all the beautiful little delights Irek has denied us."

Noticing the tears collecting in my eyes, Chip clears his throat. "It stinks in here. Let the girl shower. Then you can reconvene with your horror stories."

Ten minutes later, fog plumes across the tiny area of the bathroom in a routine I've grown accustomed to.

"You've been mouthy today, girl." Baldy plants his thumb across the thin barrier of cloth over my shoulder. Either he's gotten used to my daily yellow shower, or he's horny. "You plan to fully undress to bathe today?"

"I've grown accustomed to the cold while drying in my shirt." I grab the clean pair of jeans from Chip. They'd gotten a pair of sweats from Oleg the first night after I'd almost died of coughs and sneezes in heavy, wet jeans. Since then, I've alternated between the sweats and the jeans. I place them on the porcelain sink top. When I turn around, they're both staring.

"You couldn't have gotten me a shirt too?"

"This isn't a luxurious hotel, *Castle Girl*," Baldy sneers.

"Oleg refused," Chip adds.

Rolling my eyes, I shove my sweats down, kicking the cotton pants away from my feet. The shirt I'm wearing always dries against my skin. But when I bend over, Baldy's gaze smolders against my thong. How could he find this attractive? I'm drenched in a sadist's piss and have too much pride to give them a good look.

On graceful toes, I get into the shower. The water clings to my shirt.

"You should at least remove your bra . . ." Baldy says, readjusting the gun in his hand.

I roll my eyes and turn toward him. "I'm in cuffs, remember? You do it for me."

From my peripheral, Chip, whose conscious is less murky, folds his arms. The men exchange glances. Baldy presses his arm inward, garnering a tighter hold on the gun as he reaches forward.

"Should I?" Chip asks Baldy, gesturing toward the gun.

"Nyet, you can't aim for shit." The older man snorts. No, he wants all control. To get a good look at my breasts and hold the gun at the same time. Then his eyes swallow me whole. "I can help the little Castle Girl. She wouldn't dare try anything with this gun in my hands."

I toss my head back, the coils of my hair unmasking my face. "Yes, a poor, helpless female is what I am."

"Turn around," Baldy snaps.

"Why? It's a front latch bra," I lie, needing to keep him in my line of vision.

His pink tongue darts over his lip again. Baldy angles his right elbow tight to his ribs. His left hand reaches out, plays up the tail of my shirt, pawing at the flesh of my ass.

"Help her with the bra as she asked of you. Nothing else," Chip grumbles.

"Oh, I am," Baldy says, inching a little closer to me.

My forehead assaults his nostrils. Baldy and I go falling with him on top of me. A sharp pain, comparable to being stabbed with a needle, zeros through the side of my ribs.

"Fuck!" I screech. The bullet that went through my flesh clips into the porcelain wall. Again and again, I rear up and slaughter Baldy with my head. I flip my body around, slam a foot into Chip's face as he reaches down to grab me.

"What the fuck are you doing?"

The next hit goes into his privates. He slams to his knees, and I grip my thighs around his neck and twist. His dead body slumps sideways and on top of Baldy. The older guard groans. In a seated position, I press myself back until I'm parallel to the two. From behind, I feel for the keys in Chip's utility belt. My eyes glare through Baldy as he grunts and shakes his head. He shoves Chip off of him. With one cuff off, I grip Chip's gun and shoot Baldy between the eyes.

Brain foggy from battering the older guard's face, I jump into a standing position. I hoist myself into the jeans. I pull up the wet shirt, blood oozing beneath my left breast. A chunk of skin is missing where that mudak shot me. I drop it and hurry into my shoes.

There's banging at the door. Gripping the gun, I smile.

"What's going on in there?" asks an unfamiliar voice.

Planting myself between the toilet and the door, I unlock the knob. A Russian enters, and I shoot him in the head.

"Fuck, fuck, fuck," I mutter.

The dead man isn't wearing the standard uniform of Irek's men. Did Oleg have his own protection? He'd complained about a decrease in funding after the Resnovs terminated him. Which should indicate that he cannot afford his own detail?

Fuck it, Simeon didn't save me.

Luka is MIA.

If I die, I die.

I stalk out of the bathroom across the area where Oleg defiled me. I sift through the pictures and pick up the picture of the Invisible Thing, sliding the photo into my pocket. Nightmares were my fuel to survive, to save the Invisible Thing, and other women and girls like her. Now, I'm superwoman.

Adrenaline pumps through me as I open the bedroom door. "Where the fuck are you, Oleg?! I'm coming to get you!"

My eyes land on him down below. The banister spans across the entire length of the house. Stairs are at the far end, offering me the perfect vantage point for the man whose life I plan to tear apart.

But. He. Is. Not. Alone.

The idiot who died by my hands, along with Irek's guards, aren't the only ones. Five men, along with Oleg, rise from a table. Cards go flying as the table is toppled over.

These mudak's have guns.

Big ones.

And more ammo than the handgun I'm toting. Cursing Oleg's entire lineage, I wheel back on my heels. Bullets rain in my direction. Wooden splinters fly from the banister right before me.

"Don't kill her!" Oleg screeches. "Get—"

I slam the door to the bedroom, which seconds ago had been my prison cell.

"Okay, so you're a hothead," I tell myself, removing the clip of the .9mm to confirm the amount of ammunition I have. "You've warned Simeon of how not invincible he is. What the fuck, Asya, with seven bullets, you're far from invincible!"

A stampede charges up the stairs. I'm torn between dying and placing every last bullet in Oleg's head. And if I can't get to him?

When the table flipped, his crew were the first to show themselves. What's to say he won't keep himself hidden until the prized moment they strike?

And if I don't fucking die!

"You're fucked in so many different ways, Anastasiya," I grit to myself.

Eni-mini-mini-mo . . . I dash toward the picturesque window. Looking out, I verify freedom down below.

The door strains against the frame and hinges.

Thawp! Thawp! Someone's kicking it in.

Grunting, I grip at the windowsill. Tiny nails are wedged down into the grooves of it. Screeching, I run back, my calves touching the bed. I shoot out the window, and the lump in my throat falls. At least it wasn't bulletproof.

The door crashes open. With a running start, I jump and free fall amidst a sparkling shower of broken glass. A bank of snow welcomes and engulfs me, sending my body into instant shock.

"What are you doing?" Simeon cocked his head to the side as I lay down in the snow. We weren't children anymore. I'd claimed every part of him, and he'd claimed every part of me.

"You're telling me that you're spending how long at the Black Dolphin in another month?"

"Four years . . . I'll see you every chance I get, Anastasiya. Now get up."

"Are these four years of torture for all the times I've asked you to walk in the snow with me? Because of the book Snow Falling on—*"*

"Nyet. I have a plan." He kneeled before me. The peacoat framed his chiseled jaw. Sparks of light twinkled in his dark gaze. "I have to show my loyalty, moya milaya. When I get out of prison, I'm marrying you. Doesn't matter if you say nyet. Dah, I'll spank your ass all the way down the aisle to the altar."

My arms and legs continued to cut through the snow. "Sheesh, will God allow you in a chapel?"

He shook his head, a smile fading fast, though I'd captured the essence of it. "What are you doing, Asya?"

"Oh, this?" I glanced around me. "A snow angel. For your protection."

"My protection?" He cocked a brow. Then he claimed my thigh, stopping me from scissoring the soft, lush coldness. Simeon's knees planted around my hips. He pressed his gloved hands over my shoulders and pinned me down.

"It's a little too cold down here for you to stare at me like that," I murmured, the fog from my mouth kissing his lips.

A yelp stole across my mouth as I was launched into the air. Snow danced across his dark hair. Simeon looked up at me. "How about this? I plan to fuck you every morning, noon, and night before I leave."

"You already do," I giggled.

Simeon meticulously pulled at the leather of his glove. His thumb glided across the vulnerable silk of my throat. "We have to start searching for a better home for us to live in. And prepare you for the time while I'm away. Do you understand?"

"You mean a home for me to live in." Orbs filled with animosity, I looked away from him.

"Those angry eyes remind me of the sunrise." His voice started soft with a bit of satin, then rough, like when satin is stroked all wrong. "But you will make me bite them out of your head. Keep rolling them."

I pressed away from his chest, and Simeon clasped my wrists. The rom-coms and romantic literature I adored having him read to me were dead. We weren't children anymore. "I love our loft. I love what we have,

Sim. You gave the university two million to expand the library a few weeks ago—"

"Bratva money."

I chortle. "You're teaching there part-time. You've made friends with deans. Simeon, you're a benefactor for museums and libraries! I want to continue living at our loft."

We had created two worlds. One belonging to him solely. The other belonging to us. We were normal people.

"Shhh . . ." Simeon reached up and kissed the complaint from my mouth. He lifted me, biting softly at the apex of my sex. My pussy throbbed, my stomach flipped, and my heart flopped in my chest.

"Fuck me, Anastasiya. Right here, right now."

Suddenly, the cold disappeared. The frigid air felt warm and pleasing to my skin.

"Alright." I placed my hand across his throat. The muscles in his neck tightened beneath my hardening grip, and my sex ground down on his stiffness. "One condition."

"Dah?"

"Never leave," I murmured. "Stay with me forever."

CHAPTER 23

Simeon

I'm not drunk today.

Nyet, far too many important tasks on my agenda, such as Chutin signing his life over to me. Then my fingers will curl around Anastasiya's throat. I'll remind her who her true love is before asking if she had run to him or if he had stolen my matryoshka doll.

As her eyes fill with blood, I'll weed through the truth within all her lies.

And if Chutin stole what was mine, he will be taken to the brink of death a million times without touching peace.

And if it's a lie? Same scenario for Chutin . . . and my Anastasiya.

Dressed in all black, I sit on the balcony with my mother.

She's calmed down immensely since I tossed the vase of red roses over the side of the balcony upon arrival. Daintily cutting her eggs, she asks, "You're having tea with Irek Chutin? Have the two of you come to some sort of agreement?"

"Mom, I'm not here to discuss Bratva matters with you. How's breakfast?"

"Despite your barbaric ways," Sofiya's gaze flits over the ledge at my example, "you're my son. What are our intentions? Reaching out to him so soon after Anastasiya left?"

"A few weeks ago, I was dead to you, Mother. *Ahem*, 'you should *kill* yourself, syn?' " I cock a brow.

She clasps my hands, the bandages around her wrists on display. I take her frail, chilly fingers and place them on my jaws.

I sigh, "I know, Mom."

Sofiya's gaze shoots away from mine, then returns, gleaming azure, filled with tears.

"I know you didn't mean the things you said."

"Thank you." She lowers her eyes again. "I haven't been the best over the years . . . Your father hurt you, my words hurt you... my needs . . . desires. If something were to happen to you, moy syn, Mama would fight to the end of the earth! I would—"

I grab the knife in her hand, which had only been allowed in my presence for breakfast today. "You wouldn't rest until I was vindicated. Same goes if the situation were reversed, Mama. I'd fight for you." *Same for Anastasiya,* my conscious warns, brain at war with my heart.

"I'll miss him forever. You will have to understand that."

I arise abruptly. "I'll consult with Garbovsky for his opinion about your siblings' requests to visit."

"*You* are Tsar."

Dah, but I'm no shrink.

~

S team rises from a tea set fit for the Romanovs hundreds of years ago during the grandeur of their reign. I slide the book I haven't been able to concentrate on, on the silk brocade seat cushion. This room is fit for royalty. Fit for a woman like my gorgeous Anastasiya.

I hate it.

Everything is silk, diamond-encrusted, glass-vaulted, or red.

The red ruins the scheme of things because that very color is what this room should be painted in.

Or will be painted in, in precisely five minutes.

As Irek Chutin is escorted inside, I arise from my seat. His entourage consists of reinforcements. Ten of his closest, all brick necked, muscle-bound, and fully armed. The lack of trust causes my smile to widen.

"The new Tsar... excuse me. Not novel anymore. You've held your role, for what, almost two years now?"

He reaches me, hand extended. *Fuck you* gleams in my gaze. I gesture. A byki steps forward with a rectangular shaped gift. Red wrapping paper taunts me, beckoning me to warm my hands with Chutin's blood. The gift is awkwardly placed in Chutin's awaiting hand, promising that there will be no handshake.

I reclaim my seat.

My enemy taps his index finger over the edge of the gift before sitting down. "I have something for you as well."

"Me first." *I don't want your filthy gifts. The only recompense I require is your cold heart in my hands as I mash it into nothing.*

Chutin places the gift on the table and settles into the seat across from me.

I eye the gift and then smile at him. With the flick of my wrist, a maid begins to pour us both tea.

Irek glances at the tea, picks it up, and sets it back down. The *you-first* half-smile he offers in return is evident by his unwillingness to take a sip. *Paranoid mudak.*

"Open your gift," I order.

"I think I will." Irek plucks the box back up, gives it a little shake.

"Nyet ticking," I laugh sarcastically.

"Nyet, not with me sitting across from you, I presume. Nyet big bangs." This time, he loosens up with a chuckle before sliding his finger into the seam of the paper.

Irek tears into the red paper, tossing the Twenty-four-karat gold ribbon over his shoulder. Unlike Dominicci's men, who stood behind him to keep him safe, Irek's men take an interest. The president slows his curiosity and opens the top. Then he whistles.

"A knife..."

"Not just any knife..."

"Let me see if I have change. One of you must give me change." He smiles over at his team. Receiving the gift of a knife is taboo for us Russians.

"Won't be necessary." I shake my head. The saying goes, giving a knife as a gift turns friends into enemies, unless the receiver has a small coin to offer the giver.

"But I insist."

"But you mustn't. As you're well aware, the two of us have never been friends, never will be friends," I growl, then my voice returns to normal. "Let's resume with tea. Then we will discuss the most pertinent matter of all."

Attempting to speak over me, Irek chortles. "Someone, please, give me a coin. I've discarded less money. I can at least give you a coin for this."

Ignoring the joke, I retort, "After tea, we will discuss, *moya* Anastasiya."

"Who? Oh, the little girl. Let's discuss her." Steam fizzles from Irek's teacup as he lifts it. "Surely, such a *beautiful piece* is a worthy topic during tea. As I recall, she had a fondness for art too. Actually, the years are returning to me. I instilled those values in *moya Castle Girl.*"

CHAPTER 24

Mikhail

My aunt Sofiya had various addresses for Oleg, which she shared too quickly. She was too cooperative. I had it in my mind to ask what was behind those cold blue eyes. Instead, I rent a cross between a four-wheel drive and a hatchback and amazingly spent all morning on one tank of fuel.

At a quarter of a tank left, and one last address, in a rural area, I deign to return my father's call.

"Moy syn, I've received voicemail after voicemail from my old colleague, Dr. Dunn."

"Oh, you're chatting with friends now? How are you, Dad?" I feign innocent, toggling from the call application to the map. I'm not discussing Dr. Dunn, who'd been the hard-ass riding all the residents when I was once wet behind the ears. The Chief of Medicine continued to keep me under his wing. He offered even more support than my own father when my brother died.

"I said voicemails, Mikhail. I'm not up for conversing with

anyone. But when I receive concerned messages from a man whom I once esteemed, I react. You were supposed to begin at County?"

"Yes." I usher out a breath, contemplating my departed little brother, though fleeting. "I'm okay, Dad. Anastasiya's missing."

Malich exhales heavily. "Simeon will find her. Where the fuck are you, syn?"

"Helping Simeon . . ." I murmur.

"*Moy syn* was never a liar." His accent chimes through. It's as if he's sitting right beside me in mother-fucking-Russia.

"Sim isn't using half his brain right now, Dad." I slow around a road, windier than where Sofiya resides.

"Stop. Come home now! Yuri is the joke of the family. My beloved Igor is deceased. You're the only tie I have to this earth, Mikhail. I'm living to watch you marry, have children."

The GPS prompts me to take a left. On the screen, the passageway snakes into a smaller, curvier road.

"I have to go, Dad."

"You're a fool, Mikhail. No son of mine."

We hang up at that, at least, I have to assume the old man intended to have the last word.

The GPS calls out, offering the same prompt. A good-sized truck wouldn't gather enough clearance or width, but I begin to drive. Overgrown branches tap against the side of the windows. The wheels glide over battered roots. Five minutes in, there's a clearing. Farther up is a road running parallel to the dirt gravel I'm on, which probably leads to an easier route here. Little less than a kilometer away, a lone house stands. In the driveway are three trucks, and the sort of windowless van little girls should steer clear of.

It's the perfect remote location to hide an abductee.

"God, let her be here," I murmur.

Birds summersault into the sky in the rearview behind me as

popping sounds come from the house. Glass fragments and a figure flies from the side of the structure.

"Nastiya!" I shout, tugging the wheel to the right. Venturing off the gravel, I stall precariously close to a mound of snow.

"Anastasiya," I shout, shoving the door open. Leaning over, I reach into the glove compartment for a gun I hadn't anticipated using. Not unless it was on a man named Oleg. Immobile, she lays there. The nozzles of two Simi automatics tilt outside of the broken window. "Nastiya, fuck, wake—"

Their intent is not to kill *her*. Bullets chop at the ice near my front door. Anastasiya pops up into a sitting position. The shooting ceases.

"Not the girl!" comes a hard voice.

Then a fusillade of bullets flies in my direction, riddling the car. I zip forward, scraping the vehicle along the side of the wall as Anastasiya comes running. She opens the trunk of the hatchback and climbs in.

Her stark light brown eyes blaze through me. Even with pain laced across her face, she has this remarkable way to get under my skin. She asks, "Good Doctor, where's Simeon?"

"Sim isn't here. You have *me*." I turn forward, the muscles beneath the skin of my jaw moving in overdrive as the trunk slams shut.

"Where are you going?"

"Saving us," I grit.

She roars out in pain, then snaps, "The road is back—"

"That road leads toward those trucks. They probably have reinforcements and bulletproof windows. While all I have is . . ." I hold up the gun. Anastasiya grabs it.

"Will we fit? Oh, fuck?" She laughs as I zoom back through the trees.

"The real question, Nastiya, is, will they?"

Anastasiya mumbles about how "I'm her kind of crazy," as she rolls down the back window and begins to shoot.

Eyes darting, I drive through the dense trees. I breathe easier when a truck rams into a root, creating a barricade for the others to follow.

I glance through the rearview again. Her ass is tooted in the air, while half her body is leaning out the window. She's shouting for them to *come get us*, threatening to murder them all.

"We're good. I hope," I mutter.

"You're good. I'm not," she grits, sliding back into the seat. A streak of blood follows.

"Nastiya."

"Yes!"

"You're bleeding."

"I know." She fists the gun. "Oleg is back there, Mikhail. Thanks, but you defeated your purpose. Where is Simeon?"

I stop glaring, mash on the break, then ease around a tree. "I'm here, Nastiya. Not Simeon."

"I see." She seethes, snatching her hand along her ribcage where blood is seeping. "Again, we're headed in the wrong direction. Oleg—"

"Is back there with reinforcements, and all we have is—"

Anastasiya kicks at the chair in front of her. Her arm hangs out the window. She fires the rest of the bullets. When it's empty, she lays her head back with a huff. The air crackles between us when she meets my gaze in the mirror. An apology is practically on the tip of her pink tongue. Damn, if I weren't driving, I'd thread my fingers through her unruly hair. Do all the things that would have me tossed six feet under.

Finally, she speaks, "Thanks for saving my ass, Mikhail. I'm-I'm—"

"It's okay," I mumble at the caged animal then peel back onto the main road. "I think we're pretty much in the clear unless those guys decide to fly down the mountain. Like I said, Nastiya. You've got me."

~

S he was becoming delirious.

We were hours away.

Hours transitioned into ten minutes.

Then . . .

Through the dusk of evening, the tires trudge to a stop over the slushy gravel. Both hands on the wheel, I can hardly glance back at Anastasiya. The guilt of returning her to a monster weighs heavily on my mind. Head lowered, I ask, "You still—"

"Yes. I'm alive," she groans.

"Good. Give me a sec." I climb out of the car. Rather than the domineering palace, a lone log cabin looms ahead. We're about four kilometers past Simeon. A few minutes ago, I passed by the road, which would've led Anastasiya to *him*. Gave it the bird too. We're about ten kilometers closer to Aunt Sofiya's place. I've positioned the woman I'm madly in love with back into the middle of the fray.

Eyes shaded, I glance through the nightfall, searching for signs of life in the windows: nothing, all pitch black. I saunter toward the front door, praying nobody lives here. I saw the place, through the thicket, after taking the wrong road to speak with Sofiya this morning. I glance over my shoulder, only capable of seeing Anastasiya's shadow. She hasn't moved from her spot in the backseat.

I try the doorknob. Grainy rust peels off onto my palm as it turns. It opens. A hard sneeze barrels through me. My hand smooths over scraps of wallpaper, finding the light switch. A few bulbs across the room spark on while a few more flicker. The dim-lit room is darkened by old linen tacked to the windows. There's a bathroom to one corner and a small kitchenette.

"What the fuck are you trying to pull?" I whisper to myself. "Return the Tsarina, now."

In seconds, I'm opening the backdoor of the car and pulling

Anastasiya to my body, careful of her bullet wound. We'd stopped briefly a few hours ago. I had to get gas. She refused to let me dress her wounds.

I'll do that now.

Tend to her needs.

Then . . . talk sense into her.

"Sim," she grouses. Her mouth close to my ear, a delicious shiver almost runs through me, had she not spoken the wrong name.

"Not Sim." My lips hardly move. I press her closer to me, breathe her in. "Nastiya, we're still too far away. Your skin is pallid." I twine the truth with the lie. "I'll stitch you up before we hit the road again."

She groans the wrong motherfucking name again.

"I said, 'we've stopped so I can stitch you up.' " *Feed you. Talk some sense into you. Then we can leave this God-forsaken place.* "Okay?"

After laying her on the couch, I hurry back outside. I drive the car around the side of the structure, so as not to arouse suspicion from any of the Tsar's bodyguards. I grab my medical bag and a bottle of the family vodka.

I'll offer her enough to lighten the pain . . . and break her heart. She has to know. The beast isn't looking for her, not like I did. Not with the intent to love and help her. Not like me.

I kneel on the weathered rug before the couch. Hair shrouds Anastasiya's face. Her head is bowed as she sits. My fingers run through her thick tresses. I push them back, my mouth so close to hers. So fucking close that I hurt infinitely more than the flesh wound in her side. Her plush lips pull into a grit, and I'm reminded to mend her first.

"Drink this." I uncork the bottle, place it to her lips. Vodka dribbles her raspberry mouth, down her caramel chin. I don't lick it.

"Drink."

Alcohol rains down her throat. My fingers skate across the spilled liquid along her jaw.

Gliding her tongue over her lush lips in trepidation, she again asks, "Where's Sim?"

"You're hurt." I gesture to the vodka, and she takes another swig.

After a hard clench of her jaw, Anastasiya moans, "Thanks, I needed that. Mikhail, stop with the Good Doctor antics. I know my body. I've been shot worse. Where—"

I pluck a syringe from my leather satchel and ready a dosage, still ignoring her question. I wait a few beats as she continues to down the alcohol.

She giggles a little, eyes glittering in delight and uncertainty. "Good Doctor, should I mix vodka and whatever the fuck that is?"

"You trust me?"

"Ha, you're a man. That's a trick question if ever there was one." Anastasiya groans, climbing to her feet. Like a baby calf, her boots clamor around, gaining purchase on the dusty wood floor. In a fraction of a second, my arms steady the area where her waist amazingly zips in before jutting out into a bulbous ass and hips.

"You trust me?" My eyes meet hers.

Anastasiya's soft, tiny palms frame the back of my hands. I'm not sane enough to let go, and she doesn't stop me. She slurs out, "Mikhail, I trust you like family. But I gotta get to Sim. Have to tell him—"

"Stop." I measure out a leveled tone. "Nastiya, You've lost so much blood. Who's the man who told you to put *you* first?"

Her index finger juts into the air, sorely off her mark as she begins to wag it. "We're not talking about us. I-I-I have to—I'll be back."

Just like that, Anastasiya zips out of my embrace, headed toward the only door, which leads to the bathroom. The tips of my fingers tingle at the thought of her touch. My brain collects and files this moment for later. Right before she slams the door, she begs me to make a single call.

Again, she asks about the devil when the good guy is right before her eyes.

CHAPTER 25

Anastasiya

I know I'm dreaming. The day Anatoly attempted to rape me was a flurry, more than a nightmare. A day I'd never forget. Sixteen years old, and I'd never been so embarrassed. Simeon was a second away from condemning his father's soulless body to hell when byki stormed inside.

A slight gash pricked Anatoly's face before Simeon was snatched off him.

I blink and blink. I keep seeing them attacking Simeon. I didn't think he'd survive. But the tenacity in him. He'd ordered me to pack my things, blood dripping down his face. I'd driven us back to Moscow to his loft. Simeon was a bloodied pulp downstairs while I readied for a shower.

Leaning against the closed bathroom door, I contemplated leaving.

He wouldn't be angry. Couldn't. He never wanted this life for me. Never wanted Anatoly too close. I walked past the luxurious shower, which was so lengthy and deep, there were no glass doors. Without the strength to leave Simeon the polite way, I glanced out the window.

Long way down.

Then I climbed my tired, achy body into the shower, leaned against the wall, and let the hot torrents run down my dirty flesh.

Anatoly had his disgusting fingers inside of me.

"Grrrr!" I slap the sides of my fists against the marble wall.

The door opened. Wild eyes were the first thing I saw. Steam dissipated, and the rage in his gaze lessened. He thought something was the matter. Shock clogged my throat. I was FULLY naked!

He seemed to realize it too. There was a gleam in his eyes. He was looking me dead in the eye, seeing all of me.

"Sim," I began, glancing down at his boots. Blood was spattered on the tips and tiny drops of water joined them. He stood where the intricate pattern designated shower tile from the darker floor. Toeing the fucking line. *Voice hardly above a whisper, I said, "I'm naked."*

"You are. You were also screaming, so I came in here." His biceps stretched as he pulled the bloodied linen shirt over his head, dropping it, forgotten on the ground.

My tongue twisted. I tried my best to sound coherent. "If-if you want to get in the shower, I'll get out."

Simeon quickly undressed until all that remained was his underwear. He slowed momentarily, eyes drinking in the sight of me with wonder. Then his eyes met mine as his thumbs hooked into his briefs. My gaze darted so swiftly, the hypnotic aura surrounding him doubled down in my bloodstream.

I squeaked, "Wh-what are you doing?"

Simeon crossed the line. Water sprayed over the ridges of his muscles. All the jagged edges of him scared and enticed me all the same. My pulse quickened as he asked, "Can I assess you?"

I jutted my chin. "I'm not accustomed to you asking, Sim. But assess what?" I groaned internally. Worst retort ever!

"We aren't at the point where I take without asking. Not yet." Dark, captivating eyes descended over my flesh, leaving goosebumps. The water temperature was perfect, yet he had me scalding, frozen, exposed. "Asya, you tell me all he did to you."

The eyes of a murderer landed on mine. Simeon was not quite what I expected. Oleg would've torn me to pieces were I naked in front of him. Now, I felt Anatoly's fingers clawing into my sex.

Simeon stepped closer. His finger traced my collarbone then traveled down between the valley of my breasts. As his gaze followed the path he'd drawn, I wondered if he could feel the thunder of my heart. His finger continued to rove, ascending between my achy breasts, drifting back up to the other side of my neck. Simeon's touch raised goosebumps on my skin as he revered me like a priceless piece of art.

"Sim . . ." I gasped.

"I made a request, Asya. Tell me what he did." He twined my hair to the side, fisted it, and brought my gaze up. "I'm killing him one day. You tell me everything, and I'll ensure you're vindicated."

"Anatoly kissed me."

His body pressed against mine. Simeon rested his forehead against the wall. The tingle riding my body simmered out. An inferno radiated into me.

"He touched me, Sim."

"Where?" The sounds of his voice grew harder and scared the shit out of me. Simeon nipped at my lower lip. My brain begged me to touch him, his muscles, the tattoos beginning to flesh out across his taut skin. Touch him somewhere, but I was stuck between broken and scared.

"Where?" Simeon growled, his face a tempest of emotions.

Fury.

Impatience.

Lethal.

He dragged his teeth over the pulse-point at my neck, before letting his teeth sink in. "Tell me, Asya." He mentioned that I was his Achilles' heel while going straight for my jugular. I was afraid to tell him. Like I'd be the focal point of the rage volleying in him instead of his reason to react. He'd forget to play hero and kill me instead.

I sucked in the words. "Groped my breast. He pu-put his fingers inside of me."

The animosity transformed into a swell of passion. His lips dusted over the pain at my neck. "I'll kill him. For you, Anastasiya."

Nyet. Nyet. Let's run away.

The excruciating heat left me as Simeon reached over to grab a bar of soap. His large hands sudsed up. He pressed his fingers over my mouth, then down my neck along. When his hands moved away, my body lifted. I'd been sprawled against the wall and hadn't noticed, not until I magnetized toward him.

He repeated the process of lathering his hands. My nipples ached as powerful hands swept across my ripe breasts. My eyes flew up to his, begging for him to kiss me there—to take advantage of my emotions, to command my body for his pleasure. Our pleasure.

Simeon moved to his knees. The entire world tilted. The quartz wall I'd been posted against became the place where I laid my head, my trembling limbs, every inch of my shuttering body. Two strong hands pawed the sides of my breast, pulling them together. He groaned into my nipples, kissing them.

Burning orbs stared up at me. "He placed his filthy hands in your pussy, moya milaya?"

A ghost tightened its hands around my throat. All I had left to offer was a scarce nod. Simeon's thick chest tightened. He applied soap to his hands, and electricity fired off in the foggy air. Simeon's thick, calloused hands framed my curves, leaving a soapy trail. His hand's planted across the lips of my sex, meticulous in his movements. He cleansed me. When he removed his hands to grab more soap, I shuttered. Simeon gripped a handheld showerhead, stood, and looked me in the eyes while letting the water cascade over my aching flesh. All the shame and hurt from Anatoly's grimy fingers were replaced with a heated desire to be touched by his son.

Then something confusing happened. The walls lining my sex became heavy, throbbing, tingling, and spasming together.

"Damn, I want to fuck you so bad right now, moya milaya."

Feverish and speechless, I licked my lips.

"But you didn't say a single word, not one moan, all you did was tremble." *He shook his head.* "Next time I touch you, you'll tell me if I'm doing it right."

146

Stalk still, I watched him exit the shower, dry off, and leave. Then for a year, I had excruciating nights with Simeon so close. Until one day . . .

～

The dream of Simeon is fresh on my mind as I awaken. A lumpy pillow itches my face. I'm dressed in an unfamiliar long sleeve thermal and my jeans. A prehistoric tweed couch dips and sags beneath me. Eyes slamming shut at the thought of what transpired yesterday, I inhale frigid, dusty air.

My knight in shining armor lost his title yesterday. The role of hero was stolen by none other than *The Good Doctor*. A slight bit of condensation wisps from my lips as I run a hand over my thermal.

His thermal.

His scent surrounds me. A shiver runs up my spine, and I'm not sure if it's from the chilly morning or something else entirely.

The room is empty. Considering Mikhail may be in the bathroom, I quietly stuff my feet into my boots. I find the picture of the Invisible Thing and slip it in my pocket. With measured steps, I head toward the door. A pair of keys dangle from a rusted nail in the doorframe.

Heaping on a dose of self-deprecation, I mentally call myself *a sorry, crummy suka.* I fist the rental keys to stop the sound of them jingling together. Senses hyperalert, I glance over my shoulder while opening the front door.

Then my sad gaze pans forward, landing on warm, blue eyes, teeming with depth. I jump, caught red-handed. The air burns cold, yet the sun falls on Mikhail's wavy blond hair, a rightful halo. The logs Mikhail has cradled to his chest begin to tumble. I'd run from him last night. I stuttered and flat out darted toward the bathroom after he stitched me up, depriving him of a coherent reason.

Culpable, I dash down to grab a few of the logs.

"Don't, Nastiya." His voice caresses me like a torch, invoking

emotions: longing, guilt, hunger, shame. Softer, he adds, "Your stitches."

"I-ouch." I stand to my full height, clutching a hand along my rib.

Leaving the discarded logs on the ground, Mikhail plucks up the keys. The cheesy rubber rental-car ring suspends at the tip of his index finger as he offers it to me.

"It was cold sleeping on the ground. But I guess cranking up the fireplace is out of the question. You were leaving."

Mouth clamped tight. My head slinks up and down.

Mikhail eyes the key, a silent token of my deception. *"You were leaving. Running back to him. So here."*

Fireworks spark as the tips of my fingers clash with his. I almost have the keys in my hand when Mikhail whisks me up, gritting out, "You're bleeding."

"Mikhail, what the fuck are you doing?"

"I said, you're bleeding." His hands are firm against my hips as he carries me back inside to a wooden table. He sets me down and unzips his puffer jacket, exposing the beginning of a deep dive of muscles. *Crap.* I gulp in his scent from his thermal clinging to my chest. Silence permeates the air. He brushes my hair over my ear and runs his knuckles over my flushed cheek, mumbling about pain.

Little does Mikhail understand—I'm numb to the dull ache along my rib. "Um, I really have to go."

"I'm certain you do not." His hands plant on either side of the table ledge. He dips his head, gesturing for me to remove the thermal. Last night, I'd taken off the shirt I wore. It was soaked through. My brain had been fuzzed over, the vodka surging through my bloodless veins. This morning, I'm too damn aware of the attractive man in front of me.

"You understand how important it is for me to get to Simeon, Mikhail. I know you do." My gaze follows him as he removes his jacket. Muscles stack along his creamy, taut skin. Like fine, smooth clay, his physique forms a perfectly shaped V, traveling into his jeans. He finds his medical bag on the side of the couch. The trance breaks, and I mutter, "You know I have to get to S—"

"Who told you to look out for *yourself,* Nastiya," Mikhail barks. His broad back is to me as he sifts through his medical bag. I can pretty much imagine those charming baby blues are boiling hot sapphire.

Angered, my hands clutch the edge of the table as my legs swing. I shoot daggers at his back. "I am!"

"You are not." He whips around. The tension between us is so heavy. The sound of his boots echoes on the splintered floorboards. The leather bag is placed down next to me with a *thunk.* Grabbing a tuft of his hair, Mikhail growls, "You never did."

"Who are you, huh? The little angel perched on my left shoulder?"

"I wish." He shovels through the bag. "Stop regarding the demon on your right!"

"Simeon isn't—"

"Maybe I wasn't referring to *him.*"

The retort on the tip of my tongue dies there. I drop my leveled shoulders. Mikhail stops digging around, eyes dancing across my face. The edges of my lips furrow upwards, and his mouth blossoms into a smile too.

"Damn you, Mikhail. Stop arguing with me like we're an old couple. We'll never be—"

"An old, married couple," he huffs.

My gaze falls. His does too. His perfect ass leans against the table as he comes to a stop next to me. His hand lands on my thigh. Just like last night, I'm foolish enough not to issue a threat. My hand roams over his, fingers colliding, gathering into his larger ones. Both of us are staring off into space. His thoughts align with what should be while mine are stuck on the could have been.

Why did I recreate my version of perfection and include *him?*

"Mikhail, we can't do this. I just returned from . . ."

"Oleg."

Teeth chewing into my bottom lip, I sigh. This is the millionth reminder of how Simeon has yet to learn the name of my old headmaster.

Mikhail gives my hand a quick squeeze. Then he plants himself between my legs. "I don't want you vulnerable, Nastiya."

And you can't have me, anyway, period.

His forehead falls flush against mine, breath whispering the things that neither of us should say.

"*Good* Doctor, you're grieving—"

"I'm not fucking grieving Igor, anymore," he growls, framing my face with his hands. "Who was there for you, yesterday, Nastiya? Who?! I won't tell you the things Simeon did while you were away. How he acted! Know this; loyalty is standing right here in front of your strikingly gorgeous face!"

Mouth dangerously close to mine, I attempt to remove myself from his grasps.

I could.

I can't.

Not even my loaded precious Colt could save me. Only words will. Mikhail Resnov doesn't respond through actions. The Good Doctor sifts past my rotten core and straight to my soul and the tiny spark leading to a colossal connection that only Mikhail can pluck.

"I was there," he declares. "I'd die for you."

Pummeling at his chest, I growl, "For the past eighteen days, I breathed, I dreamt, I coveted Simeon. *I would die for—*"

In an instant, his hand collides with the side of my face, thumb trailing a thin line down my throat. Hard lips crush against mine. Mikhail's teeth sink softly into my flesh, begging for entrance. I grant him access. My eyes close at the taste of him. Kisses tease my neck. He bites softly at the curve of my exposed throat. I arch against his waist, fingers scraping into his shoulders. His skin is warm and smooth. His scent floods me with protection and craving. Each touch spirals through me. His hand burns up the inside of my thigh.

Trembling fingers wrought with desire begin to pluck at the button of my jeans. The sheer act crashes me back to reality. This is where I exit stage left. I gasp, "Stop, Mikhail, we can't. Not—"

"Okay, okay," he says, breath ragged. "I'll bandage you up, Nastiya. I'll be here for you, mend you one last fucking time. But I'm not staying in Russia. Not a second longer."

With a scarce nod, I start for the seam of his thermal, coercing myself not to inhale him again while slipping it over my head. When Mikhail touches me this time, all the fireworks in the world go off. His hands are tender, skirting like a feather over the delicate stitching.

Tender. Delicate. Simeon is incapable of such actions. My eyes warm over Mikhail, senses heightened. I find myself comparing him to a favorite canvas painting of mine. Artist unknown. Tiny blond, silver stubble graces his square jaw. He pauses from fixing my stitches to look up.

Like an idiot, I look away. There never was an us. Besides, all my mind could conceive for the last eighteen days was his younger cousin. I ignore the fiery sparks and cling to *his blood.*

The Tsar.

My obsession.

My first adoration.

The heaven and hell I've delved in, and I'm too far gone to ever let go of. Falling for Mikhail Resnov while crazy about Simeon Resnov would make me nothing more than . . .

A Castle Girl.

CHAPTER 26

Simeon

S aving Anastasiya was all that I'd ever aspired to do. Keeping her at my side and loving her. Last night, I dreamt of the day my father placed his dirty hands on her. That evening with her in Moscow at my side, where she should've been all along, I made a mistake.

I touched her before she was ready.

I let the dream rove through my mind.

Maybe she never truly was. My cousin, Kirill, who has slept for over two weeks, breaks through my contemplations by clearing his throat. When my hard glare lands on him, he nudges his chin to the food on my plate. "Are you eating that?"

"Dah." I grab the crispy bacon. It tastes like shit as I chew and shovel it down my throat. Nothing is the same.

"You going to kill me?"

I lean back in my seat, surrounded by too many fucking chairs.

The dining room could be filled with children, all the little babies Anastasiya was to bless me with. But it's not. I nod to my cousin's inquiry. "Dah."

"Sim," he groans.

"I'll kill you softly." Half of me isn't lying. For one, he's my blood. Two, he saved me from a mistake yesterday. Assassinating Irek Chutin would've been my death sentence. The death sentence of the entire Bratva. "I have no intention of murdering you, Kazen."

Kirill lifts his mug of coffee. I lift my mug of vodka. He mutters in hesitation, "Good."

"You have my word. That mudak, Mikhail, finally left. His lack of follow-through is the reason you woke up." I grit my teeth. *Where is that weasel, Mikhail?* I hadn't asked about him since the day Anastasiya disappeared. I hadn't ordered any byki to monitor him since then, either. Nevertheless, I was told he left early, yesterday morning.

Late the night before, the mudak had assumptions written all over his face, as if he thought I'd cheat on Anastasiya! I played into Mikhail's notions. I had been deep in concentration while reviewing the old Resnov Castle rosters for a missing link. I may have even fallen asleep with my eyes open. I hadn't noticed the maid's ass in my face until Mikhail brought me back to reality with his blatant accusations.

My loyalty to Anastasiya has never wavered physically.

Though I have doubted her since getting my hands on the letter she left me, no other woman in this world can compare. My next taste of the female race will be the honey between her thighs. Then she'll be dead to me—literally, *physically.* I toss back my drink, needing the burn of Resnov Water to numb my heart.

"Kirill, you woke up right on time. I don't understand how you'd think I'd poison the president's tea. What have I always told you, Kirill? What do I thrive off of?"

"The *how.*" His mouth pulls into a line. "When we find Anastasiya, with all due respect, Tsar . . ." My cousin looks me in the eye. His loyalty to me as a ruler is on the same level as it once had been. "*How?*"

How will she pay for Luka's death? Part of me, the idiot who fell for the girl all those years ago, wishes I had given her the means to leave the country, to leave me.

The demons in me will search for moya Anastasiya from the surface of this earth to the depths of hell.

And the darkness will win.

I'll find her.

I'll appeal to the Seven, especially Kirill's father, for keeping his son's death a secret. And I'll kill the woman I once—

"My apologies, Tsar." The very maid Mikhail accused me of staring at bows her head at the archway of the dining room. "The Tsarina."

My hand slams onto the table. "What of her?!"

"She's here. The byki at the perimeter confirmed it was her, driving in now."

All the muscles in me are propelled out of my seat. The suka's lips continue to move. I'm followed by my closest crew. Someone suggests having her searched before she sees me. I continue across the grand sitting room and to the doors.

"Move!" I growl at another maid in the process of opening one.

Gripping the hand-carved knobs, I pull both doors open. A car is sputtering along the road, gaping bullets at the driver's side.

The door opens, the woman, the vision who swallowed the sun and commanded its glow, climbs out. Puffy, crinkled tresses are in her face. My eyes latch onto hers. I start down the stairs. Anastasiya flies up them.

She's in my arms in seconds. I fist her hair, smell the soft soap of her. But beneath that, she's tired. I scoop her into my arms.

Kirill stares, awaiting my regard for Luka. They all stare. Without saying a single word to them, I carry Anastasiya to our room.

~

Her legs lock around my waist, cheeks flooding in tears. "Simeon, I never thought I'd come back to you . . ."

My jaw clenches. The letter sears in the pocket of my lapel as the backs of my fingers brush her cheek. I taste her mouth. I'm drunk but not too drunk to distinguish reality. She's *here*. Our tongues begin to twine, though fire burns inside of me, consuming me. The fury transitions into a supernova, warning that her life is in my hands.

Anastasiya comes up for air. She moans against my mouth. "It's been a nightmare. We have to—"

"Moya milaya, I'm so lucky to have you here, right now."

"Me too," she gasps. "I was taken—"

My mouth descends on the liar's again. Maybe the kiss will suffocate her half to death, so these hands are spared the guilt? But then my cock gets in the way. Its wishes conflict with mine.

Kill her later.

Fuck her now.

"All will be right, Asya. Not this second, but I promise you. I. Will. Make. Every. Wrong. Right."

I nip at her jugular. Funny, I did the same years ago. She'd been in the shower after my father had touched her. I shouldn't have touched her the same day. She hadn't been ready then. It took another year for her to stop trembling, save for an orgasm.

But after I'm satisfied, she will quiver at the tips of my fingers. The part of me who loved her entirely too soon will soften as her heartbeat tapers into nothingness.

I kiss her with every ounce of me. This is the last time I will love her body without Asya understanding how ruthless I can truly be.

Her fingers are silk on my jawline. "Sim, I love you. I've missed you."

My tongue twines over the sparkling tears at her cheeks. "I love you more."

My kisses form a trail of fire down her neck. I tangle a hand in her hair. Her sex welcomes me, hot between our clothes. Asya's legs lock tighter around mine. In one fluid motion, I plant her on the balcony railing.

"Sim." Anastasiya glances over her shoulder. It's a long way down. She tries to press herself into me. Distress singes across her honey skin. My hands plant around her throat, mouth stopping her cry of apprehension. I lean her body back over the ledge.

"Sim, you're drunk—"

"Hold onto me," I growl, as her heart thunders against my palm. "I'll continue to hold onto you. Like we always do, dah?"

I sit her back up on the ledge. She snatches a piece of my shirt, attempting to level her upper body as I descend to my knees. I rip the jeans from her flesh, tearing them to shreds.

Nyet panties.

The inferno building inside of my chest is almost at a crescendo. Nyet motherfucking panties! She has the audacity to create a façade with that crap automobile and these tattered clothes.

I dig in. My lips fly to her pussy. The animal in me over-shadows all thought, reason, killing my brain, and all the ways I planned to murder her.

Her fingers cling to my hair, ass rocking on the ledge. Anas-tasiya's pussy blossoms into a wet funnel, suctioning my tongue as she growls in orgasm. The fear of her upper body no longer warns about misplaced equilibrium. My tongue strokes her core, and she sighs deeply. She levels her calves against the short wall in an attempt to keep steady.

Asya's entire body reacts, shaking violently as I eat my fill of her. My cock strains as my mouth engulfs the lips of her pussy, slurping up her orgasm.

"Simeon!" Anastasiya screeches, momentarily broken. A second later, she's whimpering and hugging against my face. Her legs wrapped tightly around my head. "Sim, this is . . . scary . . . but so fucking good."

I clamp a hand along her thigh, remove her curvy legs from around me, and stand. Asya reaches for me again, and my jaw grits.

She left.

Now, she wants me to support and protect her?

"I've already promised not to let you go. You trust me, dah?" My thumb strums her clit while my other hand unbuckles my belt.

"Yes."

I cock a brow, glancing at the vice grip she has of my wrist as I toy with her pussy. *My fucking beguilement.* Slowly, her silk fingers unwind around my wrist. She holds her body in a tilted position, still hoping not to topple down to her death.

Too easy.

Gripping her hips, I guide my cock into an ocean. My hands wrap around her neck. My lips plant delicately at her mouth.

Her fucking letter. A silent vow between us that she failed me. I'm sending moya milaya to heaven today because of it. She'll have my forgiveness in death. My hip movements slow, the pace becoming her torture. I can almost taste her blood.

"Faster," she groans.

My speed increases to a punishing rate. She bucks, gasps, her declaration of love coming in a crescendo.

"Fuck, Sim!"

Was that pain flickering in her eyes?

Why should I care? She killed me four years ago. Then I was resurrected in Miami at the sight of her. My little Tsarina played the game of double jeopardy, killing me again the day she fled and left that note.

I fuck her hard, the letter before my eyes. I'll frame it. Her sorry excuse for an apology will be the reason I never let another suka bat their big, gorgeous eyes. My cock pistons through her cunt, juiced all up.

Fuck. Before her, I'd never met a wetter suka.

After her, it will be the same.

My cock sweeps into her swollen cunt, diving deeper, faster, harder. My cock twitches and convulses as her pussy walls cling tightly to it. I grunt my release, holding her tight.

Breathing yet to return to normal, Asya moans. "Shit, I . . . that was heaven, Simeon."

Dah, my sentiments exactly.

"I love you so much." My hands tighten. I let her upper body descend more, over the ledge, parallel to the ground, forty feet below. The sun shines down on all her glory, all her gorgeous curves. Heaven opens up. The light suffuses her, deeming her worthy. Time for the Man upstairs to take her. He forgives. For the first time in my life, when it regards Anastasiya, I won't.

CHAPTER 27

Anastasiya

My brain had been pleasantly fuzzy, deliciously delirious. Now, my pupils expand. I stare up into Simeon's eyes. The unsettled feeling that I hoped wouldn't become familiar to me from earlier returns. It lines the pit of my stomach with rocks. Simeon's dark orbs are glossed, but not a single tear falls.

"Moya milaya, moya Tsarina, moya everything." Voice growing thin, Simeon repeats, "My everything, my everything," his words trailing off. The look on his face is complex, thoughtful, haunted. It dims into grief like the fallen angel's last thoughts before plunging into the abyss.

He. Is. Hurting. Me.

He is purposefully using those murderous hands of his, which have claimed lives but meant me no harm, to hurt me. Realization collects like fresh rain growing stagnant down an alley's drain. Our love dies in his eyes.

Simeon has choked me while fucking. And I have loved it. Orgasming and passing out is euphoria. That's not *this*.

Fire lights along my throat. The pain is more excruciating than anything I've ever endured.

This is murder!

For a while, I stare at him. When Kosta and I lived in the states, the show *20/20* was one of my addictions. During one episode, in particular, the cheating husband was in bed with his wife. The reenactment played out where the husband was choking her to death. The forensic analysts, or whatever they're called, suggested that the wife hadn't expected a thing. She did not attempt to save herself. Her husband didn't have a single defensive wound. The analyst had a theory. She didn't expect to die.

Well, I have a theory.

The bitch loved her husband too much.

My hands fly up at the last second before death claims me. At the thought of falling, I buck.

Simeon lets me go. His hand curls through my tresses. He yanks me to the ground. A flash of relief of not being propelled to my death passes through me.

I growl, "What the—"

It's Miami all over again. He does something. Touches my neck, and I pass out.

~

N^{ow} My eyes flutter open to an immaculate ceiling. Chandeliers clutter the vast ceilings like clouds in the sky. The handcrafted crystals blur as hot tears burn my gaze. I start to raise my hands to press them over my face, to do something I haven't thought of in ages, to pray. Yet my arms don't heed to my request. *Volk!*

My thoughts fly to him. A swarm of barmy memories takes siege. The shame of Oleg rewinds. The hot sludge of his semen coating my skin moves in my mind's eye in reverse.

"Ssss," I groan Simeon's name, my sobs muffled by duct tape over my mouth. *Please, please don't let this be real. I'm home. I'm home! I dreamt that I'd driven home.*

How? My mind taunts. *How the fuck did you get home, Asya, think! You were in a room at Oleg's then—*

"You've awoken."

My head zips to the side. The voice is heavy with animosity. Yet my sight doesn't fail me.

Simeon climbs onto the bed, planting his knees along the sides of my hips. With a scrutinizing gaze, he says, "Watching tears slide down someone's face right before the end—it's all a pleasure to me. But you, my Anastasiya, you're irrefutably beautiful when you cry."

Brain still collecting information, I recall Mikhail was the reason I could flee Oleg. It all led to me returning to Simeon, who welcomed me home, gathered me into his arms.

Gentle, firm lips catch the tears across my cheeks. Meticulous, he presses his mouth against the barrier between us. Yanking at the delicate silk confines, I pull with my arms, and my soul screams.

"When I first saw you after four fucking years, Anastasiya, I wanted to tear you apart." Simeon's deep baritone drones out every word. "I told myself to gut you in half, get back the heart you stole from my chest." His hand skirts across my collarbone to my throat.

A whimper of a cry crashes deep within my chest.

"Then I saw you, and just like that, you fucking had me, Asya. You had me. And you used your deceptive tears about an innocent baby. . . about how others kept us apart." His eyes gleam with the notion that I've lied to him.

"Plllll—" I begin to plead. Simeon is always the reason between us. Yes, it might not seem as such. But he was. He found me many years ago, and he saved me. When the world up and decided our love was too vast for the earth to hold it, Simeon welcomed me home with open arms. He loved me after all the fucking cards were stacked against me. Again, I strain against the duct tape, my voice raw.

I watch as he reaches into the lapel of his suit jacket. He pulls out a scrap of paper.

"For eighteen days, I've kept this where my heart once was. A subtle reminder that you never truly gave a fuck about me, my beautiful Tsarina."

He shoves the paper in my face, too close to read. Then Simeon speaks, verbatim, " 'Though it seems I've abandoned you twice, you have to know how much I've always cared. For now, all I can give you are my—' "

My apologies with love. My mind fills in the conclusion. *That bitch screwed me, and now she's dead! I'm so dead too!*

CHAPTER 28

Mikhail

I delivered an ultimatum. Made a declaration. I kissed her with all the passion in the motherfucking universe. None of it was her saving grace. She ran back to the devil.

The bastard brought out the worst parts of her, and yet, I wouldn't trade a single argument or retort. The makings of Anastasiya epitomized perfection, and she was letting him win. Fade the glow in her, fill her with darkness.

My feet ache from the long walk. It's a long fucking way back to hell. The threat I made about leaving Russia is for naught.

I'm not conceding.

Not until . . . I'm sure of Anastasiya's safety.

The only person with wool over their eyes was me. Her undying love for Simeon—that shit hurt. But with each step I take, trekking up the lonely road toward a life I never craved, I contemplate how I will stay.

"Just to make sure she's safe," I tell myself. The textbook version of addiction runs through my mind. I fit the bill. Every box checked. My drug is outside the realm of my grasp.

Over two hours later, I'm meandering past imports, Simeon's legion saunters down the front steps.

"Kazen?" Kirill's eyes sparkle with a question. "What brings you by? Conveniently on the same day the suka arrived."

I cock a brow. "What bitch are you referring to?"

He smiles, planting his hand on my shoulder. I place my hand on top of his, squeezing his fingers together as his hand bites into my shoulder. "Kirill, I'm not a fucking pushover."

He chortles. "Nyet. I heard when Igor died that you grew a pair. You helped Vassili with his psychotic sestra? I heard you had it in you. But when *Simeon's* suka returned and the pizda I know you for returns too, dah? Show me what you've got."

I yank his hand down and toss my left fist at his nose. Kirill ducks. His fist slams into my gut. I spit blood in his face, kicking my foot out at him.

"Again, I'll ask," Kirill cracks his neck. "Why the fuck you here, Kazen?"

"Who are you to question me?" I roar. "You murder Simeon? Are you the Tsar now?"

"Blasphemy."

"Then who the fuck are you but a lapdog, Kirill?"

"Kirill Resnov is my first in command." Simeon's lethal voice comes from the top step.

"Simeon, did you murder the Tsarina?" Kirill winks at me with his back to him.

Simeon's eyes glitter. Flecks of blood are on his white linen shirt. I've heard the bastard say he prefers this attire for torture. My heart falls into my chest.

"Why would the Tsar," I begin a collected tone, "murder his Tsarina."

"Because." Simeon becomes the definition of pause for effect.

I'm a broken man, and he'll be responsible for sending me over, no doubt.

"Because, Mikhail, *my* Tsarina killed Luka. That is the only reason I'd murder her. Sure, Anastasiya has failed me, failed me lots. Beautiful as she is, I'd put her on a fucking leash and keep her, regardless of her faults. But she murdered my blood. Your blood."

"So." My hand feels like putty as I heft it up to feign nonchalance and rub the back of my neck. "So, you think she murdered our cousin, Luka, and . . ."

"And?" Simeon shrugs. "Vindication of a Resnov is the proper course, is it not?"

He steps toward me. "Feel free to refute my statement, Kazen. You're family. Don't be afraid to disagree with me."

CHAPTER 29

Simeon

I focus on Mikhail. He returned home suddenly. The wrath emitting from him is enough for me to toss his dead body in a ditch.

"Disagree. You should." I dare him, shrugging, "If your opinion differs from mine. You have that right." *Give me a reason to apologize to my uncle, Malich. The slightest reason.*

He says nothing.

I address Kirill. "I'm not killing Anastasiya today." *Maybe never. Breaking her is a little easier than living a life without her.* "She will provide you with the exact details of Luka's death. Not today. But you have my word, Kirill."

He gulps, nodding slowly. This is not the response he was looking for.

"After she provides you with details, I will advise the Table of Seven as required." I leave them to their own sad existence and head back inside. The second I left the torture chamber with Anastasiya bound to her bed, I forgot how to hate her. Now, as I head back to the room, the letter burns in my brain like a seal of her dishonesty.

How could she?

Don't fucking do this to yourself, Simeon.

Foregoing the elevator, I climb the steps to the third floor to enter the room. *Grow numb to the whimpering,* I warn myself. Her sobbing comes in a stutter then tapers off. Her breathing is rhythmic as if she's falling into a fitful slumber. I settle in a chair. A tiny smile reaches my face at the thought of her holding a knife to my throat that one fucking time I kicked her out of the bed. She had nicked me a little. After that, I placed blankets and pillows in the tub then slid Asya's loud, sleeping ass inside of it. She liked that.

Don't think about good times either. She wavered in her love, not me!

I pluck up the book I've been reading for weeks. It has never taken so long for me to finish a novel. I rub my hand over the binding. Feeling a set of eyes on me, I place the book down and look up. The pillow beneath Anastasiya's head is wet through. Her tears run along the side of her face.

"You've awoken, my pretty Tsarina," I murmur, rising to my feet. "Are you hungry?"

Her eyelids hood, transforming into slits.

I point a finger at her. "I'm the stupid one. I'm in love with you, Anastasiya. The truth is blaring in my face. All your actions over the last four years. I'm the mudak who can't stop loving you. *I asked if you're hungry! I'm not the fucking monster here. You are. Nod your head!*"

Hissing, I arise from the seat and climb on top of her. "I can't kill you. I should. Were I not the Tsar, it'd be far more than required. The Seven would kill me too. And you know what," I clasp her face. She tries to turn away. My fingers bite into her flesh. "I'd let them. Let them do us both in because I don't go any-fucking-where without you. That's loyalty, that's love, moya milaya."

Her eyes water. I glance away.

Gritting my teeth, I start again, "I've learned my lesson. So, you go no-fucking-where without me, dah." I nod her cute little head, chuckling. My laughter fizzles, growing psychotic. I reach over and grab the vodka to burn away my sorrows, sober me up.

"Listen, after you tell me what happened to Luka." I snatch her chin again. She's furrowing her brow at me. "Stop with the innocent, oblivious gaze, Asya!"

I pull the duct tape from her lips, offer her some Resnov Water. "Sim, I didn't—"

I slap the duct tape back over her lips, popping her mouth a few times. "Don't take advantage of my generosity. I offered you food. You glared. I offer you a drink. You revert to lies!"

Drowning in more vodka, I toss the empty bottle, and it shatters against the marble wall. I remove the knife from my blazer and skim it across her flesh. I don't revel in the tremble of her warm brown tone, not like I anticipated.

"What happened here?" I trace the light pink hue of fresh two-inch stitching right along the side of her breast and ribs. "Catfight?"

Eyes closed, her body shakes as more tears collect in her eyes. I press my mouth over one of her closed eyes then the other. "Nyet? Am I to assume you were too overwhelmed with the life I offered you? You left. Life not so pretty, got in a fight at a bar, club . . . oh, a strip club? You been shaking that sexy ass, those perky tits for the past couple of weeks, dah?"

At my words, I begin to pluck the stitch work. Her body tenses then vibrates. More tears fall as the wound is plucked open. But unlike her, who left a gaping hole in my fucking heart, I'll stitch it right back up.

～

I failed. I couldn't stitch Anastasiya up. With every snip of her sutures, it felt like lava was desiccating my fucking skin. The honey pool of tears spilling from her eyes sent me straight back out of the room once I left her with an open wound. I had a byki fetch a maid. I'd ordered the servant to complete the job, neatly, without inflicting any more pain, and to ensure Asya showered and was fed.

Then I ventured into the Armenian's room and let him go. Not alive. My concession would've left the Bratva vulnerable to retaliation. I shot him execution style.

Hours later, after I've had a shower of my own, I contemplate Asya while eating a cold meal. I decide to walk upstairs and check on her when my cellphone chimes.

"Fuck," I groan, answering the call. "Dah, Mother?"

"Moy syn, I've waited for you to call me."

"About what?" My eyebrows furrow. Did I miss any reports regarding Sofiya's welfare?

"Our Anastasiya." Sofiya's voice dips. "She's home."

My head tilts. Light ribbons beneath the door of Anastasiya's room. "I have to go, Mother." I hang up while my mother is jovially asking to see the woman I cannot help but love. Fisting my gun in my hand, I open the door, prepared to kill whoever came to see the girl I love after dark.

My gaze collides with something I never in a million years expected.

CHAPTER 30

Anastasiya

Heaven and hell clashed, creating a parallel universe this afternoon as I'd watched Simeon. The highlighter roved over his tattooed knuckles. Thick eyebrows kneaded pensively. The only tell that he wasn't enjoying the book, while assuming I was asleep, was the line formed by his lips. Then he'd shattered my heart beyond repair.

I'm tied to the bedpost with only a linen sheet to cover the fresh, red negligee that the maid must have assumed was suitable attire. Furious tears wash over my cheeks. The maid had stitched me up, fed me, and hummed while I bathed. When she wasn't looking, I was able to secure the picture I'd taken from Oleg's, my source of strength now.

I speculate how late it is when the doorknob rattles. The person on the other side lacks a key, but the metallic scratching sounds like they are picking it. As they enter, I can tell it's not the maid's frail figure coming. The height is all wrong: broad shoulders, slightly narrowed waist, narrower than Simeon's.

The man I pledge to never in a trillion years love has again left me in a compromising position.

I snatch an intake of air I hadn't known I needed. Looming over me is Kirill, his frosted eyes probing into my soul. The only sound is our breathing.

After a while, he bites out, "You killed *him* in cold blood?"

He leans in closer, enough to warm my clammy skin. His calloused fingers travel feather-soft over my cheek as he removes the duct tape with extreme care. The act causes fragments of my time with Oleg to compete with Kirill's demented voice.

"I'll undo your restraints. Then you can tell me all I need to know." He unravels the binding at my wrists. "Depending on if I believe you, one of us will live. I bet it'll be me."

Kirill descends on the chair Simeon commandeered earlier. He looks away as I wrap the linen sheet farther around me. "Asya, I apologize for not allowing you a moment to dress, but I've waited for answers. *My brat, not yours, has waited to be memorialized.* My ma, my fucking pa, deserve answers, and they aren't even aware Luka is . . . d-dead."

"Luka is dead?" My voice trembles. I clutch the blankets tighter around my goose-bumped flesh.

"Luka!" Kirill growls. "Don't play games, Anastasiya. Almost all my life, I've granted you the same respect, return that shit! You knew I was referring to Luka."

I tilt my head and ruminate of his words. "Luka . . . dead?"

Kirill pulls the elastic from his ponytail. It would be an intimidation tactic if you hadn't the pleasure of knowing him before his golden locks grew out. Others would be afraid right now. Hell, I'm stuck in a parallel universe. I should be afraid, but my entire body is trapped in *Disturbia*. He mustn't be ready to kill me. He forks at the wild strands then places his hair into a high bun.

"Lu-Lu- Luka is dead?" I clutch a hand to my chest, shuffling more oxygen into my lungs.

"Dah." Kirill's eyes dance across mine, searching for the same deception that Simeon expected earlier. "You—you don't know, do you?"

In trepidation, my head tracks side to side. The blanket I'd had around me slips to the ground. My trembling hands press against my face. I sob. "No, no, no . . . my brat."

"Not your brat!" he roars. Those glacial orbs have gone stale, glossing over with unfallen tears.

Hands soaking wet, I rub my forearm across my eyes, collecting the broken dam. Accusations are slung my way.

He gestures toward me. "You ruined him. Made him soft."

"I love Luka! He's my friend, *my motherfucking brat.* That's what I fucking said, Kirill! You were too, once. But Luka, Luka's dead?"

"Dah." Kirill offers a venomous roar. "What did you do?"

"Nothing."

He settles back in his chair. "What do you mean nothing? You know something. You know everything!"

"No! My last memory of Luka . . . we were driving." I have to think hard. The fuzz of a few days ago seems to clear a bit. "We-we crashed . . ." Images flit through my brain, stitching back together. I gasp, finally remembering. "He was wedged against a tree—"

"Dah, and you got out, but before you did, you shot my brat, point-blank range."

"No!"

"Funny, I don't trust a mudak who refuses to speak Russian! Like our kazen, Mikhail. You're too good for the language, but you ride my other cousin's cock." Fisting the armrests of the chair, he assesses me. "You riding Mikhail's too? Is that where you were this entire time?"

"No, you sick fuck. We crashed, then I was *taken* by Irek Chutin."

He waves me off. "Lies. Listen, I'll give you a fucking knife before I take you down with my bare hands!"

"Don't sound so noble. I'll murder you with my fucking hands, Kirill!" I spit, "Chutin took me to Oleg!"

"Nyet." Kirill shakes his head. "Took forever, but we had eyes on Irek. Simeon might have lost his life trying to murder him because of you. All lies, Anastasiya."

Jaw tensed, I stand, and he does too. "Fuck you, Kirill. I'd never murder Luka. And Chutin told me that they fixed his security systems, satellites, whatever. He said that the day he took me never existed. That he made me vanish." I raise up to my full height. "And don't talk to me about Simeon. I have more loyalty in my little toe than *your Tsar!* Simeon tried to murder me."

Kirill gulps hard, momentarily considering what I've said, then shrugs. "Keep your little sob story about my kazen to yourself. The two of you are crazy about each other. That's why I'll kill you and die. I don't give a fuck!"

"Fuck you. Fuck Simeon." My chin lifts a fraction, eyes ablaze. *"Fuck all you, Resnovs."*

"And I said, I don't care. I'll take you to Simeon. You tell him this story about Chutin and this Oleg. We confirm your story, and then you either live, or you die for murdering my brat. My brat."

I point my index finger into his chest. "Clearly, you cannot comprehend English. I said, 'Fuck you and your entire lineage,' Kirill."

We stare at each other. He's a foot taller, even without his wild shock of hair, and has enough muscles to slam straight through me. With my chin high, the lace negligee strains against my breasts, irritating the stitching at my ribcage. Damn, I wish I had shoes, and regardless of all the shit talk, I'd take the knife Kirill offered earlier.

The door is yanked open. My hand chops against Kirill's throat. I was expecting the maid, but my shoulders slump as I glare into the eyes of the devil himself.

"Leaving so soon." Simeon dominates the exit.

Kirill coughs, hands clutching for his throat. In seconds, I own the gun at the back of his jeans, leveling it toward Simeon. "Yes, Sim. Goodbye forever, bitch."

"Nyet. You and I readdressed our vows to each other a few hours ago, girl. I'm a man of my word. I won't kill you. Perhaps, in a couple of months, I'll set you aside for a little while." He takes a collected step closer to me. "Keep you somewhere nice. Give you an allowance so big you can't spend it. Come fuck you on a whim, once in a while, dah? Sounds gracious to me."

"Because I'm a Castle Girl." Eyes on him, peripheral fixed on Kirill, I step back a few paces. "A Castle Girl and all I deserve is reciprocity for sex."

"I offered you myself. All my waking hours since *you left* have been consumed with finding you. Killing all my fucking byki for not *finding you! All I know, all I fucking want, is you!*" Simeon stabs the air between us. Those pitch, dark eyes cast toward Kirill. But his blood has become the loyal soldier, still believing in a lovers' quarrel. "You apparently didn't want my love."

"How about this." I lift my head to the ceiling. "How about I loved you more than life itself, placed you in a position to be a god to me. Placed you here!" I anchor out my hand, ascending onto my tippy toes as high as possible.

A disbelieving grin adorns his lips.

"Loved you so hard. Had your fucking child," I hiss. "You think I lied about leaving you in the Black Dolphin. Guess what? I don't care anymore. Before today, I'd swear you had enough fucks to give for the both of us. When you found me in Miami, you mended my heart. I doubted us. *You fucking sustained us.*"

A look of profound fury crosses his face. "I did!"

The gun no longer weighs like power in my hands. Though I'll hate myself for it, I utter the truth. "Now, you don't love me anymore."

"I still do."

"Not so much." I continue to dig myself a grave, ready to topple into it by pulling the trigger on Simeon.

"Dah, not so much," he sighs. "Though, my obsession is at the same level. As I said, you can't steal someone's heart and expect—"

"Expect you to be constant, whereas it appears I've wavered all along. I understand. It's okay, Sim." I sniffle back tears. "Because today, I've decided that if you can live without me, *I can live without you.*"

"You have lived without me!" he sneers.

"Because of your mother!" I seethe. "Because of Sofiya. Not Anatoly. Not anyone else in this fucking universe. Your suka of a mother, Sofiya, did this to us. The result of her actions has made *you dead to me!*"

CHAPTER 31

Simeon

"My mother?" I retort, I still believe she's deceitful. Anastasiya had begun to lower the gun. Now, a renewed vigor is in her gaze as she holds the weapon toward my chest. In disbelief, I repeat, "My mother?"

"Sofiya dated an Armenian after divorcing the man who claimed to be your father. The weakling who took the Resnov name instead of forcing his wife to take his name."

My mother.

This was true. Sofiya's relationship with the Armenian was fleeting. Anatoly caught wind of her relationship, and her lover was never to be seen or heard from again. My mouth moves without warrant. "What are you saying?"

"She tore us apart four years ago, Simeon. I had a child die in my arms because of her. If I didn't have somewhere to be, I'd kill that bitch right now."

I start toward her. A bullet zips past me.

"I'm leaving, Simeon."

A story begins to stitch together in my psyche: my mother, the villain. What would be Sofiya's motive?

"Anast—"

Another shot goes off, this one piercing the ceiling as she holds the gun haphazardly up. "I'm done, done with all you repulsive Resnovs. Killing Sofiya may be the death of me. I'll worry about that later. But right now, I have one mission—to kill Oleg. Kirill, I'll leave you his fucking head if you'd like."

I glance over at my cousin, who starts to speak. Another shot rings out as Anastasiya struts toward the door. The lace gathers at her ass, descending into a G-string. She's practically, fucking naked.

"Who is this Oleg?" I growl at Kirill. I'd seen red when walking in on them. Now, my eyes fly to him for answers.

Anastasiya stops at the door, spins around, fisting the gun at her hip. "Oleg was the headmaster at the Castle I grew up in. He knows me well." She sneers, opening the door.

What did he do? I find myself asking. My stride catches up to her as she hustles along the corridor and begins down the wide staircase.

"Not this!" Asya slips a hand beneath the material at her breast and shoves a crinkled photo of a scarred figure in my face.

The image steals the air from my lungs.

"I called her 'The Invisible Thing.' But *this* is what he could have done to me, Simeon. Now, get out of my fucking way. *I don't need you.*"

She hustles to the second level. I follow. The byki in the area lower their head in respect to her lack of clothing.

Anastasiya stops to glare at me. "To this day, she was the catalyst for my nightmares—until *you.*"

I swallow hard, the apology in my eyes. "I'm—"

"I said, until you! The boy whom I met wasn't a Resnov, not on the first day. Now, he is a twisted fuck like his father. But apparently, I can't murder you." She shrugs, glaring at my guards. "I'll take the only vengeance I can."

Her mentioning my mother was enough to send my body falling into the floor, but I stand my ground. "You accused my mother, Anastasiya. Let's go to her now."

She taps Kirill's gun against her hip. "You don't fucking get it, Simeon."

"Make me understand," I grit out.

Something catches her line of vision behind me. I glance over my shoulder, down the hall on the second floor. Mikhail is exiting a room, eyebrows knit in curiosity. His chest swells at the sight of her. Jealousy wraps around my soul.

Asya mutters, "Another fucking Resnov."

I've become *them*. All Asya ever hated. She starts down the opposite hall, toward our room. I'm a second away from entering when the door slams in my face. Attempting the handle would make me look like even more of an idiot with all my guards staring.

"I don't think she murdered my brat," Kirill mutters. "Um . . . should we speak with Aunt Sofiya?"

"Why are you questioning me?" I growl, stalking over the handwoven rug.

His palms go out as a sign of peace.

My shoulder slumps against the opposite wall. I attempt to digest the last few minutes. *This is fucking madness!* The byki stand guard, awaiting an order or relief, which they will not be granted.

After a while, Kirill gestures toward his room. "May I?"

"What?" I grab a tuft of my hair.

"May I go? Can we all go to sleep? She might have too?"

"Nyet. Anastasiya's preparing," I mutter. "Previewing my gun selection." I wriggle my jaw and stand up straight. Time to give orders. "Someone, secure the last known whereabouts of this Oleg person."

Kirill's shoulder slumps against the wall. "Shit, if Anastasiya's the same kid I remember who tussled with Luka over this or that, she won't agree to any assistance."

My gaze warns that I don't give a fuck when the door opens. Anastasiya dons a black turtleneck and cargo pants. Tactical gear is splayed over her curves. She's wielding my favorite semi-automatic.

"What are you doing, Anastasiya?" I cock my head. The answer is evident.

"Not killing a messy Resnov, so the next best thing." Her mouth curves into a smile. A salute is tossed in the air, and she mutters, "Goodbye forever, *Young Resnov*."

I glare down at Anastasiya. All the blood in my veins stall. Her choice of words, "Young Resnov," came from none other than Irek Chutin.

He had her.

～

Outside, Anastasiya slams the hood of the hunk of crap she drove in. At my request, a byki had cut the wires while she'd been holed up in our room. Her foot repeatedly kicks the side of it. She's ranting about another car while byki attempt to placate her with any key she'd be interested in. I haven't said a single word. I'm simmering in the notion of my mother's treachery, and Chutin's imminent death.

"If I want nothing to do with you," she growls, battering the vehicle with each word, "then I refuse to take anything from you people. Who fucked up my car?"

A convoy of SUVs arrives, Kirill is at the wheel of the foremost vehicle. I grip Anastasiya's arm. "Let's go."

"I'm not leaving with you people."

"You took my weapons and my clothes, moya milaya. And you say you want nothing to do with us?" I lessen my grip, my eyes

179

lowering from hers for a moment. The thought of how I cruelly undid her stitches blazes through my mind.

"Should the Castle Girl walk around naked?" She stops pulling away from me and presses her body into me. "Oleg may not have fucked me, but Chutin allowed him to see me naked." Her lips brush featherlight against my earlobe then catch me between her teeth. "He could not take his eyes off me."

I grit my teeth.

"Oleg pissed all over my body, Simeon. He came too. Came like a fucking animal for hours! He painted all his spunk across my skin."

Blood plunges into my ears. I can hear it, rushing through. She wants my reaction. A broken, deranged Resnov! My arm loops around her waist. I slide her into the backseat of the closest SUV. I catch her gold-plated gaze. Mine softens in shame. "I apologize, moya milaya."

"I have more to tell," Anastasiya purrs. She doesn't scoot over.

I climb in with her sitting half on top of me. Her fingers pluck at the button of my shirt.

"I had the letter. All the evidence pointed to you. If I wasn't drunk, I was searching for you relentlessly, not a second of sleep."

"Nyet," Anastasiya strums her native language, curving the simplest of words. "Nyet fucking for Oleg. Nyet penetration. His only objective was to break me, Simeon, so that I'd return to Irek. Fall on my knees, grateful for his touch."

"I'll kill—"

"You will do nothing, Simeon. I will kill Oleg and Irek myself." Her hand splays, a gentle lover's caress down my chest. "I was celibate for four years, Sim. Maybe not this time."

I crush her tiny hand in mine.

"Did you abstain from sex, Tsar?"

The tips of her fingers are pulsing beneath the flesh. I kiss each one of them before muttering, "What? Mikhail told you he saw me—"

"Did you?"

"I've never been unfaithful, Anastasiya."

"Should have." Embers smolder behind her gaze.

"I should've fucked around?" My laughter resonates in my ears. "My drug of choice is between those thick thighs, girl! Once I'm done—"

"You should have cheated, Sim." She chortles. "I cheated."

My hand flies to the back of my neck, kneading hard, instead of around her slender throat.

"Not by choice." Her voice dips, a slight inflection, a slight tremble. "Irek had me tied up in this lace number, which he cut from my body."

I can't fucking hear this, I tell myself. It's like she's sixteen all over again. Her statement became my fuel for Anatoly's death. But I'd been there. I *knew* the extent to the pain he inflicted on her. *How far did Irek go?* I stop contemplating and focus on Anastasiya.

She needs this.

"What happened?" I growl.

"He clawed my legs apart. Oh, but he kissed me passionately."

Clenching my jaw, I bite my tongue from declaring how her revenge will be sweet. It will, but now is not the time to tell her so. All the venom radiating from her skin ceases. I stare at her a beat before asking, "Did he have you?"

"Maybe," Asya murmurs, glancing out of the window.

CHAPTER 32

Anastasiya

Everyone I know and love is dead. The boy who frightened and incited me at first sight. My sweet Luka, his Rudolf. The girl Kosta once was, although the good in her fled this earth years ago. Twisting and toying with Simeon becomes my vice for the next hour.

"You love all the details, Sim. Should I stop or continue?"

His gaze levels with mine, his tone woven with sincerity. "If it calms you, proceed."

I pause a beat. The seeds of my declaration have done more harm to the barbarian than these fists of mine ever could. It's way past nightfall, but I stop my detailed story to glance out the window. "This isn't the way. You took a wrong turn."

Simeon catches my jaw. "Oleg attempted to flee the country, Anastasiya. He has been found. Rest assured, the mudak's death has your name on it still."

A gleam is in his eyes. He's offering his services.

My tone flickers as I wonder how replaceable he is. I don't want to admit it, but he might be useful. I ask, "How much farther then?"

Simeon clears his throat.

From the front seat, a byki responds.

"Good." I settle back in my seat. "Much closer than before." *Once Oleg is dead, I'll force Simeon to part ways with me.* I wring my fingers together at the thought of having Irek Chutin all to myself. His death is mine to own. I can almost taste it.

◇

Thirty minutes later, the SUVs trail along bumpy roads in an area of old tenements. Tall, cement structures extend into the night sky. Windows stack like Legos. Apartments are close enough for neighbors to hear a heated discussion. It's the sort of place where Simeon saved me from my betting nanny. I start to unbuckle.

"Nyet." Simeon's thick arm blocks my chest.

"You found him for me is all," I grit out.

"He will be brought to you as well." He's staring face forward. I have a sudden inclination to pound my fist into the marble of his jaw. Break my knuckles a little in preparation for Oleg. And I do.

My knuckles are a fraction from his face. My fist is tightened so hard I can hear the bones crunch. "Don't," Simeon warns.

"What will you do?"

"My men are confirming if Oleg is alone or not. They'll bring him down, Anastasiya."

"I said, what the fuck will you do? If I try you again?"

He presses my fingers to his lips, kisses them before I can pull my hand away.

I maneuver around, my hip against the buttery-soft leather as I glare at his side profile. A hundred years ago, when I loved the man and not the monster, I'd seen him as art, the perfection of his structure. As an art history buff, I'd hid a notebook, dabbled and sketched Simeon. My amateur musings were no da Vinci. Too bad. If I could draw Simeon, I'd illustrate the perfect portrait then let fire lick across the canvas, finishing him off.

"What will you do, Sim?"

He looks at me, expression morose. "Probably take it."

A nerve beneath my eyelid convulses in overdrive. "You can't take it back. But maybe you could make me feel better, Simeon."

Caution tightens his mouth. Careful of my fresh bandage, I climb on top of him, press my lips against his, tasting the bad man, the Young Resnov, whose reputation as maniac and genius, once preceded him. But he was too stupid to look his mother's way, to believe her guilt for our demise. Our tongues twine, passion sparks instantly.

Lips against his, I groan. "Irek wanted this to be us. For me to kiss him while he fucked me."

Gingerly, Simeon slips me back onto my seat. The door opens. Simeon climbs out and slaps it behind him. I start out of the car, ready to dish out more hurt.

But the pain shining in Simeon's eyes distorts into wicked glee. I look up. Duct tape is around Oleg's entire face; his mouth, his eyes, and his wrists are bound. He stumbles on each movement as four byki start over. One of the men has his hands in fists, prepared to inflict more agony at Oleg's abdomen.

"Don't you dare touch him," I grit out. "He's all mine."

Oleg's face lifts. He's searching the darkness for me. I pluck at the silver tape, unravel it from those ocean blue orbs, and smile.

"You knew me by voice. Impressive." I gesture. Oleg is brought to his knees. My hand skims along his face. "Certain things—"

"How is this torture?" Simeon's steel voice cuts through the night.

I shoot him a glare. Simeon *shoots* Oleg in his calf. In the blink of an eye, his gun is in the back of his waistband, and he's signaling for me to continue. My old headmaster falls prostrate, groaning against his confines. Lights blink on in so many windows, giving off enough illumination to compete with the stars at night.

"Proceed, Anastasiya," Simeon orders.

I stare through the window.

"Residents who saw him taken from his shitty little place understood Resnovs own him now," Simeon grits. "Unless you'd prefer to take him back home, finish him!"

"Not my home."

"Then proceed."

I grip Oleg's hair, shoving his face into the dirt. "Before I was interrupted, I was saying that there are certain things about you I will always remember. Such as the thought of your semen gliding around in my fucking hair." I shove his face into the ground again. A few teeth go flying. "It made me want to fucking vomit."

Blood splatters over my skin as I smash his face into the cement, over and over again. The sound of Oleg's breath becomes faint, probably due to his broken nose. I slam his head down again. I'm suddenly in Simeon's arms.

His abrasive hand caresses my face, looking me over in concern. I blink. "Your request was torture. Not the relief of a swift death. Should I assist?"

"No, motherfucker!" It's as if I've recovered consciousness after fainting when I begin to push him away.

"Asya, your emotions are killing him swiftly." Simeon's biceps wrap around me in a bear hug. "You want to bash his brains in, in less than sixty seconds?"

"No, but I'd bash your face in if I could." There's a look I can't quite read on Simeon's face as he lets me go. I fold my arms across my chest. "You all can leave us!"

"What's your plan?" Simeon's hands move with passion. Like a professor in the center of an auditorium, all eyes are on him. "*How will he die, Anastasiya? Make it fucking count!*"

"I want to rip him in half with my bare hands," I grit. *Fuck, impossible.*

"I like that."

I glare him up and down as the lights from various windows begin to dash out. "I don't need your support."

"How will you rip him in half?" Again, as if he's forgotten how much I hate him, Simeon frames my face with firm, supportive hands.

I push away from him, stumbling to remove myself from his clutches. "I'm not your apprentice, asshole." In my haste to get away, I'm turned all the way around, glaring at the SUVs. A thought chimes in my psyche.

"You and you," I growl to two byki. "Get rope. Tie him to a bumper and a grille. Someone, find me a seat."

A dazed Oleg looks up from the ground. Dirt cakes his face as blood drips into his shocked eyes.

Darkness surrounds us, summoning me to be the cruel tormentor he was once. My voice softens, almost sensually like his hand, while playing in my hair. "What's the matter, Oleg?"

Aware of my aim, he moans, letting his face fall prostrate into the dirt again.

"You made my guts curdle with your games. Now, I will play with your intestines."

"Dah, and drive slow," Simeon says. I do a one-two step farther away from him. His love and support no longer mean a thing to me.

CHAPTER 33

Anastasiya

Clutching the sheets around me, I scurry into a seated position. I'm up in seconds, having spent too much time awakening disoriented and in strange locations over the last few weeks. I trip and fall off a platform, grabbing something slick and glossy, then screech.

"What the—" I clamber to my feet, stumbling backward. My fingers latch onto soft material, I yank. Light blazes into the dark room. Silk-blackout-curtains heap around my legs and feet as I glare out onto a balcony.

"Mudak," I murmur, eyeing Simeon. His lengthy legs are stretched out as he sleeps in a low-cushioned courtyard chair. I'd like to grab the blazer pillowing the side of his face and shove it down his crummy throat.

Memories of last night return, spotty and more vivid by the second. After Oleg's guts splattered across the street, I'd checked into a hotel. Or we, rather. Though I called him paranoid, he purchased all the rooms on the same level. Other guests were relocated to different areas of the hotel. Of course, their stays were comped.

Simeon's broad shoulders expand farther than the eye can imagine in his tailored linen shirt. A faint smile plays at the edges of his lips as he eyes me. With a yawn, he stands to his full height and heads toward the sliding glass. Voice muffled by the partition between us, he asks, "Will you open up, now?"

I shake my head, eyes flitting down to the ground. There's no looking at him. Those lips were once my pleasure. Those rich, dark eyes once warmed over my skin. The bristles of his jaw tickled the inside of my thighs.

"I've been out here all night, Asya. Please let me in." His hands plant against the glass.

Damn, now, he can see me. There's no way out of here without him seeing. I stalk across the room to the door, rise on my tippy toes, and look out the peephole. Yup, last night he'd planted byki, "for my protection."

I strut back toward the sliding glass door. A half-smile plays at his lips as he gestures toward the lock.

"This isn't how people part ways," I sneer.

His hand pops at the glass. "We aren't other people, Anastasiya."

"You've said as much time and again. I'm taking a quick bath. Then I'm leaving. If you follow me, it will be to the proper authorities."

Laughter sparks across his skin, though he holds it in. "You want Zapekanka for breakfast? Or lunch?"

An obnoxious roar rips through my stomach. I can almost imagine the cheese breakfast cake sliding down my throat. "Nope," I reply.

"Alright, you don't eat. I don't eat." He settles onto the expensive outdoor seat, fluffing his blazer again.

After a quick washup with the complimentary toothpaste and

facial products, I plop back onto the bed. He called my bluff. I'll wait him out. I pick up the remote and experiment with turning on every gadget, including a lengthy fireplace.

I fling the remote away when the television doesn't come on. I notice the balcony is all clear. I hasten over. Pressing my forehead against the cool glass, I search for the sneaky bastard.

My heart jumps. I mutter, "Motherfucker."

Simeon climbs from the side balcony of his room back to my area. He holds up a book and shrugs. *Oh, this is a test of wills?* The mudak will be waiting outside forever!

~

I try to reconfigure my nights and days back to some semblance of normal. But the next day, I awaken toward nightfall. Soft snow is falling outside of the massive sliding glass doors. Simeon catches my eye. I shoo him away. He stands up, eyes alight at the sight of me.

My heart wrenches in my chest and flops. I fist my eye sockets, though I still saw the look he had for me. The look any woman would beg for when falling in love. When I open my eyes, I notice the ice crystals in his hair, creating a deceptive halo. Simeon Resnov is no angel.

He plants his masculine arms around his thick abdomen, pretending to shake. There's a puppy dog frown on his face. Rolling my eyes, I strut toward the phone and dial the cops. The call goes something like, "I'm being held against my will."

Then I wave at Simeon and pat my abdomen, pretending as if I've ordered room service.

He settles back into his seat with the book in his hand. A highlighter wanders across his tattooed knuckles.

Why does he seem more at peace today than he has in years?

Why can't I take my eyes off him?

Why the fuck do I envision the addictive taste of his lips against mine?!

First kisses are a lovely marvel. First kisses can never occur again between the same two people. Though, every first kiss only leads to a day when there will be a last. One last kiss and a token full of memories. I'd dash it all to hell if I had the ability to.

Entranced at the sight of him, I fall into his gaze.

"Let me in, Anastasiya," his muffled voice caresses my skin.

A cold, haunting loneliness buried deep down inside wraps around me. And still, I watch him seemingly in a tranquil peace. *How? Why?* I gape at him, a plethora of emotions cloak across my skin as my limbs lock. I could watch him for hours, days, centuries, standing here. No more arguing and anger, no more sustenance or water required, just stare. My hands plant on the glass where his are. His fingers and palms jut out much farther than mine do.

"Let me in," Simeon tempts again.

At the sound of footsteps outside, I swallow the lump in my throat. Ignoring the tightness in my chest calling out to our past, I scamper across the room and peek out. The byki are trading shifts. I steel myself from another single glance and climb back into bed. This time a complimentary movie pops onto the enormous screen. Seething at the sight of a love story, I press every button conceivable to turn the channel. The image goes black, and the flat-screen ascends into the ceiling. Clean colors of the 1900 oil painting, *The Swan Princess* by Mikhail Vrubel pops into view.

Mikhail . . .

Our last encounter has my thumbs working in overdrive to remove the captivating image. I hadn't thought of him since the long ride to the palace. Simeon has that effect on me. The fucking parasite consumes all my senses.

My one, true chance at a normal life returned to Los Angeles, I tell myself. Mikhail's saving every life, and I hope to God he hasn't thought about the one soul he was incapable of rescuing. After a few more anxious fiddles with the flat-screen, it zips back down but stays black. *Good.*

Ten minutes later, there's a knock at the door, and a man with a deep voice speaks out. Again, I hurry over, this time, opening it.

The *politsyia* looks me over, chewing on a Zapekanka. "You'd have me believe you're a prisoner." He points the pastry at me. "Girl, what do you have to say for yourself?"

Stuttering over my words, I revert to full-on Russian. "Look at them! Who goes on vacation at a hotel to stalk the hallways? Those are *Resnov* guards! I'm not at liberty to leave!"

The officer smiles, hand signaling across at two carts of food. One is being picked through by byki entering and exiting rooms. The other cart is left untouched with its silver domes and lush purple pedals across white linen.

"From my observation—a penthouse suite and food for days? But at your request, Tsarina, I'll humor you." He grabs the solitary cart with all its romantic accessories, slides it past me, and then steps into the hallway. *"If you weren't a Resnov, I'd haul you in."*

I slam the door in his face and hasten into the bathroom. "I'm taking a luxurious bath, using every last one of these soaps, then I'm out of here! No more games," I growl to myself, yanking at the handle. The brute force sends the knob falling into the tub. "What the!"

More barbaric grunts are emitted as I try to readjust the knob. I hurl the damn thing across the room. Stripping from my clothes, I gather all the five-star luxury soaps and shampoos. I pitch them into the shower large enough to house a football team.

Powerless to control my own reality, I climb onto the warmed stone. "Hotter," I whisper to the automated commands. "Hotter," I shout.

A plume of steam hedges around me, licking at my skin. Searing hot water drenches down on my frame. Lips trembling, I wrap my arms around my abdomen. I can almost hear Luka in my ears while laughing, "Who's the Prima Donna, now?"

CHAPTER 34

Simeon

My fingertips tap against the side of the slacks I've worn for two days straight. Chewing my bottom lip, I peer into the window at my past, present, and future I won't surrender. She hasn't eaten. I haven't either. She slept restlessly. I only used the blanket to shield myself from the next snowfall while waiting for *her* to let me in.

Seconds ago, I heard a faint scream. I clutch my ear to my phone, awaiting an answer from the byki on patrol. The guards have sent me text messages, alternating on four-hour rotations.

"What was that?"

"I'm not certain, Tsar. Sounded like she was tossing things around in there."

I huff.

She. They aren't sure of how to address Anastasiya now. Tsarina. Prisoner. Their Tsar's forever obsession. *She.*

"Women," he chuckles tersely.

"You standing in front of the door?"

"Dah. Nobody has slept or took so much as a fucking leak, without being relieved first. You have my word."

I hang up the phone. Unless a dead mudak transitioned into a ghost and entered through a vent, she's safe. Planting my hands against the glass again, I sigh heavily.

"Let me in, Anastasiya, please," I mutter, my breath fogging against the glass. My pleas fade in seconds. *Shit, I never did enough apologizing to her.* Across the way, dense heat comes from the bathroom door. I settle back in my seat, pick up the book that I still haven't read a single page of. When Anastasiya was younger, I could dig underneath her gorgeous skin, ignoring her with a book. Yet, now, words topple from the pages, leaving each sheet as a tabula rasa. I jettison the book across the way, sitting wide-legged, waiting for Anastasiya to exit the bathroom.

My pride has been shot to fucking hell. Eyelids burdened by lack of sleep, I watch the bathroom. Steam continues to ribbon out of the parted door. When I rub my palms together, I feel the softness of her skin, the gentleness of her love. After too much time has passed, I start out of the chair again.

"She's supposed to let you in, not you take the lead right now," I warn myself, stalking to the sliding glass door. Smoke continues to float out, summoning my entry.

"Anastasiya!" I call out. *What the fuck is she doing?* I slide my phone out to glance at the time of my last call to the byki. It's just shy of three hours ago.

Ice prickling against my skin, I remove my blazer. I grip the material at the sleeve, wrap it around my hand, then punch at the window. Glass falls like hail. My shoes crunch through it. I've offered her another reason to hate me, but she should've heard this. I start slowly across the room, counting a few beats. Then I enter the bathroom, my eyes narrow at the sight of so much steam.

"Anastasiya?" I growl her name again, thoughts running rampant. *Where is she?*

Soaps and lotions are scattered across the vast marble counters and floors. I could swear I noticed a knob from the clawfoot tub in the center of the room within the fray.

At the farthest part of the room, a shower spans the entire area. My gaze trails across it, back and forth. With gritted teeth, I'm already calculating which byki will die if she's gotten out. Then my dark gaze stops on a form toward the edge of the shower. Before I can breathe easily, I'm opening the door. I look her over. Nyet blood. Nyet attempts like my mother would.

Anastasiya is sitting in a spot where none of the spouts are hitting her with water. Her lips tremble while her eyes are unwavering.

I search the perimeter of the shower. There are no knobs here. I grit out, "Off."

The water stops. I walk inside and pluck her wet curvy body off the floor, holding her against me. Anastasiya startles, her limbs jumping.

"Let me go," she begs in a hoarse voice.

"Where were you, just now?" I ask. *What the fuck were you thinking about? Oleg or the mudak, Chutin?!* Her plans for Oleg made my chest swell with pride. Still, there's no resurrecting him to die another death by my hands.

When she starts wrestling with me, I pull her into a bear hug, grabbing a towel from the rack and wrapping it around her. Inside the hotel room, icy wind washes across the space from the broken sliding glass door. Anastasiya ceases fighting. Her body trembles against me. I wedge the towel around her breast and against me, ensuring she's decent before opening the door to her room.

"Get my fucking door," I growl to the byki, sitting on a chair in the hallway.

He grabs a keycard with all access and opens it. By now, Anastasiya is clinging to me, her warm breath tickling at my neck. I hug her tighter to my chest, entering the room and nudging the door closed with my shoe. The second I place her straight onto the bed, she darts beneath the sheets. I use the towel to wrap around her hair, recalling how she never lets it dry on its own.

Anastasiya snatches the towel. Silence envelopes us as my eyes roam over her crinkly hair. She covers it with the towel and begins to blot. My eyes fall to her blistering, honey eyes, her nose, her mouth, the curve of her collarbone. The sheet she has covered herself with begins to fall. Linen grazes over her hardened nipples. Lust pools in my mouth.

Seizing the sheet to pull it back up, Anastasiya snaps, "You can go now."

"Nyet. Talk to me. Why are you—"

"I tried talking to you!"

Folding my arms across my chest, I peer down at her and snort. "That's the lie of the fucking century. You never said Oleg's name. You never mentioned—"

"How your mom is a suka? Huh? The night after that silly coronation." She glares up at me. Warmth creeps up her cheeks and spreads across her shoulders. "I'd have told you then, but Sofiya played her pity party with you and used me. In the beginning, Mother Sofiya wanted me to fuck you."

I cock a brow. "Yet you call her Mother?"

The hurled insult lights fire across her skin.

"I'm done arguing with you, Anastasiya," I reply. My voice lowers, sincere, without a tinge of cruelty like it had when she first mentioned my mother.

Anastasiya climbs onto her knees. "Remember the one time where I came into your room after your parents fucked?"

I did. I'd been furious. She had come to me like prey on a platter. Had she not hesitated, I'd have torn through her little slit and licked the pain back up with my tongue.

"You wanted to break me with your cock, didn't you?" A silly smile brightens her face further. *God, Anastasiya is as gorgeous as a sunrise.* She crawls over to me on her knees, coming up to my chest. She grips at the collar of my linen shirt. "*Mother* Sofiya wanted to teach me how she manipulated your father."

"Shut the fuck up," I grit.

"Years later, and it's finally dawned on me, Sim." Anastasiya works the buttons of my shirt. Her tongue trails over tattoos seared across my chest. "The Tsarina behind the Tsar."

I look down into her sparkling eyes. My Tsarina . . .

The little inferno of hate summons me into the bed. Though my instincts are blaring, I climb in, folding her into me. My mouth encompasses hers. I know every inch of her, though it feels like I'm tasting her for the first time. My palms brush across her curves and the soft slopes of her hips. My touch becomes a rough caress at the globes of her ass. Eyes tight with emotion, I press a hand to her face. "I fucking miss you, Anastasiya."

"I bet you do, Sim." She grips my jaw with one hand, letting the other roam across my chest. Her leg kicks up over my waist, flipping me onto my back. I laugh deep in my chest as she straddles me. Then I gaze up at her in wonder.

Anastasiya's heated core whirls along my lower abdomen while she deepens the kiss. I start to unbuckle my pants between us, lifting up to grab my gun.

Eyes on me, Anastasiya removes my weapon. My mouth laps over her fallen breast as she leans over to place it on the nightstand.

"Allow me," she breathlessly commands, arising from the bed. Eyeing her like a hawk, I zero in on the swell of her glistening petal-soft pussy lips as she takes on a wide-legged stance. My dick increases to a painful degree, ready to tear past her sweet arousal. In a trance at the thought of pounding her there, I nod. At the edge of the bed, she uses all her strength to get me out of my slacks and underwear. My erection springs free, and she clasps her fingers around it, causing me to hiss.

"Nyet, hands. Get your ass back up here, Anastasiya."

"Who said you were in charge, Sim?" She takes a lazy lick at a bead of precum.

I chuckle low in my gut, my massive shoulders rising. Slowing the direction my mind is headed, I resist the carnal desire to attack her addictive pussy. "Alright, I'm still in trouble, proceed."

On all fours, Anastasiya crawls up. Her marinated sex lands on my lower abdomen. Eyes twinkling, she says, "Damn right, you're in a world of trouble."

How do I act civilized when I can already see her lips wrapped around my cock? Anastasiya stops dragging her thumb across the stickiness to gloss her lips with it.

I hitch in another breath. "Let me in your sweet pussy, moya milaya. You're angry. I'll fix it. You want me to fuck you. I know you want me to fuck you deep."

The need to be inside of her grows frantic. Her nipples harden, and she hitches oxygen, licking at her lips. Then she reaches up, her breasts in my face again, as she ties my wrists to the headboard. "Asya, put those pretty tits around my dick. Or your mouth, you know how lovely it feels sucking me deep."

"I'd rather ride the fuck out of you, Simeon."

"Do it."

Making quick work of the ties, Anastasiya gives a good yank before retorting, "Again, you're not in charge."

"Nyet talking. Make your move." Impatience builds inside of me. "Close that pretty mouth, or I will put something in it."

I expected another attempt at a retort, but her mouth clamps shut. Her tiny hand weaves down the length of me with a satisfying moan. Her pink tongue flicks out, soft and wet at my cockhead. My dick remembers the contours of her mouth well. Growling about the constraints, I let my head fall back on the pillow, while her mouth works.

"Grrr," I grumble as cool air meets my dick.

"I said, 'I'm in charge.'" Anastasiya matches my glare, moving up to clamp her hips around me. She pushes her legs wide, and I stop favoring oxygen to watch the apex of her sex swirl around my crown. Her pussy sucks me in, then rises, leaving the head of my tautness soaking in her juices. Hunger plays in Anastasiya's eyes. She plants her silk fingers along her clit. Her lips quiver as she clamps around me as she thrusts downward. With an intoxicating grin, she does magic. My cock disappears, and I groan. My hips move in time with her movements. She leans forward, hard nipples gliding over my chest. She drags her teeth along the tender skin across my neck then bites down.

I hiss, "What are you doing to me?"

"Killing you, Simeon, like you killed me." She chews her bottom lip, thrusting harder. "Because we part ways tomorrow."

Allowing her this level of control arouses me tremendously. Her strokes are long and deep, gliding off my erection almost all the way before sinking down to the hilt. Eyes rolling back in my head, I succumb to her drug-laced pussy. That mouth of Anastasiya's always diverged from what her sweet cunt said. Insanity elevates around us, pulling us both deeper. *Nyet letting her go.*

CHAPTER 35

Anastasiya

I slam down on his cock, over and over, my fingernails clutching his shoulders. The bastard didn't believe me. He will soon. I can hardly smile, barely catching my breath as the pleasure builds. My legs cling to Simeon's waist. He has nowhere to go but deeper inside of me. I come undone from gliding over his smooth erection. Even while riding him, Simeon finds the spots that make me gasp and arch, teasing the desire from my body. His dick has awakened my craving into something that can't be ignored.

I concentrate on the pain I'll cause him as I climb and crest. The heat and freedom of fucking Simeon crash over me in a violent wave. I throw my head back in a cry of passion, biting my tongue from the automatic response. When sex and Simeon are involved, I've declared my love to him a million times over. No more.

Bucking and moaning, my pussy floods his cock. The next release slams into me. Surprise flickers in my gaze. Simeon thrusts his hips upward, abdominals flawless, as he matches my vigor. We detonate, utter ecstasy rushing across our skin, binding us together as I fall into him. My nails dig into his back, pleasure vibrating through me. I delight in his slight hiss of pain.

"I love you, moya milaya." Simeon's voice is rich, beautiful, reverberating in my mind like a therapeutic bell.

Don't do it, Asya, you can't hurt him.

Heat builds at the back of my eyelids, I sit up, tearing my fingers over his biceps, and he allows it. A canvas of viciousness and muscles beneath me. The fingers of my left hand trail across savage proof of who he is.

Skulls, guns, stars, all these tattoos are the makings of him. Smiling, I reach over and grab his firearm.

I can hurt him because he hurt me!

"Anastasiya?" The lust clouding his eyes dissipates. He snarls, "Do not fool yourself."

"Oh, I have faith you'll remove the ties. But you wanted to kill me, Simeon." The barrel trails across a perfectly defined abdominal muscle. "You clipped my stitches. That shit hurt."

Shame clamps his mouth together.

"No apologies?"

Eyelid twitching, Simeon growls, "I apologize. I had a fucking letter, Asya. Undeniably written by you!"

"For a bitch I once called Sister! Still, I forgive you. I won't kill you," I mutter, as he lifts from beneath me, sending my ass jolting on top of him. "Not a good idea to fuck with me while I hold a gun, though!"

Simeon frees his hands from the tie the second I squeeze the trigger.

"*Fuck!*" His mouth tenses.

Emotionless, I click the safety and toss the gun back onto the nightstand. Climbing off him and into a seated position, I search the bed for my towel and hold it out.

"*You,*" he mutters under his breath.

"Call me a bitch, Sim. Use your words. Use your hands!"

Simeon seizes the towel from my grasp and places it on his side, the exact place I was stitched up a few days ago. It's a good thing too because he ruined my aim. The doors burst open. Guards enter on high alert. I slink down, shielded by his massive body.

"Enjoy your evening. We're bonding." I wave them off.

"Bring me something to stitch myself up with," Simeon growls. He slides into a seated position.

"Oh, I almost forgot you were capable of stitching. Oddly, a tiny babushka did the honors for me."

"*Who the fuck* stitched you up the first time?" Simeon clinches his teeth, holding the bloodstained towel on his side. Face softening, he groans, "Listen, don't answer. Fuck the past. I want us—"

"*We* are on your rollercoaster. Let me off nicely." Burrowing my head into my pillow, I snuggle farther into the sheets. The scent is so intoxicatingly sexy. I'll sleep well tonight. This beats a goodbye kiss. I snort, "Do you feel an iota of remorse from my direction, Sim? No!"

The door opens again. A byki tosses a miniature stitching kit and closes the door. Simeon catches it in a large fist. He removes the towel. Blood streams from what I assumed was a flesh wound. *Ooops.* A chunk of skin is gone. *Darn, his custom bullet is huge.* He glares at the kit before flinging it across the way. I hide a smile in my pillow. Simeon climbs out of the bed.

"Let me off the rollercoaster, asshole!" I taunt.

A hard smile crosses his even harder stone-carved face. "You have that mouth. I could never murder you, not on account of that mouth."

"*Let me go!*"

"Not an option, girl." Rolling his eyes, Simeon turns away. He plucks up a vase on the coffee table then another shiny object. One by one, he inspects the hotel's décor.

Having watched my fill of *20/20* in America, I clear my throat. "Are you searching for the perfect blunt force . . ." *Shit, he is going to kill me,* I consider as he chuckles to himself. Not a minute ago,

Simeon declared that my mouth was my saving grace. But I no longer believe *in* him.

"What are you doing?" I shriek. I'm no match for Simeon. Kirill at least offered a knife when he almost spazzed out on me. "Are you—"

"Nyet," he mutters, lifting a metal, oblong shape, tosses it up and catches it. "You fucked me crazy just now, meaning I could *never* kill you."

Lies! I scamper across the bed to grip the gun again. Smiling at him, I let the nozzle glide around my index finger. "This is crazy. But I could pull a Romeo and Juliet. Place a slug between your eyes . . . eh, kidding. We aren't madly in love. Just psychotic. So, I'll kill you then die by the hands of the next mudak to fly into this room. I have no problem with that."

Simeon laughs low, deep. I blink a few times, holding the gun steady as he disregards me, searching across the room.

He disappears into the bathroom, returning with a face towel and wraps it around one side of the metal artwork. He stops at the extended fireplace, which is the same as in my room. Fire billows across the area. Taking a measured breath, Simeon sits on the tiled hearth. He places the end of the metalwork inside of the flame as if we're at a bonfire.

"What are you doing, Sim? I'm holding a gun."

He mutters over his shoulder, "Cauterizing the wound from my beloved Anastasiya, but by all means."

"Whatever." I drop the gun into the fray of blankets, reach over to the nightstand and grab a glass figurine. As he's starting to place the heated metal across his flesh to seal his wound, I toss it in his direction.

"Fuck," Simeon grits. The fiery metal lands on his designated target. In a tense voice, he growls, "What are you doing?"

"Contemplating!" I shout back. "As to how I'm in the room with a complete sociopath. You're burning a wound *I* gave you, instead of exacting revenge. I've hurt you more than anyone. *You have hurt me more than anyone on the planet!* Simeon, put me out of my misery."

The metal clatters against the marble floor. His golden skin is singed red and purple, where it is melded back together.

"I can't, Anastasiya!" Warm eyes smolder over me, and his voice lowers, "I'm not capable of killing you or letting you go."

Taking a measured breath, he looks me over. "I made a mistake, not finding you the very second you needed me."

"I don't need—"

"I'd call it the fucking mistake of my life. Not ripping Chutin's heart out on day one of your disappearance . . . fuck! That isn't the extent to how far I've hurt you."

Chin high, I retort. "Then what is?"

Shoulders slumped, Simeon replies, "From time to time, I thought about how fucking stupid I was for allowing you to stay."

"Should've shown me your true colors sooner." My voice grows taut. Damn, he's wrong about my mouth. I'd have murdered me a long time ago.

"Dah. Day fucking one, I should've let you go, Anastasiya. The moment you followed me back to my car. That dictated how fucking awful your world would be, and I'm a monster. A monster like my father."

I can't stop gawking at him, can't refute his statement. My gaze swallows him whole, from head to foot. The pure definition of trouble, right there. His broad shoulders are all contours and tattoos: all taut flesh, misery to the female race. For dumb girls, like me, instincts warn us, but our hearts fail us.

"From the start, I told myself not to let this beautiful, wounded bird fly off into the world. What's to say another bad mudak, like me, worse than me," he growls, tossing a fist at his chest, "would not claim you, hurt you! That still happened, Anastasiya. Oleg and Irek still happened."

But I knew them before you. I stop myself from removing the blame weighing on his shoulders.

"Now, it's too late. Before a few days ago, I could have always given you my loyalty." He huffs. "In the past, I'd doubted everyone I was affiliated with, but I'd rampage to the end of the bloody fucking world because I didn't doubt us. Then I did. Second worst mistake of my life. Not finding you sooner."

"Where do we go now?" My tiny voice echoes across the room, though all I want to say is, "Never let me go." *Yup, dumb girls like me.* Can't get him out of my head. Can't remove his essence from my heart, my fucking bloodstream.

"Away from Russia."

CHAPTER 36

Anastasiya
One Week Later

I remember gripping fresh soil. I'd sprinkled it across Luka's custom baby-blue casket. His mother, father, Kirill, and other siblings sifted the same soil through their fingers, praying for him, although, Luka's body wasn't submitted to the earth.

At the end of the procession, his final resting place was in a rich, marble mausoleum. The entire Resnov family has been placed there for decades. Mother Sofiya was too "weak" to attend. Kirill gave the sweetest speech. His wet gaze flickered over me as he mentioned wishing he had accepted Luka. Not many Resnovs knew Luka was gay, or they had their heads stuck too far up their own assholes to see it. I was shocked to see Mikhail still in Russia. He kept his distance, though, favoring his father, Malich.

For now, the Seven, all of the uncles, insist that Simeon create a plan for Irek Chutin. They promised that their patience and resources were at the Tsar's disposal.

The moment Luka was sealed in, Simeon said we were headed to the tropical island he had promised. Though numb, I warned that as long as a Resnov didn't own the island, I'd go.

Now, the sea-salted air whispers across my skin. My freshly pressed hair tickles my cheek, and I push a strand back. I lean my arms against the weathered wood. Glittering water takes up the entire sunny horizon. I stand on a wooden platform surrounding the overwater bungalow. Farther out somewhere, the sea merges into turquoise skies. The bungalow is the only structure around for miles, presenting all the luxury and peace I ever needed.

"Why are you standing there?" I groan. I glance over my shoulder at Simeon. He has a massive shoulder leaning against the open partition. He's wearing all white for a change, not with the intention of reveling in blood. The linen pants and shirt offer a delightful deception, *normalcy.*

"I was quiet."

"Yeah, you were," I mumble. *But I felt your eyes warm over me as if assessing me and protecting me all at once.* I won't say as much. We haven't fucked since I shot him, not a single taste from each other's lips. But his presence has always pleased me, going all the way back to when we met, even when I was mute.

"The chef and his team are en route, Anastasiya. What do you have in mind?"

I shrug, glancing off in the distance. "There's the boat."

"What are you hungry for? You were in your room all morning and didn't make any suggestions for last night."

"Not hungry," I sigh. His intoxicating cologne fuses with the sea air, set to levitate me toward him. Simeon saunters toward me.

"You have to eat." His hands rub down my shoulders.

I shy away. The overwater villa is big enough for both of us. His bedroom is over two-thousand square feet away from mine. "I'll eat whatever."

He claims my biceps firmly when I do another two-step. "I'll make you eat, Asya."

My lashes flutter upward, deadpan gaze on him.

He doesn't test me, inquiring, "You were thinking about Luka?"

I look away. "Yeah . . ."

Biting his lip pensively, Simeon asks, "Or were you deliberating over Irek, or my mother?"

My gaze levels with his. "No."

"You sure?" His hands travel up my shoulders, glide across my neck, and frame my face. "The second you say you'd like to return, my mother will answer for her actions, Anastasiya. I spoke with Kirill. A team is sifting through all of Chutin's political affairs and outings. We will carry out your orders for him."

I chortle hesitantly. "My desired plan of torture, sure, thanks."

"How many times have I said, 'I'd do anything for you,'? " he murmurs, temptingly close. "I've failed. *Test me.*"

Pleading ribbons his gaze. Simeon never utters or begs, but it's consuming him. Our lips are a fraction away from each other. The sound of a boat switching gears sends me reeling back in my flip-flops.

A few minutes later, the crew of four starts off the motorboat.

"Ms. Anastasiya, I have your jar of peanut butter," the chef says. His blond dreadlocks jostle softly in the wind as he holds up my craving. "Mr. Resnov, you'll be happy to know I spent all night studying a borscht recipe for later."

I pluck up the jar, prepared to mutter my appreciation when Simeon takes it from me. "She's eating real food today."

For an entire month and a half, Simeon force-feeds me a delicious array of food. After candlelight dinners overlooking the sea or late breakfasts at the kitchen table, I return to my room. Keeping down food is impossible. Breakfast is always the worst. Hallucinations of Oleg and his foul oatmeal flit through my psyche.

This evening, I groan, my bare feet moving along the smooth glass floor. A colorful school of fish is right below. In a maxi dress, I amble out of my bedroom, closing the door quickly. My body flush against the wood, I close my eyes and breathe. Good. I stalled Simeon's routine. He has a habit of knocking on my door precisely at seven. This bedroom is my sanctuary, not his. *No way you're getting inside,* I muse. My half-smile falls when I feel his gaze on me.

I peel open my eyes. Simeon is on the opposite end of the hall-way. The side conveniently marked *his side.* The kitchen and other common areas are between us. And his damn walk, he owns the vast space between us. Ceasing temptation, my vision plummets from his frayed shirt and how it caresses his muscles. The fit of his jeans is another no-go, I end up gawking at his large feet. *Mister casual, are we?* I find my voice, "What?"

Time trickles by. He had to be checking me out too. Simeon clears his throat, "We've been here for over a month—"

"Return to Russia." I stay planted against the closed door, though he's slowly passing by the kitchen island. What's worse? Not allowing him to enter or having nowhere to retreat?

"My intention isn't to rush you." He stops, leaning nonchalantly at the entrance to my hallway. *My area.* There's too much space between us.

Wait a minute! I covet space, all of it. But Simeon isn't domi-nating over me, forcing tension in my neck to look all the way up. He chews his bottom lip, and my eyes plunge again. *Fuck, what is this? A circus?* Oh crap, it's my turn to volley the ball back into his court.

"Okay, then?" I scowl. *Shoo!* As he's not a man to hold his tongue, I cock a brow.

"Does the water make you sick?"

"No." My eyebrow lifts.

"Are you . . ." One of the most powerful men in the world uses his hands to gesture in an attempt to probe me. *Wow!* What happened to choking out the truth?

"Actually, Sim, I'll head in early tonight." All the fear clinging to my skin at the thought of turning my back to him disintegrates. My hand starts for the door.

Voice made of steel, he asks, "Are you pregnant?"

I whip back around, still favoring the strength of the door for my sanity. "No."

"Assuming you're pregnant and the baby isn't mine, I'll—"

"Simeon," I cut in. On graceful feet, I start toward him. Hurt flickers across his face as I brush by. Heading toward the sliding glass doors, I pivot the conversation. "You've proven to be a crea-ture of habit. Breakfast. Workout. Shower. A new book every Thursday. Lunch with me. Harass me while I do nothing. Dinner. Repeat. It's dinnertime now . . ." *Alright, Asya, where the fuck are you going with this assessment?* Clearing my throat, I conclude, "Let's eat. Okay?"

Damn it, Simeon has a face carved by Michelangelo, and yet, for all the intricate artwork, I can't perceive an emotion. When the wide planes of his shoulders lift in another nonchalant shrug, I read him well.

And that reading scares me. I stalk out of the open area.

Outside, stars flicker in an indigo sky. The vivid moon ripples in the water's reflection. Our chef's boat lulls over the water, docking along the small pier farther out. The team is fast at work with fresh seafood on a wooden table. Crabs wiggle around in a woven basket.

Smiling comes easy. Because my heart hurts so bad this time that shoving my lips upward means nothing. Too bad I didn't have this demeanor in Cape Town. At the perfume imperium, where I was fired from before working as a maid with Kosta, I was offered a good wage. I could've made a great life had I grinned more at the wealthy tourists.

End of story.

I think about the morning after my coronation. My mind played me, inventing a foolish 'Happily Ever After.' What was I thinking?

CHAPTER 37

Simeon

Anastasiya's smile is brighter than the stars above as she chats with the chef. I'm fixated on how my destiny won't offer the slightest grin for me. Over forty-five days ago, I almost made the mistake of my life, and I can't blame her for not forgiving me. My cellphone vibrates in my pants. A select few callers have this number.

At the last moment, I stop moping and press the answer button. "Dah?"

"The girl hacked through the library Chutin will be at in a few weeks. Though security will be more comprehensive, she's confident that she can do it again." Kirill makes mention of the hacker we utilized a while back.

The kid hadn't wanted anything more to do with us after first getting into Irek's system. Not a young lady blinded by money, I'd already given her everything she dreamt of, an allowance to house her family for four years at a prestigious tech school in the States.

Since her dreams weren't greedy, I'd had an accountant add a little something extra to a trust fund for her.

"So, she responded?" I blink a few times. I'd reached out to her myself. The kid had a secure future and denied a Pakhan, even if she declined over the phone. If it weren't for weeks on this tropical island, I might've threatened her life already.

"I paid her a visit."

"What do you mean?" I growl.

"Take it easy. Dot had said she'd be tough to break. Then I met her. She was a *child*. I've never expired a kid, even if one had it coming. Respectfully speaking, she had conditions."

I grit my teeth for a moment but end up chuckling softly, aware of how Kirill's visit concluded. "What?"

"A message for you, and a message for Square Head, whom I've determined is Dot. Anyway, the girl said you were politer this time during your last chat with her. She agreed to the mission. Only wanting to know—"

"How Anastasiya replied," I groan.

"Dah? So, what is it Asya should have replied to?"

The kid had the same request when I reached out, days ago. She'd stopped me from my offering her the world again to ask if I'd told Asya about how her parents were still alive. When I told the kid it was complicated, she'd told me not to call her about anything else until I had Anastasiya's reaction. After the girl had accessed Irek's security, finding them had been my last request. She succeeded. Apparently, she didn't strike new deals without confirmation that her time hadn't been *squandered* by old deals.

Changing the subject, I ask, "Which library?"

"A library you've given generously to in the past. Not sure what business the kid is interested in, but she did the job in less than it'll take me to return through customs. Also, we have inside men willing to share everything from the president's planned speech. Everything."

I hang up the phone with the exact date of the event and an

assurance that abducting Chutin will be an easy job. But what of Anastasiya's parents?

Like Asya's letter, which tilted my entire world upside down, I had kept another envelope close to me. This one outlined Anastasiya's true lineage. In Los Angeles, she'd shot down my offer to find them. Now, the kid felt vested in knowing. But Anastasiya won't allow me close enough to break the news.

The kid had snorted and hung up in my face. I can still hear the sound of it. I'm not a fucking suka. I'm a Pakhan. Jaw stiff, I start outside again. Anastasiya is hurling a knife at a runaway crab, screeching, "Oh my God!"

"That one was crawling rather quickly," the main chef assures.

"Fast as lightning," Asya chortles. When she looks up, eyes leveling with mine, her exhilaration fades.

"We need to talk." I slide out her chair.

"Why? I helped with the ceviche. I don't need you complaining about my eating habits. I'm eating." She claims the seat, popping a chip into her mouth.

"Mr. Resnov." The main chef shakes my hand. "Welcome, welcome. Have a seat, Chief. The missus learned a few things and was a marvelous asset in the creation of tonight's dinner."

I stare at Anastasiya. She dunks another chip into an obscene amount of ceviche, using her mouth for something other than shit-talking or just engaging in discussion with me. She hates me, and the truth is all over her face.

"Can we talk?" I growl.

Anastasiya arises, and I do too.

"I'm not—"

"Feeling well?" I grit out.

"No. I mean, yes. I mean, I'm not *pregnant*." She shoves at her chair, but the back of it is wedged into a wood plank.

The wind must've carried her argument because the chef stops packing up to hold out a bottle of champagne. "The two of you are expecting! Congratulations are in order."

"She's not," I sigh, kneading the back of my neck to mask my disappointment.

"I *can't* be." Asya shoves the stubborn chair back and stalks inside.

"Tidy up and leave dinner in the kitchen," I order, then follow Anastasiya inside. She struts into her room and starts to shut the door. I wrestle it out of her hands, using my body as a wall to send her backward, before closing and locking us inside. *"Talk to me."*

Thick lips hardly move as she snaps, "I'm not in the mood."

"Because if you're pregnant, I'd be so fucking elated, Asya."

"Why?"

"I don't mind if you're having the mudak's baby, believe me." I clasp her face. "I won't ruin us this time. My mom will pay for her actions, but ultimately, I'm a man, Anastasiya. I have faults, and I'm fucking begging you to let me fix them!"

"I'm not."

"All that matters is you're pregnant with an innocent baby in your stomach. I'll be the best father. I'll love the child no matter what he or she looks like. I'll promise in blood if I have to." I move down to my knees.

"I'm not pregnant," she groans, prying my hands from around her.

I hold steady, captivated by her dancing gaze. "Is it . . . that you can't?"

"What?" Thick hair begins to cloak her face.

I reach up, stroking the strand away from her eyes. "Outside, you said you can't. When we lost our other baby, did something—"

"No. I don't know!" She falls to her knees, sinking down to my level. The water churns darkly, a swath of blackness beneath us. It seems to dawn on us at this precise instant that we were speaking of the child we lost without our baby being the facet to a revenge tactic.

"Can I hold you, just fucking hold you?" I implore. "Nothing more."

She climbs into my lap, her legs spilling on one side of me, her breast pressed against my chest. Bitter tears sink into my neck as she silently cries. For the first time in my life, I do too.

Anatoly has beaten the snot out of me. He's commanded his byki to do the same. Learning to fight back was my only option, not crying. And here I am, holding my entire world in my arms.

I'd be a liar if I said going these last few weeks without slamming into Anastasiya's pussy had not driven me crazy. With each shower, another release. Every night, it's taken more out of me not to bust down her door when I hear her whimpered dreams. I hold her until her sniffles abate. Then I lay her sleeping body in her bed with my arms around her.

~

For the next eight hours, vengeance flies out the window. It was Asya and me, and the baby I never had a chance to meet. If Anastasiya's pregnant, I don't give a fuck who is the dad, myself or Chutin.

The baby will grow up loved by two parents, one being me. Our baby will never wonder if its mother and father love him or her. All I have to do is the opposite of what my parents demonstrated, that'll set the foundation for success.

The next morning, all the air evaporates from my lungs when Anastasiya's eyes flutter open. Relief washes over her.

"Sim, you're still here."

"Should I?" I unwrap my arms from around her frame.

Her tiny hand is no match against my bicep, but I allow her to readjust me back over her waist. "No," she breathes. "Kiss me."

I start to climb down.

Her legs move restlessly. "Simeon, I'm begging you to kiss me."

"I was on my way to." A knowing moan sparks over her, and she giggles.

I climb back up and laugh a little before planting my mouth on

215

hers. "I'll start here," I say, tasting her. "But I must warn, those other lips of yours, succulent."

"Hmmm." She groans.

"I miss them as much as I miss you."

I flip Anastasiya on top. Another fit of cackles vibrates against me. Her hair fans down as she kisses me. "Can I show you how much I've missed you, moya milaya?"

Voice heady, she replies, "Please."

"Put that pussy in my face."

"Fuck," she groans, grinding against me. "You want my pussy in your face."

I grab her, lick her cheek. "All over my fucking face, my Tsarina."

CHAPTER 38

Anastasiya

Urgency, passion, and desire thread as I climb up. His cock pierces against his underwear, begging for attention. All my resolve is a bottle shaken to the brink, and ready to explode. I climb up Simeon's muscular body like he's a fucking tree, might as well be. The dress adorning my skin is shoved up over my hips. Simeon plants a kiss on the inside of my thigh, his teeth sinking into my flesh as he shoves my thong over.

His nose nuzzles my sex. The vibration of his groan has undone me. I clutch at the headboard. The first orgasm comes quickly and shamefully free. Damn it. I begged to get off the rollercoaster! Now, I'd punch, kick, and fight to the death to stay on this crazy ride. Ride his mesmerizing fucking face.

"Oh, Simeon! I love you. I love you," I grunt, slamming down on his tongue. The dysfunction of us consumes me like a wildfire. My moans have his hands claiming my hips tighter. He coaxes my curves into a rhythm. I'm gliding and swirling, dancing and screaming.

"Cumming! I'm cum...." My voice breaks into gibberish. The ache between my thighs spreads like a firework, stealing the air from my lungs, incapacitating my entire body. Arms draped over the headboard, I ground down on Simeon, growling deep in my diaphragm. *I sound like a fucking animal!*

Water drenches his chiseled jaw, along with it all the pent-up aggression. His hand slams against my ass. I'm almost tempted to ask if he can breathe, but the pain serrates across my skin, and I buck, swerving on his tongue until my G-spot is stroked.

The oh-so-magical button makes me want to crawl into a fetal position and suck my thumb for the rest of my life.

Kidding.

I climb down and grab his glossed mouth, delighting in the sweet concoction of us. "I'm not letting you go." I sink onto his cock. "I'll kill you."

In a flash, I'm flipped onto my ass. My legs fly into the air. Each thrust is pure, dripping erotica as he enunciates every word. "Your pussy is murdering my cock. So tight. Strangling me."

"Never let me go." My legs encircle his thick waist, yanking him close, never wanting to separate.

His hand clamps my neck, body melding over mine. Simeon whispers into my ear, "I got you, Anastasiya. From now until the end of time."

Again, our mouths find each other in a sweltering kiss. No oxygen is required. We thrive off each other. And when we cum, our mouths, our tongues, our bodies become a living declaration of our love.

I'm worn out, wrapped in Simeon's ropey arms. Sleep comes and goes, sex following the same routine. When I awaken after the fourth or fifth fuck, Simeon's staring at me thoughtfully.

"Asya, there's something I need to tell you . . . ." His voice trails off as I groan. He plants kisses across my nose and cheeks. "Nothing bad, I promise."

"Don't ruin a good thing, Sim. I held out for a month-and-a-half. I will double down!"

His calloused, yet soothing hands frame my face. He's not in the least bit smiling at my joke. "While you were missing, I had hackers attempt to compromise Chutin's agenda, satellites, everything. But out of all the persons assigned, one girl was able to do it."

"Okay, then we're killing Vo—that mudak soon," I gulp down trepidation and the need to refer to Irek as the wolf. "I thought it would take ages to infiltrate his—"

"Other hackers were defeated. But this girl did it, she even found evidence of the data that had been tampered with, but by then, you were back. She's good. Though, that's not what I'd like to discuss." Simeon runs the backs of his fingers across my flesh. "Once she completed her assignment, I asked her to find your parents."

I plant my palm over his hand, ceasing the loving stroke. "Parents? What an unfamiliar term."

"Asya, neither of them are dead."

I mock. "They're dead to me, dead period. No difference, Simeon."

Strong arms become my haven as I attempt to climb from the bed.

"Asya, you're angry with me?"

"No." I look up at Simeon. His firm grip isn't rough enough. Something in me misses the hard domination. The threats. The hurt that can hurl this underlying pain that only a mother and father can cause back into the void.

"Then what?" His Russian accent grows into a hoarse rasp. He's making all the right moves. He might as well sign a petition for women's liberty. I growl, beneath his touch. My eyes are begging for more than he's willing to give.

"Choke me," I murmur. "Hurt me. Do something!"

Thick eyebrows furrow together. "Nyet."

"Sim, I need you." I wriggle beneath him, in a seductive groan.

"I'm trying to have a fucking conversation with you, Anastasiya. Your parents have been found alive. All my capital is at your disposal. We can visit them this instant. I'll be by your side every second of—"

I reach up, catching his bottom lip in my mouth, addicted to the taste of copper. His cock grows harder between us, piercing the inside of my leg. Fuck, his dick is the only portion of him conceding to me.

"Moya—"

My legs fly around Simeon's waist, fingernails embedding into his pectorals.

"Hurt me, Sim," I threaten, nipping his bottom lip. "Or I swear, you're in *big* trouble."

A deep groan vibrates from his chest to my lower abdomen. Lips plaster down on mine. Losing oxygen, I feel like my brain goes dead. I arch my hips as Simeon thrusts into me. One punch of his cockhead against my cervix sends my eyes rolling back in my head.

Damn. We played normal for long enough. We cried over our child together for the first time ever. Now, I covet the insanity of him because discussing those donors isn't an option. Those bastards ruined my life.

CHAPTER 39

Simeon

My heartbeat slams against Anastasiya's back. My mouth washes over the nape of her neck. With her in my arms, I pinch at her hardened nipples, inflicting pain because my cock is worse for wear, balls too.

I'd slammed so hard in her pussy that each hit sent my balls clapping at her clit. Each hit propelled her tight cunt to suction my dick. Now she's spent, again. I thought she would sleep for ages after we had gone at it the first few times. But this was . . .

Demented.

Hard-core demented.

The tension which wound her up while I told her a small bit about her parents faded. I want to tell her again that I'll be there for every second of her discovery of them. I'll hold her hand when they offer the excuse of how she ended up in an orphanage. I'll glare at them as they ask, "Did you have a good life?" You know, the shit people hope had occurred when they didn't follow through on their end of the bargain, raising their own child.

I'll be there. But she won't hear of it, not now.

Anastasiya's body sags into the bed. She sighs. "How soon must we return to Russia?"

"Chutin will be at a library exhibit in a few weeks. It's the best scenario for him to be taken. But time is of no importance, moya milaya. My byki will hold him until you're ready to do whatever it is you have in mind."

"Oh."

"Care to share?" *You won't talk about your parents. This is us from when we were fucking kids, and I never knew of Oleg.* I'm about to threaten her to share something when her mouth curves into a dubious smile.

"Honestly. You're rubbing off on me, Simeon." Her hands fly to her face, full of gorgeous embarrassment. "I'm contemplating how he will die. Although I appreciate your mention of time, I'll take that into consideration, too."

"Ideas?" I cock a brow.

"Ha! This is not college! Where I stand in front of hundreds of students for a debate, in which you go all 'red pen' crazy, critiquing my efforts, Professor Resnov."

I smile a little. Parents aside, Asya seems to be in a better head-space. Oleg's death hadn't been a perfect conclusion. And it shouldn't be. But this is progress. "Okay, nyet critiques on my end. Once taken, he'll be off the grid. You want to go somewhere else before returning home, tell me. You want to stay here another month, a fucking year, you tell me." My entire demeanor stresses how Anastasiya is my number one priority. "As I said, time, it's on our side."

"Sim, I'll stay here with you . . ." Her tone is strummed together, reeking of contingencies. She rolls onto her back, perky breasts spearing the air. I rub a hand over my neck so as not to fall into the temptation of touching her body. That's how the truth of her parents hadn't been resolved.

She looks at me, almost as if reading my thoughts. "Sim, I need help, though. *We need help.*"

CHAPTER 40

Anastasiya

*C**razy in love.*
Mad about him.
Our love is madness . . .
This love is insanity.

A bevy of phrases denotes how psychotic love can be. Our love is off the fucking Richter scale. The type of high where neither of us wants to come down. There has to be a happy medium, right?

When I walk into the common space of our villa, all of the sliding glass doors are open. The navy-blue dress whisks around my ankles. Simeon exits his room. Again, he's replaced morose dark suits for jeans and a shirt, which rides the expanse of his chest. His eyes swallow me whole.

"Once we return," he says, "you're moving to my room, or I'm stowing away in yours."

A lazy smile crosses my lips. "Nope. I appreciate his and her rooms. Also, I doubt either of us would've gotten dressed were we to share a room. For instance, this is our first outing since arriving here. Um . . . What's with the shoes?"

He arches an eyebrow, glancing down at himself. The men's ankle boots he's wearing, give his attire a nice flare, more for the city than the ocean. I roll my eyes because it hits me. "Oh, you're afraid of sand in your toes."

The space between us vanishes in a millisecond. My heartbeat rises. The psychotic in me loves how he dominates my area. His hand has a firm hold of my throat, and he peppers kisses along my cheekbone. "Me, afraid?"

"If I say—" My entire body tenses as his sharp choppers bite dangerously close to my bottom lip. "Hey!"

"Repeat yourself, Anastasiya." Those obsidian gems twinkle, and I'm in a trance.

"You should take me over your knee . . . I said you were afraid of sand in your toes." I roll my neck.

"Dah?" He reaches around to clutch my ass, using his hands to juggle the fat flesh of my ass cheeks. "That's your statement; you're sticking to it?"

As quickly as we've taken on a roll, it ends. Simeon's cellphone goes off. He glances at it.

"More Bratva stuff?" I ask.

He flashes the phone in my face. "Nyet. Couples retreat schedule. I'm confident in Kirill. He reached out to the Seven when—"

"Couples what?" I blink. "I thought we were doing touristy stuff."

"A little of both." Simeon's hands squeeze my ass so well, my sex jolts. Then his hands are taking mine. He moves back to the open area, which leads to our speed boat, in a space that I haven't navigated since our arrival.

"Like I said, 'couples retreat.' It's a few islands over, and the timer implies we need to go, Asya."

I exhale, the ocean air is refreshing. When I'd said we needed help, I hadn't expected this.

I need this.

~

We sign up for a weekend retreat then extend it as time goes on. Activities like sky lining in the jungle or jumping from extremely high cliffs propel us to the top of stardom concerning the other couples. We become relationship goals while learning extreme-water sports together. Little do they know, the daring trust factor was never an issue.

Then there's the sex therapy with an esteemed shrink from France who made the island her home. That's where things get a little fuzzy. In a light-blue room, with shells and beads all around, the therapist asks about our sex.

Simeon and I cuddled in our loveseat. He gave an "it's amazing" grin while I said so.

"Tell me about that."

"About our sex?" Simeon arches a brow.

"Sure?"

"She has a fairly big mouth. Go ahead, Anastasiya."

I roll my eyes at him and start sharing the juicy details. The therapist volleys back and forth, attune to my chatter. Until I conclude with, "All and all, except for the one time where he tried to murder me, sex is great."

Simeon chuckles. "If we're being transparent, there was that one time when you shot me during sex. But I'm not complaining. I came *hard* first."

The therapist laughs. "The two of you are a riot. That's about it for today. I'm sure communication, our next goal, will be right up your alley."

Simeon and I stare at each other, and I gulp. But the therapist doesn't seem to notice because she sends us home with a home-work assignment about sex. Super easy.

~

Communication was right up there with *avoidance* for Simeon and me. Or rather, in the beginning, it seemed to be *my* problem. The mudak loved delving into my head. But our therapist helped me learn how to open up to Simeon on my terms.

After a few sessions, the therapist pats my shoulder while Simeon and I sit facing each other and holding hands.

"You're doing well, Anastasiya."

The beast offers my hands a firm squeeze.

"How does it feel to be open, honest?" she inquires in a tone that moves like a soft river.

"Overwhelming but obligatory," I offer a hard grin.

"Good. We're in a structured environment, so it might get a little harder before it gets easier, Anastasiya. Now, Big Guy," she says, having given him a nickname.

Simeon cocks a brow.

"Next session, we'll dig in about how you *demand* information. We will soften your approach. Anastasiya has her reading material, let me find yours." The therapist moves toward a bookshelf filled with textbooks, authored by her.

"Sim loves to read," I reply, winking at him.

A few more sessions are centered around Simeon's actions and responses to how I communicate with him. But I have to hand it to him, so far, he's surprised me. Throughout our awakening as more nurturing lovers, Simeon did the very thing I have craved since we grew up in this world.

He set aside the Bratva and placed me first.

The next few speed sessions are more trying. But we still have our sex toys.

Once complete, I utter words I hope not to regret.

Let's return to Russia.

CHAPTER 41

Simeon

Russia

Snow falls like a halo on the crown of Anastasiya's head. A line of SUVs follows us. Condensation puffs from her plush lips as she holds my hand, guiding me across an expanse. I grit my teeth at the sight. Snow blankets the otherwise overgrown grass and weed-infested field.

Our child was buried in an unmarked grave four years ago. A tenement encompasses the entire road across the street from us. It's as hopeless and decrepit as the dwelling we found Oleg in forty-eight days ago. On the drive over, Asya shared how she'd fled from our home with a gunshot wound and made it to her old roommate's home.

"There was a tree here." She spins around, cheeks singed in

shock. Frantic, she starts pointing, muttering to herself. "Where-where is that fucking tree?!"

"Take a breath, Anastasiya," I stop her. "Let's retrace..."

She moves away. "We retraced my steps from Kosta's old stoop. I counted every step! But the tree was here and our baby ..."

Gathering her into my arms, I shush her from speaking, moving a tender hand down her clammy cheek. Tears are crystalizing on her face at the speed of light.

Damn, we landed literally seconds ago. Why had I asked for this? To know where our child was laid to rest. Maybe she wasn't ready? On our travels home, the therapist's suggestions were an asset. But now, the blood beneath her skin is tinged. She's a flurry of hot and cold. My chin rests on top of her head. Her heartbeat assaults my chest, and I wait for it to normalize.

"There." I point at a wedge in the snow. It has to be a tree stump.

"Where? The tree is gone, Simeon!"

"Let's check." I guide her over in the general direction she'd frantically been searching in. She comes alive, surging forward, and my fingers grow firmer within hers, not yielding to her panic. "We found our baby." My hands strum her hair as she falls to her knees.

Eyes bright, a trembling smile curves her lips. "We found our little baby, Simeon," she murmurs up to me, closing her eyes, face curving toward my hand.

Ice stings through my jeans as I kneel down next to her. "I know our baby is at peace, Asya. May I have him moved?"

Her eyebrows lift.

Focusing on what our therapist called a positive note, I say, "This is a beautiful place, moya milaya. But I'd like our baby closer to us. With the rest of our family." As I wait for her response, my throat tightens. Although unearthing the baby should be her decision, all I thought about during Luka's funeral was about my child. How he or she had to be somewhere alone.

Asya hooks her arms around my neck, hugging me close. "I'd like that too."

~

It's hours later, and we watched in silence as a team took special care in removing a wooden crate with our baby's remains. In the backseat of the SUV, I place an arm around Anastasiya. Her face disappears into my chest. I watch a van pull off. The team will take our baby to the mortician.

"Go," I order the driver. Kissing the top of Asya's head, I tell her, "We can choose . . ."

"A casket?" Her tiny voice chimes in when mine breaks.

"Dah. When you're ready."

She sits up. "Tomorrow."

"Listen, I have something which must be done today." I squeeze her hand. "While we're en route, can we talk names?"

"Yes." A light tremble is in her voice.

"What do you think of *Ahren*?"

A genuine smile brightens her face. "Angel? How beautiful, Simeon. I love it. Alright, where are we headed to?"

"A place we will never call home again," I reply.

Her eyebrows furrow for a moment. "The home where we moved after Moscow?"

"Dah."

"Why?"

I sigh heavily. From the outside looking in, my next move might seem the worst. But I saw strength in Asya today, and she will continue to tap into that. I reply, "To right the biggest wrong of our life."

CHAPTER 42

Anastasiya

Rows of mansions line entire streets from one corner to the next. Save for a plot of land, which is devoid of anything like the one where our child once rested. Resnovs still own the area. When Simeon burned our home down with Rudolf and the other guards inside, he never allowed another luxury house to be resurrected there. Yet, Mother Nature has a way of hiding the bad, favoring the best parts. The fleet of SUVs aligns the curb. A Maybach is already equidistant parallel to where our home once was. It's too far away in either direction to belong to either of the neighbors. The windows are tinted to the fullest extent. I glance at Simeon, who's carried us when it comes to communication and openness.

But he didn't share the reason for this strange visit.

He gets out and extends his hand. "You trust me?"

"Yes," I murmur, curiosity drawn to the other vehicle again.

"Now that you're aware of where we are, I have a few more things to share with you. Wait here."

Simeon knocks on the passenger door window of the Maybach. It doesn't open. He knocks again with more patience than I've ever seen in him, which is saying heaps. The tropical island we left has brought out the best side of him.

He grits his teeth and plants his hands on the roof of the car. "Open the door, Mother."

My heart clenches. *Sofiya! Why?*

The door opens. "You appear from sparkling sandy beaches and dare to order me around! I'm the mother; you're *moy syn!*"

Silver hair spills from bejeweled pens on top of her hair as Sofiya exits. Her pale skin has an iridescent glow. While her mouth moves nonstop, I scoff, wrapping my arms around myself.

"Sim, how about the two of you sort things out?" I hustle toward the backdoor of the SUV.

Simeon starts toward me, yet his mother makes it clear, he has to choose between the two of us. He clasps her arm, growling something in her ear. His eyes beg me to comply. "Asya, I wanted us to come home to a clean slate. Please . . ."

My eyes roll away from his, and I climb into the back. Kirill clears his throat from the driver's seat.

"We had another driver," I mumble.

"Yeah, I had to deal with *that.*" He nudges his chin to Sofiya. "Had the feeling she'd be dramatic. I also assumed you'd let her win, so I got inside."

Win? I wish I could break his neck! "You're not Luka—"

"I know." Kirill moves around in the seat to eye me over. "I miss my brat."

My lips pull in with tension, then guilt settles them in a relaxed line. Kirill was never one to apologize, and we never had a problem until now. "I'm not exactly the Tsarina anymore, Kirill. Go ahead, be blunt."

"Okay. I set aside my assignments today to chauffer Sofiya. To witness this! W*omen* are so difficult," he grits.

"Women are difficult?"

"Dah." He nods. "You think Simeon requested this meeting so the two of you could have tea at your old house? Nyet! You look over there and only see a blanket of snow. Nothing more. Think, Anastasiya. Why the fuck did he bring you here without mentioning his mother to you or you to her?"

"I—"

"Get your answers, sestra."

I glare at him. "Only Luka—"

"And I miss him too. Now that he's gone, I will be there for you. Try to stop me."

I scoff.

"I'll stop the 'sestra' thing. That's your only option in this. I wasn't thinking when I accused you of . . . you know what. Now get out of the fucking car, Asya. Please, and thank you."

"That's your apology? Wow!" I climb back out of the SUV, slamming the door behind me.

"Mother, Anastasiya, I'll have your cooperation, all of it." Simeon's hand squeezes her bicep more. "Asya, you don't have to speak. Sofiya will do all the talking."

Speak? I cock a brow. *What did I miss?*

"I'm your mother!" Sofiya snaps.

"I'm a Tsar, not God. So, there's that." He clears his throat. "Mother, you have two choices. The easier of the two is yours to decide. One being, *walk* to . . ."

Simeon mentions the town where Kosta lived before us fleeing Russia. Sofiya flushes red. It took us half an hour to travel from there just now.

Sofiya snaps, "That's what, thirty, forty kilometers from here? Walk there? Preposterous, it's bound to snow!"

"Dah, the snow will be falling a little harder in about an hour, so you'd need to walk fast. Faster than you scheme and connive.

Which brings me to why I mentioned where you're to walk." He pulls out a piece of paper and hands it to her. "That's the address where your grandchild was unearthed. Four fucking years in a crate, in a motherfucking ditch, Mother."

Sofiya pinches the address between her fingers like a foreign object. "What grandchild?"

"The one you murdered."

"I would never," she sputters, moving from his grasp. A stiletto heel slips in the slick snow, and Simeon grabs her again.

"My second option, Mother, doesn't revolve around you dying by the elements. As I'd, of course, be inclined to have one of my byki watch you walk the entire way, per option one."

"I'm not walking—"

"Option two." He clutches her shoulders, softening his voice, "Tell Anastasiya and me everything."

"What grandchild?!" She slaps at his unwavering grip. "Simeon, I don't appreciate your tone. I'm a Resnov! Who would I be to *murder a Resnov?* You're my only child. Were you to have a child, I'd love him more than I love myself. More than anything. What you're saying is impossible, moy syn. Lies and manipulations at the hand of this little suka!"

Dangerous blue eyes pin me. I'd been still during their interaction, breath stalled. Waiting, not thinking, only listening, circling to the truth.

But now, I'm launching myself at Sofiya. My legs fly in the air as Simeon grabs me. My fingers push against his chest, his face. Blood swallows me whole, propelling me to the day my innocent baby was aborted from my body.

I come to in a pile of slush. Simeon rubs my face, compelling me in a soothing voice. "Calm, calm, moya milaya. You're my beautiful Tsarina. You're so strong. This has to be done."

From my side peripheral, Kirill has a hand on Sofiya. More byki are torn between touching the mother of the Tsar. They implore her to stay.

"This must be done. I demand answers," he whispers, his lips brushing across my earlobe. "You're worthy of answers. Then our Angel can continue to Rest In Peace."

"How dare you, Kirill!" Sofiya scoffs, slapping at his abrasive touch.

"With all due respect, Aunt Sofiya. My brat died. The young lady he called sestra until his last breath perished because others had a hand in these two people's lives. I have a second kazen, a little baby that I was not given a chance to hold in my arms, to play catch with or pretend tea. Forgive me later. Choice is yours."

Sofiya blinks then stutters, "How dare you mention Luka? Kirill, you're a monster. You and that suka influenced *moy syn*."

"Okay, I'm a little filthy. But don't you dare tell me not to mention *my brat*." He removes his ponytail holder.

"Kirill," Simeon grits, seemingly back in action after comforting me. When Kirill removes his ponytail, it's a sure sign reality is fading. His cousin steps back a little.

Simeon helps me up. "Talk, Mother, or walk!"

"I could never walk so far in the snow. It was a warm day when Anastasiya—" She bites her tongue.

"When the woman I called Mother attempted to kill me?" I screech.

"I was attempting to sell you, not have you murdered!" She rolls her eyes, doing a one-two step. "My toes are frostbitten!"

"Mother." Simeon's hands ball into fists.

"What will you do, moy syn? You've got a hell of a lot more to aspire to become your father. Punches won't work."

"I would never." He starts backward. "Kirill, I take it you'll follow your aunt as she starts walking. Come, Anastasiya, let's go. If she falls on the way to her destination, wait awhile. I'll have her pronounced dead before anyone comes to her assistance."

"But Anastasiya didn't die!" Sofiya stomps her feet, only to have a heel glide across the slick snow again.

He salutes his mother. "Ma, you'll get your ruby red casket and

235

blood-red roses. Though, I'll never know what color or flower my Angel preferred."

I squeeze Simeon's hand tighter and stall. "I-I."

"Dah?" He stops walking.

"This was the part that always stopped me from telling you, Sim. One day you'll regret . . ."

The Dr. Jekyll and Mr. Hyde I know him for is resurrected. Although, when Simeon's obsidian orbs dart from my face to his mother, I see his dilemma. He's torn.

Torn between us.

Torn between vindication for our sweet Angel.

"I'll talk!" Sofiya reels on her heels, arms around herself. "You're my beautiful baby, Simeon. If you lost a child—"

"We did!" My throat scorches from the shout.

"If you lost a baby," she addresses him only, "then I beg your forgiveness. Right here, right beneath the heavens."

She spins around, looking up. The sky opens up. Instead of a lightning bolt, soft snow crystals fall. Sofiya clutches a cross at her neck. "Resnovs are blessed, moy syn. Other factions have more death. Kirill, I will miss Luka forever, my nephew. But—"

"Why?" A voice that sounds uncannily like mine inquires. The volume of my tone sends birds in flight around us. Overwhelmed and overtaken by her flair for dramatics, I shout, "Why, Mother, please?"

Sofiya blinks. "I love you, Anastasiya."

And when I think she's about to play off my vulnerability, Sofiya ceases from her deflection and continues. "I love you but . . ."

The contingency rings loud. *Love me without restriction*, I demand. *Fucking love me.* I stare at the woman who was to replace my parents. I'm not so callous to believe that it doesn't take the same essence flowing through one's veins to have unconditional love. Simeon is my drug for anxiety, fears, any negativity. But a mother's or a father's love would've created a different woman in me.

Sofiya could've been *that for me*. The reason why I flourished and prospered. The reason why I could have been a little less crazy. Shrugging, I repeat myself, "Why?"

Condemnation billows from her mouth in a deep huff. "You *are* a Castle Girl. You were born with an assignment, one which you failed to fulfill."

"What the fuck are you talking about, Mother? I asked Anatoly for her," Simeon grits, pounding his own chest. "Anastasiya was given our blessing. She became mine. She became free."

I want to smile. The selfish man, who always loved me without contingency, wants to believe I'm free. Hell, not even I want that. I'll never be free because his love is my drug.

"Oh, moy syn, Anatoly blessed her, dah. But no one asked me. Before you were, *I was* Tsar."

CHAPTER 43

Simeon

Ask me if my mother is out of her fucking mind. As a kid, I'd
say nyet. I'd present facts:

Anatoly manipulated her.

Brainwashed her.

He ruined a certain part of her cognition. *Not all of her, just the
part designated for a really good man to love.* Shit, even I saw Anastasiya as a blessing and not just a piece of pussy I couldn't let go of.

Ask me about her sanity today. My mother has lost it.

"What do you mean, you were Tsar? Make this shit make sense
now or walk!"

A flicker of a smile creases her mouth. "I could come to Anatoly
with a cup filled with poison and tell him so. Tell him he'd be dead
before he finished, order him to drink of it. He would."

Around me, all the men are staring at the ground, unsure how
to respond. Anastasiya is glued to her ranting.

"Our Asya was to have that hold on you, Simeon."

I glare at her, the declaration echoing in my ears.

"Oh, nyet, my beautiful boy. She would never kill you. She did succeed in loving you enough. The little Castle Girl didn't have it in her to follow through with orders."

"The revealing dresses," Anastasiya snarls. "The 'talk to Simeon because his feelings are hurt.' He was my friend. He was fucking traumatized by you and Anatoly."

"Let me finish." My mother lifts her stilettos again, and I'm slightly satisfied by her being agonizingly cold. "You forced this upon me, all of you!"

"Then finish," I speak up.

She lifts her gaze and mutters to herself, "Alright, why the hell not? My brother was loaded, drunk, and high on cocaine when he raped me before the eyes of Vassili, his mother, and Grigor and Danny. God, in that moment, he did not see me as his sister but as an ally of Vassili's mother. *His enemy.* I hated the very blood in our veins for it. Then I found out I was pregnant."

Somehow, I glance over at Anastasiya. Her tiny arms are wrapped around me. Our roles have changed. She's offering all the necessary support I attempted to aid her with a while ago. *That mudak raped my mother.* I could always tell when she was lying. One time, I had snapped after Anatoly had come to see her. She'd replied that these things had to be done. But that was a lie. She loved it. Somewhere along the lines, she learned to *love it.*

"Abortion was never an option. A Resnov more Resnov than us all. We had created *perfection.* A pureblood. And *I* was its mother. I was blessed with a pregnancy and then blessed with a *male* heir. Anatoly was so proud. And he loved *me* for it, for you, Simeon. I was rearing the next heir, his son. Because of that, Anatoly would do whatever I said. Whatever I wanted. *I* had the power. *I* was the true leader."

I bite back the bile rising in my throat. "Keep going," I growl.

"I'm freezing!" Sofiya's teeth chatter, and she shakes. "Let's discuss this without all these extra—"

"I'd like to stick around, Tsar," Kirill states.

I nod. "Everyone stays."

"Absurd." Sofiya shakes her shoulders, and snow descends. "When I went to Anatoly, in tears, and told him what beauty we made. Simeon, you have no idea how much Anatoly loved you. Blood of his blood. Our blood."

"Loved him!" Anastasiya gasps. "Anatoly punched, kicked, *attacked* Sim every chance he got—"

"I said he loved him!" Sofiya snarls. "Loved our boy more than the rest of his children. Because our syn was a *pure* Resnov."

"I'm sure you gave Anatoly that idea. Like drinking poison, right?" Asya grips my hand to show our solidarity.

My father loved me? I assess Sofiya for lies, but she snaps, "Anatoly loved him. But Simeon had to grow to be great. The Resnovs have to be devoted to our own ascension. None of Anatoly's other children could compare to ours. That meant a father who didn't spare discipline."

"You're vicious," Asya says crossly.

"I am. I molded my son into the next in succession. Anatoly had to hate Simeon. And I had to assist with that by fucking my brother. So, there's that."

"I bet you learned to love it," Asya growls.

"You're saying that monster loved me?" I ask. People love things and other people. It's a concept. This is unfathomable.

"Dah. Then Anastasiya came into our lives. A vessel. Like I said, you were to help me curve Simeon a little further. The perfect Tsar, unyielding."

"I would never," Anastasiya mutters.

"How?" I ask. The workings of my mother's psyche are beyond conceivable.

"As Anastasiya has already expressed. Look pretty, console you when I curved Anatoly's action."

"When you controlled your brat?" I retort.

"Sim, this is not for the male species to comprehend." Sofiya shakes her head. "The art of the female. You'll be happy to know that our Anastasiya has only ever had your best interest at heart, which brings us up to speed. It's unfortunate. She was to be my protégé. I'd shape and control her. She wasn't pliable enough. She was too interested in falling in love than learning true wiles. Her innocence did captivate you. But that was only one part of the plan. Captivation. Influence—*my* influence."

"I'd never!" Asya growls.

"Thus, we are here! Because you never fulfilled your duty, Anastasiya. You became their family. Luka and Kirill's little friend. Simeon's love." Sofiya's eyes blaze through Anastasiya with more to tell.

What more?

I glance at Anastasiya, and she's as oblivious as me and the rest of my byki.

"When you say Anatoly blessed her, that was all. I *allowed* Simeon to love you and keep you. Then I dropped a little notion into Anatoly's ear. I'd grown tired of waiting for Anastasiya to mold to my will. Like inferring that perhaps our Anastasiya was not a fucking virgin. He was to test you."

I'm in my mother's face in a second. "He touched her!"

My mother's face tilts. "It was a simple test. You came running."

Anastasiya grips at my hand, pulling me back.

"Anatoly fingered her cunt. Get over yourself, moy syn. You begged for this farce."

"Shut up already!" Anastasiya shouts at her while heaving against me with all her might.

"Nyet. Keep magnifying your punishment," I threaten.

My mother's entire body shakes. With her hands fisted at her sides, she declares, "I want to die. The man I loved more than life itself is dead."

"What happened to Anatoly raped you? To the disgust?!"

"We. Fell. In. Love."

"Oh yeah? Anatoly had a whole lot of love to give, suka. You love no one!" Asya snarls.

"How dare you, little girl! I thought Simeon might not understand as a man. Don't be so daft, Asya. Connections, Asya. Anatoly touched you, and Simeon was ready to die because of it. Don't be so full of yourself. He touched you for me."

Asya gasps, "What if—"

"Nyet, my daughter. You failed me." Sofiya points a stiff hand at her own chest. "Anatoly taught Simeon *tough love*. Instead of being a facet for moy syn to reign with time, you weakened him! Your disappearance was the final key to his training since you weren't manipulatable. You've always hated the Bratva, Asya."

My woman nods. "But I stayed for Sim."

"Correction. *Had* you stayed, you'd have become a variable. A division. You'd do anything for Simeon, and he'd do anything for you. Such as discounting all the work I did!"

"So, it's all about you, Mother." I glare in disgust.

"Dah, if you believe so," she mumbles. "I suppose the death of my grandchild is also on Asya's head. Had she been trainable then I wouldn't have needed to—"

"Kirill, you get the names of every Armenian out of this woman as she walks, and you take a long fucking drive. Now," I growl to my cousin, cutting off my mother's blaming words. I never met my Angel. I will never forgive Sofiya.

"Dah, Kazen," Kirill grunts.

My fingers brush along Asya's frozen ones. "Let's go."

She nods.

My mother flies into a rage. At my command, the byki hold her back. I continue to address Kirill. "Tell me the second my mother falls to her knees. The moment she lays in the snow. The length of time it takes her to stop breathing."

"How dare you, Simeon. You were coached to be the perfect vessel! I made you," Sofiya hisses as I open the back door for my woman. "Get back here."

"All this time, you were my first real mother. First real mother!" Anastasiya shouts.

"I was the best mother you could ever have!" is the last thing my mother hurls at Anastasiya as I slide in the seat beside her.

Dysfunctional as it may be, I needed this. I look her over, regretting yet believing she needed it too.

"How do you feel, moya milaya?"

"Alive." She lets out a pent-up breath.

"Good. The Armenians will be taken care of. And speaking of Armenians . . . I cannot promise that I'll ever apologize to Rudolf's family. It would paint the Bratva in a weak light. But you know my sentiments, Anastasiya."

"Yes," she murmurs. "You're remorseful . . . in your own way."

"Good. One more person left to go. Then we can start our happily ever after, dah?" Again, I look her over. I hate to acknowledge that my mother's last statement was a low blow. Everything she said was like a serrated knife through the heart. But when Anastasiya is ready to learn more about her parents, the truth is hers to be had.

She smiles at me. Eyes twinkling, content. "Let's get all of this over. I think an HEA is in the cards—no parents included."

"HEA?" I arch a brow.

Though this day was trying, there's a sparkle in her eye when she says, "Means 'happily ever after,' Sim. You're the literature freak, remember?"

CHAPTER 44

Anastasiya

Have you ever had one of those dreams where you'd stay asleep a while longer if you had that type of control? It's enticing, dangerous, sexy. You'd awaken later, panties soaking wet. But for now, you were torn between the delight of staying a while.

Simeon's broad chest epitomizes power against my back. Desire stirs warm in my core while he drops kisses on the nape of my neck. The rough padding of his fingers shapes my already hardened nipples into taut, focal points of delicious pain.

As I moan, I connect gazes with someone watching us.

Black leather strains over the muscles of a man, standing at our window. A leather mask covers the stranger's entire face, only leaving gorgeous blue gems and a pleasantly twisted mouth.

I wonder who he is. My curiosity melds into deja vu. Simeon's fingers trail down my throat. His mouth nips at my neck so delicately. Every time I open my mouth to warn him of the voyeur, only a moan floats from my lips. With each moan, the magnetizing stranger appears closer to us. When my mouth opens to speak again, the stranger's tongue brushes mine. His mouth tastes of champagne. I pull away slightly, turning my attention toward Simeon, whose fiery kisses weaken my legs. Shutters ribbon across my skin as the stranger nips the junction of my neck and shoulder. His hand slides up my stomach, steadying me before descending toward my breast.

"Sim . . ." I breathe heavily, hearing the undoing of a belt buckle behind me. This is a dream, I tell myself. Because Simeon doesn't share. Or maybe I'm imagining us in one of those erotic stories I beg him to read to me.

As I attempt to think it through, they descend on their knees with me sandwiched between. My eyes close. The sumptuous feel of lips trail against my neck, spine, breasts, and lower back. I lean against the stranger, scraping my nails across Simeon's shoulders as Simeon breathes in my sex.

Again, I call Simeon's name, but his mouth is playing a game, teasing, flicking, tasting my inner thighs, everywhere except for satiating this carnal need. I know that the second his mouth brushes across my clit and throbbing lips, the danger stirring in my stomach will disappear. I'll welcome Simeon's touch and the stranger's touch.

Simeon's mouth frames my pussy. The stranger wraps an arm around me, kneading my nipple. My body starts to turn around. I tell myself to stop, but those champagne kisses intoxicate me.

"Sim . . ." I groan as he positions himself behind me. His hands drag smoothly down my spine. My arch is refined as his cock enters me.

Suddenly, the stranger is sitting before me, fingers massaging at my scalp as sweltering heat builds in my core. The outsider runs his hand along my frame. My senses are flooded as his fingers draw along the inside of my thigh while Simeon fucks me from the back. Then he drags his fingers over my clit, swirls my juices around.

"Yes! Keep fucking me. Just like that," I groan, training my eyes on the voyeur's baby blues. His slick finger caresses my mouth. I bring his finger to the back of my throat, tasting my juices and slamming back on Simeon.

"Don't stop fucking me, Sim," I groan, noticing how I'm only regarding the man I love.

Pure lust shines in the stranger's eyes, telling me exactly what he wants.

Simeon's thrusts become measured. My slick walls suck in his cock, exhilaratingly slow. At the same pace, I lower my head into the other man's lap. He poises his shaft at my hungry lips. The urge to suck his cock is unbearable.

Simeon forces himself so deep, stretching my trembling walls. Mouth wide, I take more of Blue Eyes.

Each punch of Simeon's dick into my pussy, and I'm choking more of the stranger down. Our groans increase. Simeon's pace is urgent. His balls applaud my clit with each thrust.

My mouth works at the voyeur's cock, his fist in my hair. My senses are heightened. A tidal wave courses through me as Simeon recklessly dives in and out, sending the stranger's member bashing into my tonsils. My mouth feels lovely, expanding to capacity. My walls stretch to the same rhythm and depth. The dual sensations flood my mouth with saliva and my psyche with dark erotic thoughts. It feels like I'm being consumed from the inside out as they play my body any which way they crave.

With so much cock in my mouth, I strangle instead of screaming at the top of my lungs. The Tsar's pace becomes barbaric. A thrill runs through me as both men tense. Cum volleys deep into my core and shoots down my throat.

"Simeon!" I shout, the thick, creamy cum glossing my lips.

Simeon falls into me, seemingly unaware.

The man in front of me, grips harder on my ponytail, bringing my face up. The mask has disappeared from his heavenly features. His gaze cuts through me. "When I cum, you swallow all of it, Nastiya."

~

T he erotic dream fades fast. I slam into a seated position. The nickname, "Nastiya," rings in my ears, fading to black. It's replaced by Kosta's snide words: "Will you become the little fuck toy of all the Resnovs, too?"

Rubbing a hand over the back of my neck, I hurry to a standing position.

"What the fuck was that?" I ask myself, my bare feet meandering around the expensive carpet. They say dreams mean the opposite of reality.

Kosta's super dead.

Simeon is too jealous. *We* are way too jealous for a threesome.

But Mikhail . . . that was way too much love.

I almost sprain my ankle, turning to glance at our bed. Relief floods through me. An early riser, Simeon isn't in the room. After leaving Sofiya to walk in the snow, we finalized Angel's arrangements.

"We didn't even have sex last night," I murmur, pacing again. But that should be a plus. We comforted each other.

"Okay, today, I'm meeting with the liaison to the Castle Girls, then Sim and I are completing one of our communication assignments." My pace falters instantly. *This sure as fuck won't be a topic of discussion.*

A knock at the bedroom door sends my shoulders jumping. "Calm down, Asya," I groan, then speak up, "Yes?"

A maid enters. "Tsarina, may I be of assistance?"

"Yes," I reply anxiously, then scale down my nerves by waiting a beat. "I'm scheduled to have lunch with . . ."

"Faina?"

"Yes," I nod, chewing my lip. "She's the liaison, who attempted to meet with me months ago." I stop speaking, wishing Luka were here. "Tell Faina I'll meet her at the hospital in lieu of lunch first. Please."

"Anything else?"

I close my eyes and sigh deeply. "As a matter of fact, yes."

The maid blinks a few times. Her wane fingers fidget as she awaits my response.

My voice perishes to a scarce octave. "Is there a doctor or midwife in the general vicinity?"

"Dah." Her frail hands stop their nervous dance, and she smiles up at me. "I will go—"

"One more thing," I call her back, my eyes closing momentarily as I sigh.

CHAPTER 45

Mikhail

After all the time I waited patiently, she came to me. Drinking in every inch of Anastasiya, I feel behind myself for the brocade couch, sitting before my legs can buckle. This is Los Angeles all over again, except I'd been running after her. Anastasiya leans against the closed door of the palace bedroom, no desire to close the space between us.

"You were supposed to leave, Mikhail." Her plush, pink-tinted lips pull into a line.

"You're highly aware of my reason for staying." I swirl the glass of scotch in my hand, having poured myself a drink mere moments before she arrived. Crystal-like residuals, my preferred substitute for Nastiya, eddy in the dark amber.

"I assumed you had more brain cells." Her fingers clash with mine as she snatches the drink from my lips. "What's in this?"

I snort. "You give a fuck today, I see. For sixty-four days, how many of those minutes, seconds did you think of me, Nastiya?"

The glass goes hurling into the empty fireplace. "Once, Mikhail."

"One single occasion." I fork a few fingers through my hair. My eyes are a fury of truth. There is no need to declare my every waking moment was spent on *her*. "Damn, that drink would come in handy right about now."

"*Good Doctor*, that's who you are," she begins in a collective voice. My eyes are on her peep-toe shoes. Black, glossy toenails peek through. Far away, she resituates herself in a wide-legged stance near the door. "When I think of you, I pray for the best, Mikhail."

"What's best for me? Seems the two of us have vastly divergent notions of what the other one needs." I start out of my seat. Sharp, honey eyes zero into my skin.

Lips curved into a half-smile, I elect not to unsettle Anastasiya any more than she already is. I head toward the bottle of scotch on the dresser. Picking up a silver spoon, I open up a pill bottle and begin to crush the contents into a new glass. "I'm gonna go out on a limb here and ask you a silly question."

"How about returning to your life."

"In the past sixty-four days, because clearly, I counted them, did Simeon see you crying in the shower? Breaking down, tears in your eyes?" I glance over my shoulder to eye her. Vivid images flit across my face. Sentiments won't fail me even past the memory loss of ripe old age. "Sim aware of everything?"

Her thick, pouty lips draw into a line. "Yes! Is that what you need to hear, Mikhail? Simeon supports me?"

"Is that a yes to the former or the latter, Nastiya? Yes, to you breaking down at the thought of showering, and yes to everything it encompasses?"

She leans against the wall, the side of her tiny fists slamming into the wood. *Tap. Tap. Tap.* "It's a solid yes, Mikhail."

"At the cabin, you scurried off—"

Anastasiya cuts in, "I didn't."

"Alright, jetted away once you were stitched up. Not a single word. But before, when you got in the shower. You broke. I was there for you." My fingers curl under, impressing upon my palms at the thought of how I came running. My vision of perfection, literal and physical, had shattered. "You wanted to cleanse the dried blood. Then you broke down, a sopping mess."

She whispers, "Sim's aware of what Oleg did."

I nod. The amber is a perfect rendition of her eyes as it splashes into the glass. I can feel her behind me, closing in, doing all the things she should have done months ago. Drawing toward me instead of falling into Simeon's snare. Her hand is over mine as I grab my drink.

"Go home, Mikhail." Her breath tickles the center of my back, warming through my shoddy V-neck. "Save people."

"I want you." My voice volleys, tone laced in darkness I've kept underfoot. "I gave you alcohol for the pain. Stitched you up. Hardest thing I've ever done. Had you so motherfucking close. My hand was a fraction away from your breast as I mended your warm brown skin. Let's not mention—"

"Then don't!"

"No, I think I will. I was the nice guy. You cried in the shower. I helped you. Wrapped you in towels. Cut down the cold chill. But you tell me to save people. All I ever wanted to do was save you, Nastiya."

I move around, arms encircling her waist before she realizes how taboo our nearness is. I bring her body flush to mine, leaving no space between us. "I've brought the dead back to life, kick-started hearts. Focused long and hard before telling mothers and husbands the person they loved most in the world died on the table."

Through a flurry of lashes, her honeysuckle orbs look up at me.

Her voice hardly meets my ears. "You will continue to save lives and comfort people."

"Why? For a man who's desperately saved lives, and called orders, which weren't as effective, I haven't saved the one who meant the most to me. I dare you to tell me we hardly know each other, Nastiya, I will." I stop, my lips in a hard snarl.

"Shut up!" She growls.

My eyes bite closed at the thoughts of the taste of her mouth.

Her face softens in contemplation then blazes darker. "The longer you stay here, Mikhail, the more at risk you'll be."

"So be it." I plop back onto the couch and down the entire glass. "That's why I lace my drinks. Lowers my moral compass. I'm waiting for Anatoly to possess Simeon, change him into the para-noid-schizoid he was destined to be."

"For what?"

"So, when Simeon loses his fucking mind, I'll strike, and the Seven will see no fault in me."

"God, Mikhail, how many of these damn drinks did you have? It's midday." Anastasiya struts over. Her fingers strum through my hair. She yanks my head up. "You're an idiot. I thought of you once. Are my lack of feelings for you worth your life?"

"Dah."

"I'm so done lending a hand. You saved me, but we'll be together soon at the rate you're going. Dead together, asshole."

My eyes rove over Anastasiya's skirt, her ass, her hips as she sashays to the door. The shape of her has me in a trance. Suddenly, I'm in the cramped bathroom at the cabin. Water raining over her heated flesh, drawing her body out of the shower as she cried about the sadist, Oleg. *We were leaving this dark, seedy world. I tasted it.* She was in my clutches, ready to let it all go.

"Wait, Nastiya." My voice dips in emotion. "You and I were supposed to chat that next morning, sweetheart. I was going to tell you that Simeon was only looking for you to kill you. To murder the woman he claimed to love. That I loved you. Those were my only intentions. I'd tell you about Sofiya."

"Heh, I appreciate the intel on Simeon. I've had it to here with Sofiya," she murmurs, facing me.

"Sit," I pat the seat beside me, "for a few. You owe me nothing. I'm asking you to, Nastiya."

"Good Doctor," she groans.

"C'mon, stop stressing the 'good' crap. You'll let me say *goodbye*, won't you?"

Chewing in her bottom lip, Anastasiya hesitates. Confusion flushes her skin. I'll seize this moment. We are not Bratva, she and I.

She isn't the Tsar's Tsarina.

She hates this world. During our walk in Vegas, after she told me to look up, our story didn't end there. No, it had only begun. We walked the seedy strip. Her eyes a bright, unquenchable light, her aura unmatched, as she became mine. True love gives strength. It perceives something in a person that no one else does. Being passionately loved is courage. My love for her will create a braver woman, help Asya let go. Simeon dims her shine, ruining her. No more. I'll continue to feed that shine.

CHAPTER 46

Simeon

Seated in my office, I slide the paperwork regarding Anastasiya's parents back into the top drawer. My curiosity is piqued, but I'll respect her wishes. I return my attention to my cellphone. An arms dealer is prattling about what he's bringing to the market.

"Dah, I agree with your proposal," I reply, into the speaker, when he lets up on the fast-talk.

This is my first day back in the office. So many things to do, yet I've delegated my time to align with Anastasiya's return from seeing the Castle Girls. The Bratva will not come between us.

The arms dealer continues to try and upsell me when I was already sold.

I cut in again. "I'll have one of my guys schedule a meeting." I glance at the open door to my office to see a vaguely familiar face. The maid whose ass came to fruition in my face while Mikhail slung accusations at me has a hip leaning against the doorframe.

Eyeing her curiously, I continue into the receiver, "Don't waste my time. Dah?"

"You have my word," comes a second before I hang up the phone. With an eyebrow lifted, I gesture for her to enter. There are many servants here. The older ones are readily recognizable as the turnover margins are low because the incentives are high. I can't recall seeing the eager blonde more than a time or two, one of which included her as being a vessel during the argument with my cousin.

"I have news to share about the Tsarina—"

My hand cuts through the air. "That won't be—"

"She's pregnant."

My mouth moves into a straight line as she mentions that another maid requested a home visit about an hour ago from the doctor on the premise.

When she's done sharing, my mouth twitches at the side. "Had you waited your turn to speak, you'd have heard my entire state-ment, which would've indicated I don't appreciate gossip."

Her eyelashes flutter, confusion converting into a twitchy smile. "I assure you, it's not hearsay. A midwife was on the premise for—"

"You are dismissed."

She stays put.

I clear my throat. The byki at the door enters.

Sighing, I ask, "Miss, what is your name?"

"Claire."

"Claire is fired."

"What? I don't—"

The byki's gun goes off, traces of brain and blood jut from the side of her head as a .9mm bullet exits the other side.

"You'll excuse me as I leave you to have this cleaned." I stand up, walk around the table, and exit the room.

Discord will not be tolerated. The dead suka had an underlying

255

motive in sharing information about Anastasiya. People like her and Kosta don't belong near my Tsarina or me.

My mother is another example. However, she astonished even me by seeking shelter in a cave with Kirill having to watch her all night. I hadn't made any stipulations, but I was told it was the worst night of her life. She began walking again at first dawn, only to arrive about thirty minutes ago. Sofiya is now cut off from all funding due to her.

Kosta, Sofiya, the likes, they're all lumped into one big bag of shit. The type of people I refuse to fuck with.

"Where is Anastasiya?" I ask another byki at the end of the stairs. While I'd rather respect her wishes to tell me she's pregnant at her own time, I'm anxious.

He sends out a message and then says, "The Tsarina went to Mikhail's room a few minutes ago."

Don't get jealous. You trust her.

Not him.

I contemplate allowing her space. All those trusting exercises roam through my head, and when I come to, I'm at the door to his room. Knocking is all I can consent to.

"Come in," Anastasiya calls out.

I wriggle my tensed jaw and enter.

They're sitting on loveseats across from each other. Asya smiles up at me, her legs crossed respectably, but with those hips and thighs.

"Sim." She pats the seat next to her. "You won't believe what Mikhail had in mind for us. He suggested a welcome home party."

"I did." My cousin offers half a smile.

"I was persuading Mikhail otherwise. But he was relentless. Said he's heading back to Los Angeles now that everything is right between us. We all know you aren't big on parties. And the two of you aren't so close."

"Nice gesture, but nyet." I eye her, my heart swelling with love. "Anastasiya, may I?"

"Well then, no party." She arises. "Mikhail, if I don't see you after I return from an outing this evening, then there's always next time, right?"

"That's right." He pounds a happy fist into the air.

I cock a brow, but she's up. My eyes shower over her flat abdomen. I take her hand and pull her out of the room, closing the door.

"You're pregnant?"

CHAPTER 47

Anastasiya

Simeon is on his knees before me, hands clasping my stomach. His head is planted against my belly, then he pulls up my shirt and plants kisses over the taut surface.

"Sim," I groan.

He's far from listening. He mentions how I don't have to answer, and a maid told him without prompt. Now, she's dead.

"You killed her." I clutch his jaw, looking down at him.

"Nyet."

My head tilts. "Well, is the maid dead, Sim?"

"Dah. Not my fault."

"You're a monster." I remove myself from his embrace and stalk down the hall.

He's up in seconds, planting an arm around my waist and guiding me into a library, one of many in the palace.

"Asya, I won't have anyone around who is against us. She's deceased. End of story. I wish she hadn't said a word, but I'm fucking elated."

I can't stare at him. Leather and lemon-scented wood cleaner funnels down my nostrils.

"I . . . I never." I gulp down the lump in my throat, running my fingers over worn encyclopedias. "I never got a chance to meet the other girls I was supposed to the day Irek had me taken. I can't be late."

His massive shoulders fall. "How far along are you?"

Gaze leveled with his, I reply, "I'm not ready to talk about this, Sim."

His hands go to the top of his head. "Don't go. Not right now, moya milaya. It's not my intention to compromise your Castle operation. Talk to me, baby, first. We made that promise."

I head for the door, my argument with Mikhail fresh on my mind. Simeon's hand goes to my shoulder. His chin rests on top of my head, his arm claiming me from behind. A huge hand splays across my stomach. "Everything will be okay, Anastasiya."

"See you tonight," I murmur, peeling his fingers from over my stomach. I open the door, scurry down the hall, and hustle down the steps. I'm not bold enough to glance over my shoulder.

Sunlight streams in as a byki opens the double doors.

"May I have any keys. I need a drive." I shrug.

Kirill is tossing a set of keys into the air as he stalks up the steps. Under his eyes, the skin is darkened from lack of sleep. "Nyet keys. I'm driving."

"Seems like you just arrived . . ."

"Dah," he sighs. "Sofiya had us holed up in some sort of cave. She fended for herself. Might've been entertaining to watch, had I not been with her. Then I drove at a snail's pace at dawn. She made it."

It doesn't hurt so badly, not now, with my concentration on how I left Simeon. It was an asshole move. But the revelation will still be thick between us when I return. Overwhelmed, I shrug. "So the witch lives?"

"Dah. I'm aware of your agenda, Tsarina. Let's go."

"Whatever, Kirill." I groan. "I can't be late."

He pulls out his phone. "We should be on the early side."

"Good. Get me out of—"

I'm spun around on my shoes so quickly I land in Simeon's arms.

"I don't give a fuck if the baby is Irek Chutin's, Anastasiya. It's my second chance. *Our* second chance."

My eyes brighten. There are people around. A very powerful man like him doesn't claim someone else's child. Especially not to an audience.

I shove a shaky hand through my hair. I feel like an ass. The second I began to dress after learning about my pregnancy, the midwife mentioned Mikhail. She'd said it was an honor how I chose her over him. I literally went to another man seconds after learning about being pregnant. At that moment with Mikhail, the shock ceased to exist. Now, the revelation of a baby growing inside of me charges the air, and Simeon has made all the right moves.

With a deep controlled voice, he again implores me to open up. "Asya, I was denied the opportunity to be there for you last time."

My lips part, nothing spills out. It wasn't his fault for not being there. I run a hand over my forearm, vulnerable to the idea of had he known. Would the Black Dolphin have continued to be his home for the next three and a half years?

"You," he points to a byki. "I'm declaring to this woman that I will be the best father. I want a son or a daughter, both. I'll be blessed with anything my Tsarina has. You're my witness. Kirill—"

"Stop," I hiss.

"Kirill, if I fuck up, shoot me here!" Simeon places his stiff index finger to his dome. "Murder me, Kazen, no consequence."

"Simeon, I don't want you to die!" I gasp. "I love you."

"And you're keeping *my baby? And I mean mine as in fuck genetics, fuck the notion of Chutin being . . . I'll be there always!*" he grits. "You're keeping my little one, dah?"

Voice strangled, I gasp, recalling all of my taunting on the night

Oleg's intestines splattered half a mile down the road. "Simeon, Irek never . . . he . . . didn't. He's not the father—"

The world stops spinning, tilts off-kilter, flung the opposite direction. Simeon spins me in the air. His face is in the crook of my neck as my legs fly. As I land, I teeter on my heels. I look up to see Mikhail at the window. He instantly steps away.

Like every time before, the Good Doctor vanishes from my thoughts. Simeon commands my attention. He's elated. I'm afraid.

~

The ride to the prestigious hospital is where the uber-rich visit. That is, if their diagnosticians cannot pinpoint their ailment in their lavish mansions. Groundbreaking research occurs here, and the Castle Girls, the ones who were deemed the least likely to thrive, are inside. I wriggle in my seat. Mikhail springs to the forefront of my mind. I shoot him down, *bang, bang,* with thoughts of Simeon.

I love Simeon with all of me, but I place my arms around my abdomen and determine the insanity we have for each other will never match the love a mother has for her child. Is our connection sustainable? Would Simeon truly be a good father? My fingertips trail across my lips where his public dedication fanned into a promise of adulation.

Antsy, I glance over at Kirill, who is exceptionally quiet. "So . . ."

"So . . ."

A smile blossoms on my lips. "You said Luka and I were irritating as children."

His cold blue eyes warm over me, sparkling at the mention of his brat. "I did. Wouldn't take it back either."

I wag a finger at him. "Kirill, you're stubborn."

He grunts. "Speaking of stubborn. When we arrive, you're not to leave my sight."

"Why? Shouldn't you take a nap?"

"Nyet. You want to have a private conversation with any of your friends, forget I'm there."

"Wow, you left no room for compromise."

"That shit is for you and Simeon. He may be showing his nicer side as of late—"

"Do you think it will last?" I blurt. Why, I have no idea. Kirill's loyalty will forever abide in Simeon. I could goad Luka half to death, but Kirill is not Luka. Both of them were truly older brothers to me, while one was my best friend, the other offered cold protection.

"With you, Dah." Kirill's gaze locks onto mine for a millisecond. "I do him in if he fails, remember?"

"You wouldn't." I roll my eyes.

"Dah, you're right. I wouldn't. *Sim wouldn't either.* The little baby in your belly is the next Tsar or Tsarina, and my loyalty is now yours," he assures. "One day it will belong to . . ."

"My child." I gulp. *My baby will be Resnov.*

"You worried about the Seven?" he inquires quickly then continues. "Don't. I ensured them Chutin was behind Luka's death. None of my uncles thought to blame you, anyhow. They knew how much the two of you meant to each other."

CHAPTER 48

Anastasiya

The liaison, Faina, had turned out to be more than a female the Bratva hired for the Castle Girls. She was one of us. Faina had an owner quite like mine, referring to the clause in our contracts that outlined our educations. While Chutin preferred I dabble in the arts, *Garbovsky* required his chattel to have degrees in therapy.

Yes, that Garbovsky. The one whose grandchild played the piano. The one who assisted Sofiya in her *delusions*. His girls were educated, and he didn't meet them until they'd graduated from university.

Faina was just shy of her first degree when all the Castles were dismantled. She had never met him. Some would call her a Castle Girl success story. Now, the Bratva is paying to further her education.

With coffees in hand, Faina and I walk. Kirill at our rear is quiet as a mouse, except for when Faina shares about a young woman's owner. One young lady is still in therapy. She'd broken her legs from the fall. He'd stiffened as Faina shared the story. Now, we're headed for one last introduction.

"There is one young lady the resident psychiatrist hasn't finished assessing yet," Faina says.

"I thought they were all doing as well as could be expected. Wounds healing. They are transitioning back into society. How has she not been assessed?"

Faina pushes red strands behind her ear. "Alonna is her name. A few of the others shared she'll respond to Loni." Faina sips her drink. "Loni won't say a word. She's still in ICU. Her previous owner um . . . I'm sorry."

Faina touches her chest at the mere thought of Alonna.

"She had what?" Kirill bites out. Then his eyes lower, and he mutters, "Forgive me, Tsarina."

"It's okay." I nod to him, then return my attention to Faina.

The gorgeous redhead blinks back a glossy gaze. "She had intensive skin grafting on her back, minor grafting on the side of her face."

My heart softens. Kosta's face had been mutilated too.

"Loni's treatment plan is more extensive than any other, Anastasiya. Suffice it to say, you and I are lucky, fortunate."

"Take us to her," Kirill orders, as if my 'okay' gave him a voice. I'd ask him what happened to being my shadow, but I thought I'd seen warmth in his eyes earlier. Now, they're a smoldering cobalt, ready to avenge or protect.

Once at the door to the room, I address Kirill. "We don't know Loni's frame of mind. She may hate men or be afraid of them."

He gives a gruff nod. "I'm not moving from this spot."

I open the door, letting myself in and closing it behind me. Though I doubt Kirill would've gawked at her like a science project, Faina was given this role for many reasons. One, her educational background, and the most important, she is a woman. And clearly one of us.

The sterile-scented room doesn't have a single sentiment on the wall. Alonna lies in bed. White gauze covers much of her body. Pops of rich bronze skin peep through at various areas. Lengthy individual braids wiggle out from a cap supporting her scalp.

Heat burns my eye-ducts, but I meet her chocolate gaze. Not expecting a response, I begin in a soothing tone, "Good afternoon, Alonna. I'm—"

"I know you." Low, deathly words slither out toward me.

My pupils search over her. *No, this cannot be right.* The Loni I knew had been the youngest Castle Girl I'd ever seen in the place. Before Kosta became the bitter woman Oleg and Kahdar created, she'd mentioned Loni.

I brought her chocolates. She'd grab them with her fat, small-fisted fingers as a toddler. The truth slams into me hard enough to send me flat on my ass. I widen my stance and offer her a soothing smile. "Loni—"

"Here I am. I've waited for you to arrive."

I bite the bile down my throat. "Chutin—"

"You called him Volk. I distinctively recall that before you left."

She hadn't even been my age when Volk came to see me the first time. She'd been still so young when I left at the age of twelve. I guess, five at most.

"I liked that name, Volk. It fit well." Though her voice can only rise above a whisper, it's deep in thought. "I was the last purchase from his father."

Tears wet my eyes. "Loni, I'm so sor—"

"Don't be. You brought me Colombian chocolates."

"Did Oleg?" I try to speak, throat clogged.

"Yup. I didn't make Irek's father happy. Enter Oleg. But that occurred after you left. The other girls who jumped with me, they were all owned by a Chutin, Anastasiya. Not just you." She says it with no bitter malice in her voice whatsoever. "Oleg paid less than

265

the amount of a few scraps of copper for us, once we broke for him."

Meeting her harrowed face, she attempts a smile. She tries to talk about the chocolates again, but it is so hard for her to do. She'd mentioned she was Afro Columbiana once, and that was why I had that weasel Volk purchase the chocolates. He'd buy me anything. But he knew . . . he had to have known I wanted them for his father's matryoshka doll. That sick fuck.

Shame tightens my throat as I say, "Oleg was fired a lot sooner than the Castles were closed."

"But we looked like this." She can hardly move. Her gaze slithers over her bandages. "Dah. The new headmaster found us in a secret compartment a few months in, at least, I think. Oleg didn't feed us daily, anyhow."

"Why didn't he say something?" I murmur.

"Not certain. Didn't want to be to blame for breaches of contracts. We found out that we had food in our individual cages that entire time. You saved me, Anastasiya."

"I'll-I'll be back." I open the door, murmur my apologies, and close it behind me. Kirill is still standing where he promised. I hurry to him. Baffled, Kirill uncrosses his arms, and they fly around me. He might not be Luka, but when I close my eyes, I feel my brat.

Kirill grips my cheeks. "Sestra, stop it."

"I asked for this too late." My voice breaks. Mikhail Resnov can't save me, and my delayed reactions murdered more Invisible Things and Alonnas than conceivable.

"Simeon's baby is in your stomach."

I sob, "I'm not—"

"You have the future Resnov ruler in your stomach. Don't cause the baby any stress. Do you hear me?" he grits through clenched teeth.

A ball of sobbing mess, I nod.

"That little baby growing in your tummy is already a spirit, already feels your emotions. You got that?!"

"Okay."

Kirill's hands unclamp from my face. His square jaw nudges toward the door. "Looks like you left in a hurry."

"I did. I'll be a little while longer with Loni." I wipe my tear-streaked eyes. "In the meantime, you make the call to Simeon. He said time didn't matter. Tell him, I'm keeping Chutin until the end of forever." *Me and the rest of the Castle Girls. Let's see how he likes that.*

CHAPTER 49

Simeon

These past few months were a blessing and a curse alike. My most valuable possession returned to her rightful place at my side. So, when Kirill calls, my heart launches into my throat. My second-in-command is highly competent, reaching out when issues arise. To see his number on the caller ID when he's in charge of keeping Anastasiya safe, my baby safe, has me answering him on the first ring.

I place the contracts onto the table, fisting the phone at my ear. "Whatever the fuck you're calling me for, better be good news, Kazen."

"That depends on you, Sim." At his use of my name and not Tsar, the air growing stale in my lungs expires.

"What is it, then?"

"Asya had a quick message for you. I guess it couldn't wait until she saw you. She's keeping Chutin forever—verbatim."

I cock an eyebrow. *"Keeping him?"*

"Oh, um, it took me a few seconds to understand her statement. Your Tsarina is crazier than you, Kazen, bravo! I take it she wants him tortured until his heart gives out or the apocalypse comes."

Jealousy, second nature to me, fades, and I smile. "That's what she said. My beautiful Tsarina . . ." I murmur. "Then you have the best doctors on hand for when he's brought to us."

Not me.

Us. Anastasiya and I.

"Mikhail?"

"He's going home tomorrow."

"Sim," Kirill sighs. "You watching him like a hawk? He disappeared for a little while when Anastasiya first went missing. He was visiting his mother's grave. He's not like us, Kazen, but he's blood."

"Shut the fuck up, alright," I cut in. "He's a Resnov. I'm not murdering my blood . . . without cause. Before you left with Asya, Mikhail shared he's leaving on his own accord. None of my men have been assigned to him since he made you a sleeping beauty for a while."

My cousin growls into the phone. "I don't recall the Tsar being a comedian."

I almost break into a grin. Before hanging up, I retort, "I don't either."

In Los Angeles, I groveled, said I'd change. Then I'd told Vassili the exact opposite. All I had to do was give Anastasiya the illusion of what she thought she needed and hide my barbaric ways. There is no way in hell I'm giving up that part of me, but I'll be a better man for her. I'll protect, be strong, and love our baby. A father is his child's first hero.

With that in mind, I request an architect and interior designer, then I call for my cousin, Mikhail. It was true. I had removed the bodyguard assigned to him when I'd assumed that he couldn't have had a hand in Anastasiya's disappearance. Nevertheless, discussing as much with Kirill brought something to my attention. Like the day she and Luka's car wrapped around that fucking tree, he was gone the day she returned and much of the day before that.

Where was he?

~

Hours later, I'm swiveling side to side in my leather chair when my deadly glower lands on my older cousin. Earlier today when Anastasiya had exited his room, I hadn't noticed the puffiness beneath his eyes, nor the sheen of silver whiskers at his jaw.

"Sit." I gesture.

He offered to have a party for me? For us? Why? Does said inquiry align me with my distrustful, deceased father? I don't give a fuck if it does, but out of respect to Uncle Malich, I'll ease into my concerns.

"The president will be under my protection in about two weeks."

"Under your protection?" Mikhail lifts an eyebrow then thinks aloud. "You mean under your protection as in you plan to torture him? I assumed all the Chutins had an arrangement with our family for ages . . . shit, even I know that."

Mikhail grabs a tuft of his blond hair. I wait for him to continue speaking. Similar to Don Roberto Dominicci, who only learned to shut his fucking mouth the day his lineage was cut in half, all my enemies use their mouth to dig their graves.

"Is that a good idea?" he gasps.

"Why would it not be?"

He sputters on his words. "Simeon, I have no real ties to the Bratva. You say it's a good idea, you're my little cousin, but what trumps that is your status as my Tsar."

"Dah, I'm your Tsar, aren't I?" My glower lands on him.

"Yes," Mikhail stresses.

I reach over to my top drawer, my eyes still on his. *Sim, don't fucking do it. He hasn't crossed the line since the jet ride to L.A. Asya seems to like him, almost like Luka, I guess,* warning myself to be easy. I yank open the top drawer and pull out a bottle of Resnov Water.

"Let's have a drink, shall we," I test him. Mikhail swims like a fucking fish in alcohol since Igor's death. I pour two glasses, sling one across the table.

His hand stops the cobalt glass. A little of the vodka sloshes out. My drink is almost to the rim, too. We toss them back.

"Ready to reacclimate yourself to society—leave this underworld you were born in?" I pour us more.

"Yeah."

Hmmmm, he had an opinion about Irek Chutin. Now, he's clamming up. I refresh our drinks, letting the clear liquid pool at the rim of the glass now.

Mikhail downs his, and I down mine.

We're at the end of the bottle when Anastasiya pops her head into the room.

"Sim . . ." Her face blossoms into an uncertain smile. "What are the two of you doing?"

"Drinking," I reply.

"He's testing me," Mikhail sniggers.

"Simeon, why are you testing your cousin?" She clears her throat.

"Because I . . ." Mikhail begins.

CHAPTER 50

Anastasiya

When I returned to Loni's room, I started to apologize. She refused to believe I had wronged her in any way. We parted ways on the grounds that I'd come back in a few days, and she agreed to participate in the psychological assessment that had been ordered for her.

Now, I'm staring between the one man who's claimed my soul and the other who just offered a vastly different universe. I've told myself a thousand times to ease into a conversation with Simeon about my sordid connection to Mikhail. Take some of the blame by sharing how I once compared him to Volk.

Chaos, Armageddon, and hell all wrapped into one shiny, red ribbon. I'm not strong enough for that shit.

Clearing my throat, I ask, "Simeon, why are you testing your cousin?"

Seconds transform into hours, years, a millennia while I wait, then funnel back down into nothingness.

"Because I . . ." Mikhail stutters. "I'm leaving, and contrary to his steel exterior, my little cousin loves me."

"Okay, well, you've had enough." I place on a smile. Our fingers clash as I remove the glass from his hand.

"I could use more," he slurs.

"That's up to you. But right now, Sim and I need to discuss a few things." I hook my arm through Mikhail's. Funny, the stars don't shatter in the sky when I touch him in Simeon's presence. With an affable smile, I lead him toward the door. I shut it behind him, close my eyes for a fraction of a second, and gulp down the shame of running to him earlier.

Upon turning around, Simeon is swiveling in his chair. The predator feigns innocent, though his intentions are transparent.

"What were you doing, Sim?"

"Drinking with my kazen. You have eyes."

"Oh, I have eyes." I roll them at that, strutting around the table. His hands slide around me, kneading the flesh of my ass, and I sink down onto him. Gripping his short, black hair, I pull his eye level from my breasts and to my face. "Hey, you sarcastically replied how I have eyes. Sim, look me in them when I'm talking to you."

His voice is lethal enough to make me squeeze my thighs around him tighter. "Who do you think you're talking to?"

"You. I'm the big boss." I smack his lips with a kiss. "Wow. I taste alcohol, enough to get me—"

Simeon grips my wrists, bringing them behind me. "Nyet. You're carrying my child."

My gaze falters. My worries about having a baby in this underworld are ready to erode the progress we've made. Shit, today, I'd begun to loosen the foundation we built on the island.

"Hey, hey." His grip on my wrists tightens, his other hand testing the tautness of my throat. "My fucking baby, Anastasiya. I

273

will never question you about our baby. I will look into our son's or daughter's eyes, no matter the fucking color, and tell that kid how gorgeous she is or handsome he is because he was lucky enough to come from here." He plants his hands on my flat abdomen. "You mean more to me than anything in this world. So, what the fuck does that say about your womb? The innocence growing there?"

I'm drowning in his sincerity. "But . . ."

"You're loyal, Asya. You had a baby for me once. This is my baby. I won't say it again."

Bottom lip trembling uncontrollably, I open my mouth to speak. Simeon catches my jittery lip in his teeth, squeezing hard.

"Are we bringing up this discussion again, Anastasiya? Are we?"

"Simeon—"

"Because as I see it," his demeanor becomes smooth like wine, "*my baby* is here. You have a job to do, create a healthy start. My job is never to forget our baby is a gift. Be the best fucking father I can be. That's my gift. Don't deny me, Asya."

"I'm not," I stress the words. "Sim, the baby isn't Irek Chutin's."

His smoldering gaze roams over me. "Then what the fuck is wrong, moya milaya? Uncertainty is written all over your face."

I crush a few fingers into my hair, clamping at the strands while heaving a sigh. "Us. Simeon."

"You doubt us?" His muscular frame, beneath me, seems to deflate. "For all the power I wield, turning back the hands of time isn't one of them, Asya."

"We drown in each other, Sim. Quick to explode, quick to forgive."

"No more." He frames my face. "Anastasiya, we've demolished the highest fucking hurdles. Now, all I need is your promise of forever. In return, I'll be who you need. Keep being my good girl, the one who saw the best in me from day one. Do that."

"I just get lost in my head sometimes, Simeon. Thinking about the past," I stress, with a deep breath. The years fly through my mind. Not all of them have been perfect. Mikhail had got into my head. Truthfully, I granted him the key, my mind a muddled mess from Volk. Throat tight, I say, "Sim, I love you, madly."

Heated tears burn my eyes as a smile breaks across my face. His knuckles become silk along my jawbone, thick chest heaving a sigh.

"Let's be great parents, moya milaya. We've broken promises to each other, but this one we will fulfill together as man and wife. Okay, krasivaya?"

"Are you proposing?" The damn breaks, I sob through the laughter.

"Dah, and here's your chance to say, dah, too." He grips my face again, shaking my head for me.

I dart out of his clutch, chuckling harder. Rivers of happiness blind my eyes as his fingers move feather-soft around my waist. Through broken, elated words, I declare, "Simeon, you are a beast! What happened to a new ring, a new plan?"

"Pay attention, girl." Simeon leans back in his chair. On the tip of his pinky is a classic, white-gold band with the softest most intricate waves.

"How?"

"I've always told you the *how* is—"

"You were talking about torture, Simeon." I snatch his hand toward me. I deftly wipe away the tears. My heart is warmed over a thousand times, viewing the inscription inside. When I read the declaration, another laugh bubbles through me. "Very dominating, Sim. But I wouldn't have it any other way."

"Good. I've had this ring in my pocket since we left paradise, Anastasiya." Simeon takes my hand, placing the statement of his adoration there. It's free of grandiose diamonds, a perfect snug fit. My not-so-gentle giant places my finger to his lips, and for the first time in forever, all the seeds of doubt fade into oblivion. He reads the inscription aloud:

"To my heartbeat. My entire world.
Not even death will part us, moya milaya."

CHAPTER 51

Simeon

Night of the VOLK

Standing in the mirror, I wrestle with the bow tie of my tuxedo. Through the reflection, Anastasiya's voluptuous hips splay against the wall behind me. A silver dress brushes her curves. A slit dangerously ascends her left thigh. On her tiny feet are the type of million-dollar crystal stilettos that send my cock rising in my pants.

"Why are you dressed?" I sound more accusatory than I had meant.

"Ha! How about I look gorgeous. In a few months—"

"You'll be infinitely more striking." I'm against her in a second. "When I get my hands on your ass and tummy."

She purrs against my mouth. "Sim, I'll remember verbatim what you said. Ass and tummy—even when I have more of the latter."

My fingertips skim over the slit of her dress and along her flesh. "Again, I ask, why are you dressed? You hardly kept breakfast down this morning."

"Because payback is—"

I press my mouth against hers. My tongue glides over her bottom lip before my teeth sink into the thick flesh.

"I'm going, Sim."

"Nyet."

"Morning sickness won't stop me."

"Technically, it's been morning, noon, and anything you eat sickness." I softly wrestle her body against mine. "You tell your Tsar the plan. I'll fulfill it for you."

She sneers. "Nyet."

"That mouth is the crux of all the discipline I'll give to you once I return from the gala," I retort. The one instance she speaks Russian is to defy me.

"Simeon, nobody is aware of my plan."

"I'm your man," I growl.

"Tough shit." Her hips lead her toward the bedroom door. She grips both handles, pushing through, head higher than any other royal.

I stalk after her. Anastasiya pauses long enough for me to flank her side and take her tiny hand in mine. But I don't stop there. I squeeze the life out of her little fingers.

She grins up at me.

"So, the remainder of the plan?" Beam inquires.

"You will know when you're told." I snarl.

The twins share glances. Others call them creeps. I call them loyal and easily read. Although now, their faces are clear to all the guards surrounding us.

This is Italy all over again. The sadist in me withholding Dominicci's demise until the last moment.

But this time . . . even I don't know the plan.

~

My resources acquired the perfect spot to abduct Irek Chutin. He was supposed to be brought to one of our torture houses, prepped for me.

Prepped for his last breath.

Enter Anastasiya.

She requested to attend the gala, coveting the sight of Chutin in his natural element and the seconds leading toward the capture. Dah, my fault. The second I took her on missions, I indeed told her that removing a target from their natural routine was a passion of mine, second to the torture itself. All a mind fuck.

For the next few hours, we're incognito on the second level of the building. The Bratva also has the intel on Chutin's guards and their rotation. Anastasiya revels in every second of watching the mudaks meander down below, while I'm on high alert.

I brought a pregnant woman into a very dangerous situation. *And she would try to murder me, had I locked her ass up and proceeded with the fail-proof plan.*

"Sim . . ." Anastasiya grips my arm. She's glaring down into the fray of Moët drinkers and haughty conversations. "Do you know how badly I want you right now?"

A flood of desire hardens my cock. I grip the railing, attempting to keep my focus. "Nyet. Not here, Anastasiya."

She plants her warm, soft body behind me. Her nipples dig into my back. Anastasiya slides her hand in front of me. "Why not here? I distinctively recall how hot and bothered you were when we attacked Khadar."

I chuckle deep down low and tip back the drink in my hands.

"Is it because I'm pregnant?"

"Nyet." Dah, fuck yeah. She has a little baby growing in her belly, and she needs to be safe.

"You sure?" I allow her hands to pull down my zipper and knead at my cock.

"Anastasiya, you keep at it, you're going over my shoulder, and . . ." I'd lock her in the trunk to keep her safe, but my baby comes first.

"And?" she inquires, stroking my balls.

My body tenses, but I grunt, "Home. End of fucking discussion."

She ascends on her tippy toes, kissing my neck and capturing my earlobe in her teeth. "Not the end of the discussion."

"Don't make me regret instincts. You're pregnant. You should be waiting for your little wolf to be thrown at your feet. Kirill has a doctor preparing a room for you to dismember—"

"I never said anything about dismembering Chutin, Simeon."

I turn around, ready to inquire for the thousandth time about her intentions when she descends to her knees.

"Have a little fun with me." She winks. "Before I enjoy the first man who ever claimed he loved me."

My jaw clinches, and I capture her throat, forcing my cock to slam all the way in. Through the fan-thick, long lashes, Anastasiya looks up at me. Her pink, luscious lips draw tight across my rigidness.

"Fuck your clit," I growl, urgent to slide my seed down her throat and regain my focus. But the longer she sucks sloppily at my cock, the more my brain hazes over, and my eyes roll back.

Asya moves her fingers beneath her silk dress. Her other hand is firm against my balls. Entrapping her face, I slam into her depth.

"Shit," I hiss. "When I cum, you cum."

Her tonsils squeeze at my cockhead, tongue slithering around. The sensation curls my toes underneath, and I forget all, save for her. The depth of her mouth is so tight.

"This is what your mouth was made for, Anastasiya." A smug smile lifts my lips as I grip her hair and fuck her face. My dick swims in her euphoric funnel.

Her wet mouth moans around me, pulling in the length of me. In and out, my cock smashes at her tonsils. She switches hands.

Her slick, sticky fingers work my balls as her other hand screws between her thighs. Each thrust tests her gag reflex, sending her deep throat squeezing. The rhythm of her hand hypnotizes my balls until they begin to twitch.

In a low, barbaric tone, I order, "Drink."

CHAPTER 52

Anastasiya

The place where the Bratva obliterated their opponents is an actual castle. And I don't mean the fine, ancient establishments where us Castle Girls were blinded by opulent tapestries. I mean a falling down, fortress of gray stone. Many of the various wings have crumbled to the ground. A tower to the west vaults into the sky.

At the tippy top, there are cells. Each one smells of mold, stagnant rainwater, and death. I'd replaced my stilettos for tennis shoes, but even in a long coat, I huddle in the blanket Simeon gave me. The chill jars my bones.

He runs his hands over my shoulders. "You could go—"

"Say it," I dare him.

"Home." He does.

The doctor, sifting through a cart of terror items, glances between the two of us, clearing his throat. His pale skin matches that of the stone walls. His disinterest is even more pallid.

I'd been antsy while taking Simeon in my mouth before. The

strength of his cock had calmed me. "Sim, I asked for this. I'm not sparing his life."

A deep breath draws from Simeon's massive chest. "My only concern is you, moya milaya. When you went after Oleg, you were high off emotion. You haven't had bad dreams in a while now. We can leave, let Kirill handle this."

The sound of footsteps ends our conversation, growing louder, nearer. My heart constricts in my chest. I can do this. I'll set eyes on Irek Chutin and . . .

A body tumbles across the stone ground before us. Five byki, including the twins and Kirill, have animosity-charged gazes on him.

A cloth covers Irek's eyes. The penguin suit he wore tonight is splotched with blood and dirt. He grips the ground, calling out, "I have money—*lots* of money."

My entire face trembles at the thought of how little Oleg was charged for the Castle Girls. The echo of distant coins clatters to the ground before my mind's eye. Oleg's words lick against my ear: *"This is the price of a Resnov Castle Girl when I make a bargain with a Chutin."*

"We are leaving now." Simeon grips my shoulders, and I spiral back to reality. "I don't like this, Anastasiya, when you get fucking locked into your head."

"Hello, imbecile! I have money." Chutin crawls in the direction of Simeon's voice. A byki issues a kick to his stomach, which drops him like a slithering snake. Dust floats up, accenting the streams of tears on his cheeks.

I push at Simeon, finally able to react, drawn to the Volk's tears.

"Anastasiya," Simeon grits out. "I don't—"

I haul off and shove my unyielding mountain again. The adamant beast squares his shoulders as I growl. "I asked for this!"

"Moya love?" Irek turns his cowled head in my direction. I spoke, and he knew me by voice. "Moya Anastasiya. Please."

The world tilts on its head. I go to my knees, removing the

canvas bag from his face. Weary blue eyes plunge me further into an alternate dimension. "Moya Anastasiya . . . I'm sorry."

He places his arms around me, hugging me tightly. All the rage in the galaxy is bottled in Simeon's stormy eyes. Kirill heads toward us. I hold up a hand.

"Go ahead." I find my voice. "You're sorry, right."

"Dah." His soiled palms, soft as silk from lack of fighting for his supreme existence in our *lawless* world, caress my cheeks.

"And you have money?" A voice so foreign echoes in my ear. But it's *mine*.

Those baby blues begin to roll. "You know I do. Ten times more than these savages. I was without you for so long. I regret allowing Oleg to take you. But simply put, you required training. Come home with me."

His delirium, or overconfidence, sends me clasping my arms around my belly as I chuckle. "Kirill, do you have money?"

He removes his ponytail, past the point of anger.

"I said, do you have—"

"Here." Dot hands me a hundred note.

"More than necessary, but thank you." I take the paper, tear off a fraction, and hand it to Irek. "Loni believes she's worth more."

Animosity swelling, I tear more money. It falls like useless ribbons between us. "So did the girl who was in the same cage as her when she was sold to Oleg. So did your father's plaything, so did The Invisible—"

"You suka!" Chutin raises his hand to slap me, but I pull the Colt from my coat pocket, nudging it against his nose.

"Probably a good idea that you carry on in your mission to hit me," I hiss.

We're at a standstill.

"Because you will come to learn that I have no intention of shooting you and/or harming you, myself, Volk."

Damn, I slipped in the childhood nickname. Chutin's eyes burn wild. I rise. Simeon clasps my forearm, assisting me.

"Young Resnov." Irek shrugs. "The offer still stands. Your little Bratva is no comparison to me. Let me make you richer."

Simeon kisses me. "I'm ready to go," I murmur.

"I had this suka. Fucked her good." Chutin spits at us.

"Lie if you like, Irek. You told me I was no Castle Girl. It might have been the only truth you ever uttered," I retort. Simeon exceeds my expectations. With an impassive glare, he does *not* react.

I kiss him again. "Thank you for having faith in me."

I turn to Kirill. "Is everything prepared?"

"Sestra, your will, will be done." He holds up his hands, signifying his role in the mission has come to an end. "The doctor will fulfill every request."

The old man stands on feeble legs. "I have my bag of tricks and a few assistants to aid around the clock."

"Then carry on, please."

"What the fuck are you doing to me?" Chutin shouts.

I start down the steps. The twins give their excuses as they hurry by.

"Am I missing something?" Simeon cocks a brow.

"Dah." I make use of his language and wink. "You're missing everything."

He's teeming in questions as we continue down the stairs. The second I reach the solid ground floor, Simeon yanks me around, a lot less than he would if I were not pregnant.

I sneeze. "I hate that place."

"Well, my team loves it." Simeon glances around at the quiet twins. Kirill hasn't made a peep. "All of you delight in torture. Dot, you favor fillets of skin. Kirill, you make a body a punching bag, Beam—"

"Pakhan," Beam cuts in. "Your tactics are fine by me. It's the Tsarina whom I fear."

"Did I say you could speak—" Simeon cuts himself off. "You all know?"

284

Kirill chuckles. "I had nothing to do with this, Kazen. Honest to God. I was searching for Sofiya when you all went to Italy. I heard you refused to share your plan until the last second. Well, this girl tortured us with it."

"What is the fucking plan?" he growls at me.

"Dildos." Beam swallows, shaking in disgust. "Lots of dildos and any other objects Anastasiya and her friends deem appropriate."

Simeon's shocked gaze slides over me in horror.

"Yes. He likes to fuck. So, he will be *fucked* until his rectum falls out. Irek will beg for death, but his body will have to consent before we do. Loni and a few others applauded this idea." I pat his shoulder. "Men."

CHAPTER 53

Simeon

S ix months later

A nastasiya blushes. The glow beneath her honey skin
suffuses her. I stand behind her with my hands dripping in
massage oil. Me worshiping her body has become a morning ritual
for us.

"You're obsessed," she murmurs.

"Moya milaya, I've learned the hard way, your absolute refusal
to accept anything other than my best is why we are here." My
dripping, wet hands splay across her eight-month, full-grown belly.
Kneading in the oil, I stop on the tiny mark where I'd wickedly
unraveled her stitches. I'd never been so jealous in my entire life.

Her eyes sparkling at me, Asya says, "You made mistakes, Sim. I
did too."

Our fingers roam over her belly together, connecting as one, coming to rest at her belly button. She cranes her neck, nuzzling her mouth against my chest. "Now, we've created a better future. We're living in it. Besides, I returned the favor with a harsher battle wound."

Laughter curls from my abdomen as she winks.

Staking a claim to her stomach again, I banter, "My son is in here, listening to that sass mouth of yours."

"Oh, this mouth, that licks your scars and tattoos and—"

"Hey," my voice levels into a powerful growl.

Unraveling her body from within my arms, Anastasiya turns around to rise on her tippy toes. Soft, tiny fingers glide across my jaw, then she groans. In the background, her cellphone vibrates on her nightstand.

My glower trains across the room to the electronic device I'm ready to pitch against the wall. Aware of my intention, Anastasiya grasps my arm. "Hey, I'm a woman. We can have this argument about my mouth, later, in bed."

"Now works for me." Lust clouding my gaze, I glance down at my growing erection.

"Oh, no, Simeon! Not now. No matter how much I'd rather stay here all day with you, reality called." She waddles past me on graceful toes toward the cellphone to silence it. "We have a Bratva meeting in less than an hour. We should get ready."

"The Seven will wait." I grab a slip of silk, removing the cellphone from her hands, and position myself behind her again. "May I?"

Anastasiya chews her lip. "We should—"

"They will wait."

She scoffs. "All week, I've reminded you about the meeting *they* asked for. Last night, I couldn't sleep. This morning—"

"You mentioned that meeting until I traveled under the sheets." I palm pussy, massaging softly. Her lips grow hot and heavy beneath her panties. "I made you forget about it. End of discussion."

I secure the blindfold over her face, dropping a kiss on her collarbone. The Table of Seven can request all the meetings in the world. I'll trump every single one of them. Though, I understand Anastasiya's concern. They demanded debriefings like crazy during Anatoly's rule. I'm almost three years into my reign before the Seven solicited this get-together.

"Take a walk with me, Asya."

Her chest swells in a sigh. "I can't deny you."

Slipping my fingers in hers, I guide her out of the room and down the massive corridor. Three doors over, I let one of her hands go, open it, and then lead her to the center of the room.

"You ready?"

Anastasiya sucks in a nervous groan. "Diamonds and gifts won't help. *They* requested the meeting because of *me*."

The blindfold glides from Anastasiya's eyes, sliding along her collarbone. The silk frames her all the way to the floor. For every second of it, she stands in awe. Asya gapes at the sight, and I stare with abandon at her belly. Fuck, the first time she shouted that the baby had kicked, I was at her side. The movement was too tiny to feel. Now, my son packs a punch. My eyes glue to her as she does a 360 turn, slow, eyes roaming over a furnished nursery.

Voice teaming in sentiment, Asya speaks, "You gave me flowers after you returned from Mexico. I remember being livid because your flight was delayed. One day, you promised to exchange the flowers for our baby."

"True." I focus on my realized dream, and the endless love destined for us so soon.

"After we made up," she blushes, memories of sex in her eyes, "while we were laying together, I told you about the nursery. All the things I probably never had, not that anyone can recall that at such a young age. All the possessions I wanted for our child just because I had no mementos for myself. That conversation was years ago, Sim. You remembered."

"Dah. I remember everything about you." The backs of my fingers roam across her cheeks. "The bad because I won't take you for granted anymore, moya milaya. The good because I don't give a fuck how old we get. I'll go senile and won't forget you."

"Oh, Simeon." Tears shine in Anastasiya's eyes as she comes into my arms.

~

The meeting came together in a secret room, encased in marble. My half-brat, Vassili, sat at the opposite head of the table across from me. Uncle Malich is to his side. Around the table were the rest of our uncles. I reach over, mouth brushing Anastasiya's earlobe, and prompt, "Breathe."

Underneath the table, she grips my thigh, a not-so-subtle reminder of the argument we just had. We were content, yet late to the meeting. Then the second we stood outside of the doors, she became the wrecking ball. I told her to 'fuck the Seven.' And she reminded me to *use* my advanced degrees. We aren't perfect. I squeeze the meat of her thigh, too.

I rise to my feet, calling the meeting to order. First, we discuss the Colombian cartel, whom I assisted in accessing Dominicci's territory. Then I mention other successes from my reign, my gaze landing on my woman. Enough to ask if I'm using my genius.

She hides a smile, delicately rolling her eyes away. I'm fucking winning if I do say so myself.

"Profits are up," Vassili edges into the conversation. "You've done well, brat."

"Thank you, Coach Karo."

"Dah," Malich nods his head. "You all toast. I'm outta here. Let's call this meeting adjourned."

"Don't be so melodramatic, Uncle. Join us." Vassili pats his shoulder.

"We have a few concerns, Tsar," calls another voice as Malich starts up.

The Seven is down a member since I stripped my mother of her Bratva rights and assets. She still had a voice in the form of Kirill and Luca's father. The snarky growl I offer Linden grows tighter. Malich huffs, reclaiming his seat. Uncle Linden, my mother's youngest brat, who took it upon himself to shelter her, clears his throat.

"By all means," I reply, as Anastasiya gives me a nervous pinch. This is day one. She's going to fucking slaughter me while listening to Linden bumble around.

Linden sits forward in his seat, glancing around to ensure he has all his brats' attention. He does. Except for Malich, whom I'm astonished decided to grace us with his presence from Los Angeles. My favorite uncle leans back in his seat, head to the mural-encased ceiling.

Linden begins, "Chutin's stand-in has done an impeccable job guiding our beloved Russia. The candidate we set in motion has grown more influential for the next vote."

"Sounds like a win?" Malich mutters.

"Malich," another of my uncles clicks his tongue. I glare at him. While I was Anatoly's right hand, he never spoke, not a single word. He continues, "We're still concerned. Chutin is legally dead. What if—"

"He won't be found," I grit out. Then I sit back. The air is thick with division. Once they finish exercising their mouths, I *will* shut this motherfucking conversation down. Although patient, chatter assaults my ears. I'll allow my irritation to rise, collect, then I'll strike.

Malich raises a hand, stalling the shifting tide of the argument. "Well, there you have it. We all agree with Simeon's expertise. Irek Chutin won't be found. Meeting adj—"

Linden snaps, "Speak for yourself, Malich."

Vassili cuts in. "I'm also in agreement with Simeon's competence. Are we ready for the next topic or . . . ?"

"Nyet," Malich holds up a hand. "Our brotherhood is making more progress in the last two years than it has in ages. All you old farts, take heed. Simeon has—"

Linden gasps. "Aren't we all curious about what happened to Chutin?!"

A chair scraps against the ground. Anastasiya arises. I hide a smile, confident my woman would handle this.

Linden shoots her a glare, urging me to jump across this table and squeeze his throat. I blink away thoughts of watching his pupils turn to bloodied jelly.

"Listen up," she says. "Chutin received due punishment. I don't mind sharing; however, I know how fragile the male stomach is. *Shall I proceed, Linden?*"

"You can't be serious, Tsarina."

I slide a knife onto the table. "I advise you not to address your Tsarina, in such an informal manner, Uncle Linden. Adding her title, after utilizing an improper tone, will prompt me to have your fucking tongue."

"Sim," Anastasiya groans. Her honey eyes swim around the room. She's badass, but frozen in intimidation

I bark at her, "Then you correct him!"

"I meant no harm." Linden licks his lips. "Please, moya Tsarina, your reference to the male stomach? Is it any worse than the bomb planted in that Italian by our Tsar?"

I slide my knife back into my belt.

"You'd have to be the judge. The Italian is dead." Her shoulders square. A cool smile teases the corners of her lips.

That's right, moya milaya, I think, *be fearless. We're lawless, not them.*

"As for your president," she says, "Chutin's rectum fell out about two months ago. I instructed the supervising doctor to reattach it and tighten things up a bit. Every morning, noon, night, upon completion of his meal, or not, he gets a different sized cock stuffed in his ass. And I'll tell you, most of the time he needs a good stitching afterward. I have a few friends. They're worse. Shall I continue detailing their requests, which are crueler than sodomy, nyet jelly?"

Choked gasps invade the room. She holds up her slender fingers, recounting other suggestions. Her use of the Russian language is flawless.

Anastasiya glares through my uncle. "The mudak has yet to die. He's no murderer, so I'm not obligated to pass such a judgment. Oh, also, my friend Loni likes to—"

"That-that will be all," Vassili gags.

"Jesus," Malich mutters. "I was an ER doctor for almost thirty years—"

"Will it suffice? I doubt Irek has the physical mobility to run, let alone hold his shit! Most of you attended my coronation. I said it then, I am the *Just* Tsarina. If you'll excuse me."

I smile, glancing around the room. "She's more vicious than me, dah?"

CHAPTER 54

Anastasiya

Blood runs along my fingertips. I snap, letting go of the rose bush where I had intended to hurl breakfast.

"Ginger?" an all-too-familiar voice asks as I gulp the bile down. I turn toward Uncle Malich. With a genuine smile, I hold out my arms. He embraces me in a way that I'd presume a biological father would. Squeezing me, swaying a little, then smiling at me as he lets go.

"You showed those mudaks." Malich grins.

I look into his sincere gaze, seeing Mikhail through him, and my heart squeezes a little for the first time in a while. It's crazy how I thought about him more after he left. "Thank you, I tried."

"Nyet, don't speak Russian, Anastasiya." He winks. "You've preferred speaking English since your return. Truth be told, I slipped into our native tongue as a young doctor on a few occasions. But if English is your preference, then don't get me in trouble with Simeon."

"I—"

He wags a finger at me. "You walked into the meeting, ready to keel over, let them rule. Then you remembered the girl I met on your thirteenth birthday! Gorgeous, all the boys in love with you. You've grown into the *Just* Tsarina. Mikhail told me so the night of your coronation. You'll have to forgive an old, depressed mudak for not attending."

I chew my lip. Had Mikhail told him about my coronation speech and my disdain for using our language? Attempting to shovel away thoughts of him, I ask, "Uncle Malich, is it too cheesy? *Just Tsarina?*"

"Nyet."

I pause a beat. My eyes keep falling from his gaze. I glance across the quiet courtyard, then ask, "How is everyone?"

Malich begins with his grandchildren from his departed son, Igor. He's still snarky about Yuri.

"Oh goodness," I laugh a little, holding the underside of my belly. "One day, he will come around."

Grunting, Malich takes my hand and leads me to a wrought iron bench, carved in the shape of roses. "If Yuri gains back a few pounds and removes his head from his ass, that's the day he'll come around."

"Uncle," I chide. "He's our sweet Yuri, maybe not so cuddleable. What of Mikhail?"

Internally, I'm shaking like a spindle. Is it wrong to ask of Simeon's older cousin? *Yes!* The guilt floods in at the thought of our time at the cabin. Can a woman have room in her heart for two extremely different men? Most certainly not in her life. I know that now. After telling myself a thousand times he needed a crutch because of Igor, I know it was true. I was this crazy ball of mystery, guns blazing where I went, danger, and he clung to that. And I clung to the warped mindset that I'm still learning to get over.

Oh, hell, yes, I'm over Volk. His torture is my therapy. I only saw him the one night but reading updates on how he's faring suffices.

It feels like I wait forever before Malich responds. "Haven't seen my son."

"Since when?"

"Last time you saw him, Anastasiya." Malich pats my knee then stands up. He holds out a hand for me. "I have a request to make of you and Simeon."

I glance where Malich nudges his chin, and the man who stole my heart at the beginning of time is sauntering over. As we begin to walk, Malich mumbles about how Mikhail travels through South Africa via Doctors Without Borders.

My tender giant meets us halfway. He wraps me in his arms, pressing his lips to my forehead. "You good?"

"Yes, Sim." I cling to his massive chest.

"Uncle," Simeon begins, hooking his arm around my waist. Though ready to burst, I still feel small in his arms. "Did you give moya Tsarina one of those encouraging chats?"

Malich tsks. "After Linden's whining? You know I did. But Anastasiya doesn't need an old man like me for motivation. You're a courageous young lady, the better half of this beast."

Simeon gestures toward an envelope in his hand. With my mind still ruminating on Mikhail, I only hear him mention *Mother*. "I'm not ready to learn about . . ." I bite my tongue, seeing the familiar handwriting as Simeon tears the envelope in half.

Simeon cups my cheek. "When you're ready, Anastasiya, we will cross *that* bridge. But this is from Sofiya. Linden gave me the letter after his audacity in the meeting."

"Yeah, I see." I clear my throat.

Malich looks between the two of us. Shrugging, I say, "I thought Sim had paternity information for me. I'm sorry, I—"

"You're not ready?" Malich clasps my hands. "When you're ready, you have a family to support you, Anastasiya. You have Simeon. Me. Your son, which is why I'd like to speak with you both."

"How can I help you, Uncle?" the Tsar inquires.

"Simeon, Anastasiya, I would like to be there for your son. My family has decreased in size. Families are meant to grow and flourish. Let me be there for the two of you."

"Awe, thank you, Uncle Malich." I wrap my arms around his neck and hug him again. Simeon shakes his hand. If I had a solid understanding of what parents were, I'd say Malich was Simeon's best model over the years. No matter how far away, Malich was the anchor Simeon could reach out to for wisdom and understanding.

"Maya sem'ya - maya sila i maya slabost'," Malich relays the Russian proverb. The adage clicked in my brain once Simeon and I started fighting for each other, instead of against each other when angry. He was my weakness, still is.

My family is my strength, and my weakness . . . The proverb roams through my mind as my hands glide over my tummy, ready to nurture, protect, love. I may have followed Simeon's path into the Resnov Bratva, but one day, I stopped being neutral about it. The brotherhood's importance to him had to become significant to me. Now, I'm at Simeon's side where I should have been from the start. Because a woman cannot support her man standing miles away.

EPILOGUE

Nine Years Later
Simeon

"Who called you 'zanudnyy?'" I growl, clasping my son's chin in my hand. Wriggling my jaw, I let go of Little Luka. He's not a *wimp*, and I cannot murder an eight-year-old mudak no matter how much the kid might deserve it. "Daddy's sorry. Little Luka, what did I tell you about ignorant people?"

"Well, Mommy says that's a bad word."

Little Luka picks up a scone next to his teacup and takes a bite. We're sitting inside the very establishment that my father denied me a chance to visit as a child. The Russian tearoom is carved in opulence, and my son deserves the best.

My abdomen vibrates as I chuckle. "Mommy's mouth is . . . full of roses, moy syn. Anyway, real Russian men have father-son teatime. That's what real Russian men do. You understand?"

Kirill sniggers under his breath. The complementary suit jacket he's wearing is too tight under his armpits. I laugh tauntingly at him. "You know I told them not to give you your size, right? Next time you waltz in here, underdressed, I will," I mouth the threat, hands over Little Luka's eyes.

My cousin laughs again, rolling his eyes while lifting his arms like a chicken. The confines of the suit stop him from flapping. He then grabs the tiny teacup, no finesse.

"That's the difference between us and him." I rope an arm over Little Luka's shoulder, slump down a little to his level, and gesture toward Kirill. "Ignorant people."

"Mommy said—"

"Uneducated people, moy syn."

Little Luka's cheeks puff out in a huff. "Mommy also said not to ridicule someone to their face. Daddy's sorry, Kirill."

I shake my head, denying my child's statement.

"Little Luka," Kirill cuts in. "How did you handle being called a *wimp?* Or should I do the honors?"

My cousin darts out of the chair before I can react then pats Little Luka on the shoulder. "I love you, kid. See the two of you later. Sim, your requests are complete."

"You mean, delegated?" I arch a brow. He shrugs, the answer on his face as he saunters toward the entrance, removing the suit jacket with effort.

"What did Kirill do, Dad?" Little Luka asks. His inquisitive blue eyes, just like my mother's, peer up at me.

"That's what a brat is for."

"But Kirill's not your brat."

"Little Luka, you have four little sisters. Daddy and Mommy's friends are your older brats. We are a brotherhood of sorts. Next time someone refers to you other than the name your father and mother gave you, remind them you're a Resnov." *Or I kill that mudak for being disrespectful.* I smile in thought.

"I did, Father. I told him I was a Resnov." Little Luka huffs. "Then he told me his last name."

"What was his last name?"

"Yahontov."

I click my tongue. "Means nothing. Next time, you tell your friend—"

"Not my friend."

I laugh a little, seeing so much of Anastasiya in Little Luka, even at a tender age. "Tell the little mudak to tell his father your surname, okay?"

"Ooh, I'm telling Mommy you cussed."

I shrug. "Tell her. But you do me that one favor, understood?"

"Dah."

I wink.

"So, what was Kirill doing for us?"

"Why do you have a thousand questions for me, Little Luka?" I laugh, rubbing his shoulder. I finish off my tea. "Listen, syn, don't ever stop asking questions. Kirill handled family business. Now, let's go wake up Mommy and your little sisters."

～

At the palace proper, a stampede commences. Little Luka bounds to one side of the grand staircase, promising to tell Anastasiya I said, "mudak." My daughters dash down the other side.

The girls span in ages seven, five, and two three-year-olds, who blessed us with a double dose of unconditional love.

"Hey, hey, Simone," I call out to the oldest. "What did I tell you about your siblings?"

"Oh, Father," she moans, slowing her pace so that she gets between the two little ones. Simone takes their hands as they grapple with each step.

I drop to my knees. My five-year-old jumps the last step, torpe-doing into my arms. Then I fall back with her.

"Girl, what have you been eating?" I ask as we're wiped out on the ground.

Alex beams down at me, her eyes a marriage of my pitch-colored ones and Anastasiya's honey gaze. "Oh, Daddy! You're strong. I know you are."

Seconds later, the rest of my daughters topple on top of me. Pretending to struggle to a standing position, I grab one around the waist, another over my shoulder, and situate Alex in my other arm. Simone laughs up at me.

"These babies." She rolls her eyes with a smile. "Daddy, you can carry Mommy too."

"I'm not so sure that Simeon can carry all his girls at the same time," Anastasiya calls down from the top of the banister.

"Dah, he can, Mommy," my oldest daughter retorts.

"Simone, Daddy's in trouble for saying bad words today," Asya says. "Would you like to be in trouble too?"

"Nyet." I reach down and place my daughters onto the ground. "Daddy's not in trouble, Simone."

"How is that so?" Asya glances up at me, eyebrow arched.

"Because I chose the perfect day to speak freely to moy syn." I clasp her in my arms. "Little Luka has a family tree to construct for school. Meaning, Mommy has to share a little something about herself."

My Tsarina wriggles from my clutches. I hold her tighter. "You promised."

"Dah, Mommy, you promised," Little Luka chimes in.

I stroke her cheek and whisper, "You can break a promise to me. Not your son. Not at his age."

She nods.

I let her go, starting for the stairs. The letter the young hacker gave me over eight years ago, still lays discarded in my office. The mouthy kid is Central Intelligence now and an asset to the States *and the Bratva.*

I turn around. Anastasiya is running her hand over the twins' faces, telling them Dedushka will be down in a second. I note the pensive hold she has on her smile. She's not prepared to learn about her parents. I walk over, tip her back, and kiss her hard on the lips. A round of complaints, laughter, and mock disgust goes in one ear and out the other. "You are my Tsarina." I whisper how she's my everything, over and over again. I'd declared the same words the day I almost murdered her. I love her just as hard, yet now I funnel that love the right way.

Her breath whispers across my skin, heart hammering against mine as I hold her close. I'll never forget our wedding day and how beautiful my Anastasiya looked. She was a gift from heaven I never deserved. My cousin, Mikhail, told me so too, but not to my fucking face. If he had, he'd be dead now. He had sent me a card regarding my pending nuptials, making it clear he was in love with her and that I better treat her right. He didn't attend the wedding, and we haven't seen him since. As long as I never see him again, he will live, though I did appreciate his honesty.

I kiss down the curve of Asya's neck, teasing and nipping her sensitive spots. "You can stand?"

"Yes, Sim. I can stand." Laughter bubbles from Anastasiya's soul as I let her go. Every time I hold her in my arms, it takes all of me to let her go. She takes a few dazed steps. With one last look, I hustle up the stairs, heart full, chest heavy in love.

ANASTASIYA

How many women can say they've known a man all their life, *and* he still leaves her breathless? Simeon's lips were ardent. Each caress of his mouth along my skin stole at my oxygen until my lungs were void. He models love for our children. In the bedroom, he leaves me without a doubt that after birthing his offspring, I'm the epitome of his adoration.

I dote on the twins, hefting them into my arms. "Let's go see where lunch is?"

My plucky five-year-old pouts at me.

"C'mon." Simone takes Alex's hand. "Mommy can't hold us all."

"But your *dedushka* can," Malich calls out from down the hall.

Somewhere along the line, he went from Godfather to Grandpa. Our only hope at grandparents for our children was Sofiya. Simeon's mother can write enough letters to fill the Black Sea, but it's not enough. I'd forgive her for Simeon. I tell myself that, and I tell him that because I love him. He won't forgive her because of our sweet Angel.

"Still jet lagged?" I ask Malich as my oldest girls cling to each side of him.

"Daddy and I tried to wake you up before tea, Dedushka," Little Luka shares. "But we heard you snoring across the corridor."

The old man giggles with him.

"Alright, young man." Malich ruffles his hair, causing Little Luka to laugh. "You snort-laugh like my Mikhail did at your age, Simeon too. Dah, I heard your father snort-laugh a few times, when he wasn't so angry."

"Hey," I cut in with a smile. It's been ages since Malich mentioned his eldest son, who hasn't returned to Russia. "Little Luka knows nothing of his father being angry."

"Dah, I do." Little Luka's head bobbles, cerulean pupils sparkling. "Daddy said that word earlier. That very bad word."

～

A few hours later, my palm plants on the smooth, marble slab. My thumb caresses my oldest child's name. A flush of heat runs across my face, tears springing forth. Little Luka leans against my hip. His head burrows in my rib. "Don't cry, Mommy. You said Angel makes you happy."

I blink tears away as Simeon speaks to our son. "The strongest thing a man can do, moy syn, is cry. Anyone tells you otherwise, you come to me."

"Daddy's right." My unsteady tone finds a morsel of strength as Simeon loops an arm through mine. "Alright, children. Mommy is sharing a little bit of herself she never has before, take it easy on me."

I reach into Simeon's blazer while looking into his eyes, feeding off his power. I clasp the envelope and pull it out. The edges are worn. It takes everything in me not to shred the paper as I had with the money as a statement to Chutin. A little less than a year into his sentence, Irek ran into the wall one day before his scheduled torment. He bashed his skull repeatedly. I had warned the doctor not to stop him from committing suicide, though I had orders for a byki to shoot Irek four years into his sentence.

Four years, Irek had me in a trance, from age nine to twelve. The bastard did not last to die by a single bullet.

I blink a few times, opening the letter.

"That can't be right." Simeon peers over my shoulders.

"What?" My eyebrows knead as I read the tiny blurb. Whoever wrote this, gathered information, input and output, nothing more.

Francisco Roman–Italian, 10% Dutch. Entrepreneur. Married. Children. Last known address. Alive.

Annika Wright–African American, with a static breakdown of various African ethnicities. Army Reserves. Last known whereabouts. Alive.

"Oh, I'm *not* Russian," I mutter.

"Nyet, well that too." Simeon grabs the paper. "You're a Roman .
. ."

I take it back from Simeon and ball the paper up. "Alright, children. The man and woman who created me were named Francisco and Annika."

I know my son will have a thousand questions for me. Malich stops toppling with the little ones to ask. "Simeon, what's—"

"She's a Roman," Simeon repeats.

"I said, *we're dropping it* after I opened the envelope. I don't care who—"

"What's a Roman?" Little Luka asks.

"In this instance, a last name, like Resnov."

"That's quite true, syn," Malich mumbles.

"You don't care in the slightest?" Simeon stares at me.

"I said I'd open the paper. Whatever the contents, I'd read it." I gulp.

"What's a Rom—"

Simeon kneels to Little Luka's level. "You know how Dad told you to mention your last name to that bully. In the world Mommy and Daddy were born in, a surname holds power. That's a very powerful name, Little Luka."

"Like Resnov?" our son inquires.

I kiss Little Luka's forehead. "Malich, do you mind?"

Simeon levels a gaze at me. I meander from the Resnov mausoleum, across the marbled slab steps, hugging myself.

"Sim, the pain from my parents' neglect stopped ruling my life after Simone was born, okay?"

"Okay."

"Shit, I don't believe you're parroting my 'okay' means this discussion is final."

"Why do you get to cuss?"

I chortle. "Hello, our children are over there. Apparently, Roman is a big deal. Francisco hasn't searched for me. Look, it says he's been married to the same woman and has children older and younger than me. He may or may not have ever known about me. So, who cares? Why raise my expectations? I'm not meeting either of them. Do I make myself understood?"

In an instant, Simeon has pulled me around a huge tree. He plants me against the bark, his hand squeezing softly at my throat, gaze leveled with mine. "I'm the man; you're the wife."

"I know," I grit.

He nips my lip, then drops a kiss, blotting out the pain. "Good. You don't have to meet the mudak. Choice is yours. Doesn't make you any less of a Roman. So, now, I will tell you, my Tsarina, we do not associate with them. Unless you—"

"I will not." I scoff. "Had it not been for Little Luka, I'd never know, Sim."

"And you're content with that, I get it." He places his forehead against mine in thought. "I doubt we will ever have a problem with a Roman. My antics with Dominicci elevated their status to the ruling house in Italy. You think I'm a fucking beast, but those Romans all are."

"Alright, as your Tsarina," I glare up at my husband, "I appreciate the intel. As your wife, whom you've helped overcome abandonment issues, understand that I am happy. Don't piss me off."

"You're happy?" He clasps my throat tighter, gaze zeroing on my lips.

"Sim . . ." I murmur.

"Anastasiya, when I get you home, I'm fucking that bad mouth of yours."

I pant as he clutches my breasts, his mouth burrowing between them, biting across the curve of my melons.

Head falling back, I moan. "Oh, please. We're going to make another baby; you keep talking to me like that."

"You keep blessing me with beautiful, healthy babies, Asya. I'll keep loving you, lawlessly."

Lawless love. I like that. It's as enduring as unconditional. But my miniature shadow and my beloved brat's namesake says, "Yuck!"

"Mommy and Daddy love each other, Little Luka." I sigh, as Simeon lets me go.

My guard has shattered, Simeon's too. He's transformed since being the depraved beast I returned to. He's so much more now, for our children, for me. Though Little Luka stares up at us, Simeon's obsidian orbs eye me hungrily, while abounding in emotion. His love for us defies all laws.

SUBSCRIBE TO MY NEWSLETTER & BE THE FIRST TO KNOW ABOUT "DIABLO INSIDE"

Thank you for reading *Lawless II*. I hope the ending wrapped up perfectly! Sim and Asya finally have the happiness they deserve. Anastasiya is definitely not interested in reaching out to her family—whatsoever. **But be prepared for the spin-off, "PURE SIN," which will include her father's family, the Romans. That Italian Mafia Romance will launch in November.**

For now, Mikhail Resnov is living his life . . . broken hearted.

Kirill is doing well too ;)

Subscribe to my newsletter. Also, I hope you'll take a second to review on Amazon, Goodreads, and BookBub. Reviews are social proof to potential readers, and reading them encourages me to continue writing . . .

Keep reading for a very short sample of "DIABLO Inside." My main character, Dominic Alvarez, is so hot, he's deadly!!!

ABOUT THE AUTHOR

Amarie is the author of stories from dark to light, erotic to semi-sweet, heck, she will even attempt to tickle your funny bone on occasion.

Sign up for my newsletter for information on upcoming releases. Have a chat with me in my Facebook Group (I'm less prone to shyness there lol, and often share new works in progress there first!)

Take a second to stalk me:

DIABLO INSIDE

Every single page of Diablo Inside is scorching hot! The sex, the anticipation, the murder. I don't know if I should fear Dominic Alvarez or fall for him. This is your next stalker-romance addiction! I can promise you.

XOXO,

Amarie

Blurb

ARIA JONES

A monster has Miami in a state of uproar. The media calls him El Santo, I prefer El Diablo—the beguiling angel who fell from grace.

Yes, his beauty and charm is unparalleled.

But his truth has been uncovered.

By me.

My obsession with Dominic Alvarez will be his demise. I crave everything about ensnaring him.

Looking into his captivating dark eyes, crushing his even darker soul.

I refuse to become like the others- the women whose hearts stop at the sight of him.

The women lost themselves in the allure and temptation of El Santo before they could feel the danger at the tips of his brutal fingers.

I'll save them because when my twin needed me most—I failed her. The time for redemption is now.

EL SANTO

Seduce them all.

Frame their vivacious curves in the palm of my hands.

Make their souls mine.

It's what I was born to do.

But here comes a cunning mouse, playing in a snake den. A good girl with bad aspirations.

Aria Jone lives inside the walls of her pretty head. That's where I will be—in her head.

I'll sit at her table, sleep in her bed, take her heart.

Once I glean the secrets behind Aria's jaded gaze and discover her greatest fears, I'll collect the little lamb like the others.

Collect, crush, and make her mine *forever*.

ARIA JONES

Raw fear licks the nape of my neck. With each breath, I drown in the past. *Sounds of an Ice Cream truck, laughter, The Oldies—family reunion music—funneled my ears. In hesitation, I watched my younger sister take the hand of a stranger whose smile surpassed the Texas sun. They were getting chocolate sundaes for us and coming right back . . .*

I warn myself to touch something, pursue reality. My clammy

palms press against the cool, veiny marble countertop. ReAnna and her abductor disappear, rich opulence returns.

"Aria, don't let the past fuck with your head," I tell myself, surrounded by massive slate-gray walls. Custom everything and stainless-steel appliances align the kitchen. The sliding glass door, which frames a breathtaking view of Miami Beach by day, is veiled in nightfall. Hearing heightened, I call out, "Hello?"

The top floor of a sky-rise luxury apartments is where I call home. The only dwelling on the level. My poor, rich roommate—emphasis on either term has never worked a day in her life. When Miranda's funds decreased, she sought a roomy. Though our home is a sanctuary, it's Saturday night. Countless Cosmopolitans, couture dresses, and posh lounges are her religion.

So, if someone responds to the greeting, you're screwed, Aria.

Fisting a chef knife, I add a tentative threat: "I have a . . . gun!"

My fingers drag across my tresses, tangling in thick roots, desperate for of a touch-up. I'm bare foot. My camisole and pajama pants boast the black girl magic tag. My demeanor? Not so much.

Faint steps echo out. Adrenaline rockets through my veins. "Miranda, if that's you . . ." *You will see the side of me I hide from everyone else.*

Barefoot over cold, opulent limestone, I navigate through the vast expanse of the home. I stop in the hallway, which leads to my side. Miranda kept the balcony wrapping around the east, north, south. While I possess a lone terrace, for early mornings from my art room. Light bleeds from that very door.

Jutting the knife downward, I snatch open the door, to catch Messy Miranda. She's so worried about my pockets, I've caught her snooping around my area since signing the lease a half year ago.

"Miran—" Alarm seizes my throat. My gaze collides with olive green gems, whisking me to my first obsession. No amount of therapy ever remedied the guilt. Older siblings have an unwritten obligation. *I failed ReAnna.*

During some flashbacks, I lose sight of them in the commotion, of a hot summer's day. Or I freeze. Either way the ending is spun, ReAnna is never to be seen or heard from again. Breathing spiraling, my hand extents to the doorframe.

Touch reality or faint. My seesawing vision slows as my fingers clash against the ornate, glossy frame. Exuding false confidence, I demand, *"How did you get in here?"*

Despite my past, I'm not crazy. Miranda draws imaginary lines and counts beans. Her fixation on division made me anal, too.

This is my haven.

Miranda has hers.

The attractive Cuban dominating my art room doesn't belong here.

He's thick. A dangerous kind of thick that can bulldoze straight through me. Taller than my musings from afar. A leather jacket forms along his imposing shoulders and biceps, tapered down to a narrow waist. Dark-wash denim encase muscular legs and a scrumptious ass—I know, I've seen that ass from afar. He's the entire package, every physical attribute on any woman's list. The sight of him heats up the adrenaline already coursing through me.

His face is flawless deception: angelic, devilish, and sends goosebumps rising on my arms. Summer-kissed skin, sharp jaw. Dangerously delicious stubble accentuates a beautiful, *hostile* mouth. The Cuban ruined the lives of women, with that mouth. Probably stole kisses while pilfering the last ounce of air from a woman's soul. The rich depths of his green eyes took ages for me to stare into once I captured him in photos. All of which . . . I've seen from afar.

"I said how did you get in here?" Never mind the delirious question of 'how,' as oppose to 'why,' I'm astonished I can utter a single word.

The breeze from the balcony jostles his loose, chocolate brown curls. He nudges a perfectly contoured chin toward the balcony.

"We're on the highest level in the building!" I argue.

At the standing desk, the Cuban picks up a photo. The image captures an attractive vessel. *Him*. Mouth twisted, he flicks the photo of himself toward me. It dashes at my feet. Then another and another.

My first obsession fucked my mind over—ReAnna's disappearance.

My second fixation is piling at my feet.

Photos glide across the floor. All of him. The camera lens worshiped his angles. His face. His chiseled chest. The Cuban god. My fascination will take him forever, if he plans on flinging all the photos to me.

"Those are my personal property," I grit out.

The man pulls from a rolled cigarette. A sweet, musk scent fizzles from captivating lips as he plucks another photo. He flicks it into my general direction.

"They are mine!"

"Are they, Aria? Or shall I call you, *LeAnna?* You changed your name, *chula.*" His warm, alluring tone puts smooth malt whiskey to shame. In quick strides, his boots walk over renderings of his face. He stops in front of a canvas painting, which had taken an entire week to create from another photo. The Cuban snatches it from the easel, staring at the creation of himself. My panties percolate at the sound of a low, angered growl building in his throat.

I sigh, calming my desire as he continues to stare at the painting. Bold brush strokes matched his swagger. I'd spent more money on pallets of gold and mocha to paint *him* in these past months than I did in my entire undergrad at NYU. There are a thousand transitions of his photos into my favorite medium—paint—in this room. So if he plans to pick them all over, it'll take forever too.

I don't mind forever, as long as he doesn't murder me . . .

My hips widen as he drags from his handmade cigarette, then quietly rips stitches down the center. "This your property, Aria, *si?*"

A gasp ribbons up my throat. "You need to leave—"

"Or, what? You call the cops?" His thick eyebrow juts.

Focusing on the painting, he lights one side. Cinders curl into an insignificant flame. Letting the scrape fall, the Cuban crushes the furious little spark with his boot.

"Let's call the cops. Tell them how *you* stalked me." He pounds his chest. "Took photos, painted me without consent, *si!*"

I gulp as he enters 9-1-1 onto the cellphone screen. The quiver of need racing through my body dies again. He has that effect on me. I run hot, then cold, before trepidation triumphs. He poises his finger over the call button, and my jaw clamps.

"Eh, is the authorities our next course of action, Aria?" His Latin accent twines my name sensual, slow, making me painfully aware of how enthralling the devil is. Though his stance is threatening, I'm continually reminding myself not to . . . fear him. Never mind the natural reaction: desire.

"We call the cops, mami. You say I'm breaking and entering." His chuckle is a low rumble in his colossal chest. "But this room depicts something else altogether."

Heat flushed, I level my gaze on the notorious killer. Not afraid to lose myself in the pits of his eyes, not now. "You're the stalker. *Murd . . .*" My voice breaks, he's a murderer, who collects beautiful women.

The cigarette dangles at the tip of his lips. He huffs a breath, smoke clouds the magnificent structure of his face. "Aria, you're gorgeous, deranged. Not a compelling combination. This will end bad for you."

"You're a sick fuck, Dominic *Angel* Alvarez. You know my name, *I know you!*" I grit out, finding the voice I neglected when ReAnna vanished. "You're—"

My body is planted against the wall. Haunting, shadowy green eyes glare down at me. Red heat radiates from Dominic's taut skin.

"What were you saying?" His accent, I've heard a million women gush about, twists. "Repeat yourself, Aria!"

"Kill me," I threaten. "More paintings of you are here. More photos than you can conceive of finding after disposing of my body."

The backs of Dominic's knuckles are a soothing leather across my cheek. At his subtle touch, I shake like a spindle. An enigmatic pull tethers us. Exhaling, I realize this is the first time he touched me. Before, Dominic's intensity sent me reeling back.

My gaze zips away from his hypnotic orbs, which have hints of honey in their filthy, green depths. Those eyes are how the women submitted to the ultimate predator.

"Kill you?" Dominic calls me crazy beautiful, serenading me with an imaginary Spanish guitar.

When I tremble, he stops murmuring sweet words in my ear. He rubs his index and thumb finger together. "You're crying, Aria. Look at those big brown eyes. You weren't aware?"

A mouth worthy of reverent love tips into a grin.

"You weren't aware you're crying." He knots his fingers into my hair, baring my throat and vulnerable pulse to his lips. More Spanish words float from his devious mouth. He presses his mouth along my cheek. I become attune with the flush of my tears. This is how the other women die, so caught up in the rapture of him, they lose themselves.

As I've said, I know these things.

I've watched, waiting for Dominic to break another pretty soul —because I'd pounce before he consumed her.

His gaze dances over mine, leveling me, spearing me against the wall further. "*You* begging me to tear you apart, Aria?"

"No," I whimper.

"You're crying. I have yet to rip you to shreds. Should I break you, *chula?*"

My heart shutters to a stop. There was one thing in this world I obsessed over before the sight of Dominic Angel Alvarez.

The disappearance of ReAnna.

For the rest of my life, I'll obsess over her. Had I not breathed life thirty minutes prior to her, would shame claw so deep? Too late for questions, too late to save my twin. Now, I've vowed to rescue Dominic's women.

"Mami, should I show you what happens to bad girls, si?"

"Try me!" I cling to convictions I never knew. This second obsession of mine won't extend as long as the first one. Justice will be served, with my death. Aside from the photos and sketches, I have notes, a virtual journal set on a timer. The media calls him El Santos. El Diablo's more appropriate. Dominic's balls are in a vice grip and he doesn't know it. Fuck spending another breath on this earth. My life can conclude now.

Grab DIABLO Inside on Preorder now!

Or check out Fearless Series featuring Vassili Resnov!

If you're up to date with all the Resnovs, then might I suggest, Devil In Her Bed. Although 'DIABLO Inside' is a complete stand-alone, some awesome characters from 'Devil in her Bed' will make an appearance.

Thank you so much for reading the Lawless Series, don't forget to leave your review.

CPSIA information can be obtained
at www.ICGtesting.com
Printed in the USA
LVHW011701200820
663740LV00006B/998